MURDER
at the
COURTHOUSE

Center Point
Large Print

Also by A. H. Gabhart and available from
Center Point Large Print:

Small Town Girl
Love Comes Home
The Innocent

Hidden Springs Mysteries, #1

MURDER
at the
COURTHOUSE

A. H. Gabhart

CENTER POINT LARGE PRINT
THORNDIKE, MAINE

This Center Point Large Print edition is published
in the year 2015 by arrangement with Revell,
a division of Baker Publishing Group.

This book is a work of fiction. Names, characters, places,
and incidents are the product of the author's imagination
or are used fictitiously. Any resemblance to actual events,
locales, or persons, living or dead, is coincidental.

Scripture used in this book, whether quoted or
paraphrased by the characters, is taken from the
King James Version of the Bible.

The text of this Large Print edition is unabridged.
In other aspects, this book may vary
from the original edition.
Printed in the United States of America
on permanent paper.
Set in 16-point Times New Roman type.

ISBN: 978-1-62899-796-5

Library of Congress Cataloging-in-Publication Data

Gabhart, Ann H., 1947–
   Murder at the courthouse / A. H. Gabhart. —
   Center Point Large Print edition.
       pages cm
   ISBN 978-1-62899-796-5 (hardcover : alk. paper)
   1. Large type books. I. Title.
   PS3607.A23M87 2015b
   813´.6—dc23
                                                    2015032953

To my husband, Darrell

MURDER
at the
COURTHOUSE

❧ 1 ❧

Miss Willadean Dearmon found the body on the courthouse steps at exactly 8:59 a.m. Miss Willadean appeared at the courthouse every weekday morning at that exact time, barring holidays, major illnesses, or snow over her boot tops. As far as anybody knew, she didn't actually have a schedule written out, but were her day divided out on paper, that's what it would say. *Courthouse steps 8:59 a.m.* Out of bed at 7:30, bran cereal and whole wheat toast with a smidgen of orange marmalade at 8:00 while listening to the local news to see if anyone she knew might have passed on during the night. A fresh dab of rouge on her cheeks and a liberal coating of her favorite cherry-red lipstick at 8:35. At exactly 8:47 she closed her front door behind her, patted her pinkish-gray hair into submission, and headed toward Main Street. On the first of nine chimes from the Christian Church bell tower, she stepped through the courthouse entrance as the office doors were swinging open for business.

Not that Miss Willadean had any business to transact. She didn't own a car and could only pay her property taxes once a year, but she liked to stop by the county clerk's office before many customers showed up so she could exchange a few words with Neville Gravitt. She told friends it was her Christian duty to brighten up the poor man's day since his wife succumbed to cancer two years back.

But this Tuesday morning in the second week of May when Miss Willadean climbed the courthouse steps, a man sat slumped against one of the stone columns that held up the porch entrance. The possibility the man might be dead never entered Miss Willadean's mind. After all, this was Hidden Springs, Kentucky. People died in hospitals or at home in their beds or easy chairs. Once, a preacher had a heart attack and died in the pulpit of a church out in the country. But folks didn't sit down and die on the courthouse steps. It just wasn't done.

So when the man didn't pay a bit of notice to her, Miss Willadean assumed he had overindulged in strong drink. That was enough to tighten her mouth into a thin, straight line of disapproval, but added to that was the fact she'd never laid eyes on this particular man before in her life.

Miss Willadean prided herself on knowing everybody in Hidden Springs. Everybody. She not only knew them, she knew their middle names, their children's and grandchildren's names, what street or road they lived on, where they worked, and if they skipped church on Sunday. Folks said Miss Willadean probably even knew what brand of toothpaste you used. Little escaped Miss

Willadean's notice or, once noticed, remained a secret for long.

The discovery of this stranger was no exception. She paused only a second to glare at him before she hurried on up the steps. Her sensibly low heels clattered on the polished tile floor as she rushed down the hall straight to the sheriff's office without even slowing to peek in at Neville Gravitt.

Deputy Sheriff Michael Keane looked up from his desk as Miss Willadean came through the door, her arms flailing as though she had to fight her way through the air in front of her.

"Miss Willadean." Michael jumped up to hurry toward her in case she stumbled in her headlong rush into the office. A mottled red was inching up her corded neck, and her eyes were bulging, not to mention the fact that she was at their office at least five minutes earlier than usual. "What's wrong?"

She sputtered a few words that didn't exactly connect with one another, and Michael worried she might be having a stroke.

"Easy, Miss Willadean." He put a hand on her shoulder. "Sit down and we'll get you some water." He glanced around at Betty Jean Atkins, who stopped filling the coffeemaker and reached for a bottle of water.

Miss Willadean refused to move toward a chair. Instead, she jabbed a finger toward the front of the courthouse and found her tongue, which never stayed lost very long.

"I don't want any water. I want something done about that . . . that drunkard out there on the steps. Imagine, inebriated at this time of the morning. He didn't even have manners enough to speak to me." She bristled and yanked down the corners of her pink knit suit jacket. "Acted as if he didn't know I was there."

"Who's that, Miss Willadean?" Michael asked.

"Well, I'm sure I don't know. A stranger if ever I did see one. Who in Hidden Springs would be found in that condition on the courthouse steps this time of the morning?"

Michael could think of several possibilities, but he didn't name them. The less said around Miss Willadean, the better. She had a network of friends who could spread rumors and gossip faster than he could walk the two blocks from one end of town to the other.

"I'll go take care of it." Michael kept his voice low and even. Sounding in control made his job easier. Plus, it didn't hurt that he stood a couple of inches over six feet and had steady blue eyes that somebody once said made lying to him impossible. He didn't know about that, but he did know that calm worked best in most situations.

Miss Willadean's eyes settled back into her head and she quit punching at the air long enough to smooth a stray wisp of hair back into place. She

12

glared up at Michael. "I should think so. And right away. You've wasted enough time talking already."

"Yes, ma'am."

That placated the woman somewhat. She was right. He had wasted time talking. The drunk had probably staggered away by now. Routine. Then again, it could be something out of the ordinary. After all, Miss Willadean didn't know the man. That was definitely out of the ordinary.

He gave the old lady one last pat on the shoulder. "Sit down and rest a minute."

Miss Willadean didn't sit down. He hadn't really expected her to, just hoped she might. Instead, she followed him back through the hall toward the front door.

Stella Pinkston stuck her head out of the county clerk's office to give Michael the eye. Stella said being married didn't keep her from appreciating a good-looking man when she saw one. She peered up at him through bleached-blonde bangs and gave him a suggestive smile. "What's going on, Mike?"

Michael was crisp with her as always. "Just a drunk out front. Nothing to keep you from your work."

She batted mascara-coated eyelashes at him as if he'd just offered to meet her upstairs in the hallway behind the courtroom when court wasn't in session.

When the click of her high heels joined their little procession toward the front door, he held in a sigh and did his best to quell the irritation that rose inside him. He tried to carry out his duties in a professional manner, but in Hidden Springs, that wasn't always possible. Somehow everything had a way of getting turned into a sideshow. Even something as common as a drunk.

He'd been back in Hidden Springs working for Sheriff Potter for almost a year, after spending too much time trying to enforce the law in Columbus. In that city, on the streets in his beat, bad things could happen any day or night. For a while, he thought he could make a difference. He could make the streets safer. Maybe not the whole city, but his beat. He could slow down the drug trafficking, help kids see that school might be their ticket to a better life, protect the store-keepers, do some good.

Early on, in a weak moment, he'd shared his aspirations with his partner in the city. Even now, five years down the road, he could still hear Pete Ballard's raspy laugh. "Tell me again, kid. Which was it you graduated from? The police academy or the seminary?" Pete had been working a beat longer than Michael had been breathing.

Michael hadn't backed down. "You don't have to be a preacher to want to help people."

"You've been looking at way too many recruiting

posters. Lost kids coming up to big, strong police officers to ask the way home." Pete shook his head. "You better stop believing in fairy tales. One of them little darlings comes up to you nowadays, they're liable to spit on you. Or worst-case scenario, try to shoot you. That happens, you'd better be ready to pull your trigger first."

When Michael set his jaw and kept his mouth shut, Pete punched his shoulder. "Look, kid, no need getting your nose out of joint. All of us start out floating a little off the pavement like as how we're the second coming or something. 'Course I never had much of a line to the big guy upstairs. Too much static on my end, I guess. Maybe your connection will be better."

Somehow he and Pete had learned to be partners. The wet-behind-the-ears kid with big ideals and the burned-out cop who'd been kicked in the face a few too many times by the public he'd sworn to protect. But Pete never stopped trying to toughen Michael up. For his own good, Pete said. To keep him alive.

Then one day Michael found himself in pursuit of a kid caught shoplifting at a corner grocery. Pete had long since surrendered his running ability to cigarettes and couldn't keep up. The chase ended in a deserted warehouse with Michael in shooting stance, yelling at the kid to put his hands up. The kid turned to look at him. Desperate eyes in a girl child's face. She didn't look over thirteen. After a long moment, she turned and ran on into the shadows.

He hadn't fired his weapon. He hadn't even shouted at her to stop. He let her go. Purposefully. With intent. He hadn't done his job. Not that anybody had known that. Nobody was in the warehouse but Michael and the girl. When Pete came panting in a few minutes later, he guessed. Told Michael that kind of thing was going to get him killed. Maybe get them both killed. And Michael couldn't say he was wrong.

So Michael had come home to Hidden Springs where he spent his days on the job breaking up a drunken fight now and again, tracking down folks who wrote checks for more than they had in their bank accounts, or directing traffic on PTA meeting nights or after high school ball games.

He liked the small-town pace. He liked being able to figure out who was going to make trouble before they had time to make it. He liked being a peace officer in a place where it seemed possible to keep the peace. Where he didn't have to pull out his gun to try to stop the craziness on the streets. Where he didn't have to think about seeing the face of a desperate child in his sights. The occasional vagrant wasn't all that big a problem. If the man was still there, he would roust him up and usher him back to the jail behind the courthouse.

Michael pushed open the door, spotted the dark red smear on the pillar behind the man slumped on the steps, and knew at once that lack of manners had nothing to do with the man not speaking to Miss Willadean.

⊰ 2 ⊱

Michael blocked the path out the door and turned to the two women behind him. "Stella, why don't you take Miss Willadean back to speak to Neville? I'm sure he's wondering why she high-hatted him this morning."

Stella raised her eyebrows at Michael, but she did as he said and took hold of the old lady's arm. Miss Willadean allowed Stella to tow her two steps back toward the clerk's office before she put on the brakes. Michael could almost see her thinking Neville Gravitt would be in his office all day, but if there was someone in Hidden Springs she didn't know, it was her bounden duty to find out his name and his business.

She shook off Stella's hand. "I will not. I'll stay right here and be sure you do your job, Deputy. It's my right as a tax-paying citizen."

Michael knew when he was beaten. There was nothing for it but to pull out his radio, push the button, and open up the line to the office with Miss Willadean's ears tuned to every word.

"Betty Jean, get hold of the sheriff and Chief Sibley and tell them to come on down." He paused a moment. "And bring out some of that police line tape."

"Police line tape?" Betty Jean's voice crackled through the radio. The static didn't hide her surprise. "You mean like on TV? Do we even have any of that stuff?"

"The bottom shelf by the door." Beside him, Stella and Miss Willadean both looked as baffled as Betty Jean sounded. "I guess you might as well go ahead and call the state police too." Michael hesitated again, but it had to be said. "And get hold of Justin Thatcher."

When he said the coroner's name, Stella's eyes widened, and she was almost pretty.

"What do you need Justin for?" Miss Willadean's voice went up a few decibels. "You don't need a coroner to tell you the man's inebriated."

"No, Miss Willadean, you don't." He put his hand on her arm and spoke gently, almost as if he were breaking the news about a family member. "I'm afraid the man out there isn't drunk. He's dead."

The color drained away from the two spots of rouge on Miss Willadean's cheeks, and she swooned. Michael caught her easily. Beside her, Stella let out a gasp, but Michael wasn't sure whether it was because the man was dead or because she hadn't thought to swoon before Miss Willadean did.

Neville Gravitt, who must have come out into the hall looking for Stella, rescued Michael. He shoved one of the chairs that sat along the wall under Miss Willadean. Michael lowered the limp woman down into the chair and looked at Neville. The slightly stooped, graying county clerk met Michael's eyes. While Neville Gravitt didn't have much imagination, he had enough to know what Miss Willadean would surmise when she opened her eyes to see him tending to her. So the hint of desperation that appeared in the man's eyes was understandable. Nevertheless he loosened Miss Willadean's collar and sent Stella after a cup of water.

Michael went out the door to get a closer look at the man slumped against the column. He was, as Miss Willadean noted, a stranger. Michael squatted down and lifted the man's hand. Not long dead, but definitely dead, and not from ordinary causes like a heart attack or stroke. Not with the smear of dark red on the column behind him and a slowly coagulating pool of blood around him. He didn't know how Miss Willadean had missed that.

Michael pulled out his radio again and told Betty Jean to bring a camera when she brought the police tape.

She came right out to see what was going on.

It was so quick that Michael was sure she couldn't have made the first call.

When she saw the body, she got pale around her lips, but she didn't come anywhere close to fainting. Not Betty Jean. She might have gotten her job in the sheriff's office because she was the sheriff's niece, but she was good at the job. Hardly anything anybody did surprised her. Even better, she was a computer whiz and had no problem handling the folks who raised a ruckus about paying their property taxes. A couple of years older than Michael, she was a few pounds on the heavy side and unmarried in spite of being a faithful subscriber to *Brides* magazine.

She handed Michael the camera and tape. "I guess Miss Willadean will have enough to talk about from this to last her the rest of her life."

Michael didn't bother agreeing as he focused in on the corpse.

Betty Jean hadn't moved. "She'll probably even get her name mentioned in the *Gazette*."

Michael looked up from the camera to glance uneasily across the courthouse lawn toward the street. The *Hidden Springs Gazette* office was a mere half block away. Hank Leland would be there in two minutes flat if he got wind of something going on at the courthouse. All that had saved them so far from curious onlookers were the empty sidewalks and the fact that most people parked in the lot behind the courthouse and used the rear entrance.

Michael looked at Betty Jean. "You better go make those calls. It wouldn't do for Hank to find out about this before Chief Sibley or Sheriff Potter."

Betty Jean shook herself a little, as though coming out of a trance. "Right." She took one last look at the man's body. "A funny place to pick to die."

"I don't think he did the picking."

"You mean . . ." Betty Jean stopped and took another look at the blood on the post and step.

"You better go make those calls."

With a quick nod, she headed toward the courthouse door. When she pulled it open, Judge Campbell's voice boomed out his usual good morning as he showed up for work. Then the door shut again, clipping off the confusion of voices answering him.

Michael was surprised nobody had followed Betty Jean outside. Neville must be guarding the door to give Michael time to do what needed to be done.

If only he felt more certain about what that might be as he took a few pictures and then gingerly felt the man's pockets without disturbing his final resting position. A roll of bills and some change. No phone. No wallet that he could feel. No business cards. Nothing to explain why he was dead on the Hidden Springs Courthouse steps.

Michael hadn't worked a murder in Hidden Springs, hadn't actually ever worked a murder. He and Pete had come across a few dead bodies in the city. Suicides or overdoses mostly. Some accidents. A child hit by a car. Another kid thrown down the stairs by his drunken father. The kids were always the worst. Preacher Dan who ran a ministry for street kids called them throwaways. Kids nobody wanted. Kids nobody would miss.

Michael couldn't say he missed them since he hadn't known them. But he had grieved for them, for the loss of hope and innocence. For how easily their life flame had been snuffed out. And their lifeless faces had a way of popping up in his head at odd times to bring back the sadness. They were there now as he stretched the yellow police tape around the porch pillars, the World War I monument, and a conveniently located tree.

Michael looked at the body against the post and wished he'd told Betty Jean to bring out something to cover it up. Somehow it seemed obscene to leave the man exposed like that where everybody could stare at him. Even worse was the feeling the man was staring back.

"You can't see 'em as a person," Pete's voice echoed in his head. That's what he told Michael whenever they found a body. "There's too many dead people to cry over them all. Better to concentrate on what happened to them and why."

Michael tried to do that now. He blocked out the thought of the man eating breakfast awhile ago with no idea this day was going to be his last. The almost surprised look that death had frozen on his face didn't matter now. What mattered was why the man was there on the Hidden Springs Courthouse steps where folks didn't get murdered. At least never until today.

Murders rarely happened anywhere in Hidden Springs. Winston Lakes shot his son-in-law a few years ago, but everybody knew why that happened. There were only so many times a man could stand seeing his daughter get beat up, no matter the consequences. Then that tourist had shot his wife before he killed himself out at the campgrounds on the lake. That was while Michael was in the city, but Aunt Lindy had written him about it.

Maybe that was what happened here. Maybe it wasn't a murder at all. Maybe the man had shot himself. A hard theory to hold on to with no gun in sight and the fatal wound not visible. Obviously shot in the back. On top of that, a man who shot himself had no reason to look so surprised. None of that kept Michael from wanting to think it possible.

"Neville tells me there's a body out here. What in the name of Jehoshaphat is a body doing on the courthouse steps?" Judge Campbell's voice boomed loud enough to alert half the town as he came out of the courthouse.

The judge always talked that way. He claimed it won him votes because nobody ever had to ask him twice what he had to say. Michael couldn't say he was wrong. The judge had won three consecutive terms as judge-executive of Keane County.

"I don't know, Judge. I was just wondering if the poor soul shot himself."

The judge looked a little green around the gills as he stared down at the body. "Why in the world would he come here to do that? Unless it was some kind of political protest or something. You think that could be it?"

Michael couldn't believe the judge was being serious, but it wasn't exactly a time for joking. So Michael only said, "I don't think so, Judge."

Folks started flocking into the courthouse yard, attracted by the judge's voice and the yellow plastic strips flashing in the sunshine. Chief Sibley and his son-in-law, Paul Osgood, arrived in their patrol car with the roof lights flashing. Buck Garrett was right behind them in his unmarked state police car. His blue light went round and round on the dash. Every store on Main Street emptied out.

Hank Leland came running and pushed through the crowd to edge up close to Michael, the only county or city official he knew would actually speak to him. The others gave him rehearsed quotes. Carefully.

"Can you believe this?" Hank peered toward the body. "I guess I should have been suspicious instead of relieved when Miss Willadean didn't show up at 9:22 to tell me what stories to put on the front page this week."

"Your news instincts must have dozed off," Michael said.

"Dozed off?! I must not have any. Look at that. A stiff on the courthouse steps half a block from my office. What's going on, Keane?"

"You know about as much as I know, Leland, and probably will know a lot more than me before the day's over."

Hank grinned. "Not me. I'm hopeless. I didn't even pick up my camera. I had to give Harold Hoskins five dollars to go back and get it." Hank looked up the street toward his offices. Harold was nowhere in sight. "I guess I should have made it ten bucks."

"Or picked somebody who can move faster than Harold." Michael shook his head at Hank and walked away. He still wanted to check for some kind of trail or clues, and with this many people converging, he needed to look fast.

The judge was ahead of him, stepping over the yellow police lines to walk across the portico and stare down at the dead man.

"Don't move around in there, Judge," Michael called, but it was too late.

The judge glanced down at his shoes, swore

under his breath, and scooted his feet on the concrete as he walked back toward the courthouse door, leaving a bloody smudge with each step.

After that, the only good thing to happen was the coroner showed up with his body sheet before Harold got there with Hank Leland's camera.

⚛ 3 ⚛

As more people gathered on the courthouse lawn, what had been an interesting sideshow turned into a three-ring circus. All they needed were bleachers for the spectators and a spotlight for the performers. And a ringmaster. That was what they needed most.

Michael felt a lot more like a spectator than a ringmaster. But even if he couldn't direct the show, he could act like a police officer and do something instead of simply taking in the sights. He headed over toward Paul Osgood and Buck Garrett, then changed directions when their conversation turned into a shouting match about who got to tell who what to do. They hadn't even looked at the body yet.

That was their problem. His was making sure nobody else followed Judge Campbell's lead and climbed across the police lines to get a closer look at the body. The judge had left tracks across the porch and no doubt right on into the courthouse. The chance for gathering any useful evidence was getting slimmer by the minute.

At least he had taken pictures of the scene before the circus started. He held up his camera and took two more of the body. Then just for the heck of it, he turned the camera on Paul and Buck up in each other's faces. Buck Garrett's muscles strained against his state police uniform. He could easily make two of Paul Osgood, who looked more like somebody's idea of an accountant than a police officer, but in a war of words, Paul might come out the winner.

Michael looked away from them to focus in on Sheriff Potter bustling up the walk, one of the Grill's white coffee mugs in his hand. Before the sheriff could notice him there and ask why he was playing with his camera at a time like this, Michael turned to find Hank Leland in his viewfinder. Hank had sneaked inside the yellow police line to edge up behind the coroner examining the body. Hank spotted Michael taking his picture and gave him a goofy smile. Then Michael snapped a shot of Judge Campbell coming back out of the courthouse, presumably after cleaning his shoes.

Michael turned the camera on the crowd in the courthouse yard and took some random shots. Nobody could be left in any of the stores or offices in all of Hidden Springs. Even Reece Sheridan had come across the street, and hardly anything but the promise of good fishing stirred him out from behind his lawyer's desk these days.

When Michael spotted Anthony Blake in the crowd, he wondered if they'd dismissed classes at school so everybody could share the excitement. But of course, it wasn't school that had been dismissed, just Anthony who had dismissed school.

Michael frowned. It was part of the boy's last deal with the court that he not skip school. Sometimes Michael wondered if the kid really wanted to stay out of jail.

At sixteen, Anthony had already been in and out of trouble a half-dozen times. Nothing major, but he seemed to be working up to it. Anthony must have felt Michael's eyes on him, because he jerked his head around to look directly at Michael. Something near panic flashed across his face before he ducked behind the World War I monument.

Michael started across the lawn toward Anthony, but Sheriff Potter stepped in front of him.

"What in the world is going on here, Mike? Why didn't you call me sooner?" The sheriff's fleshy face was red and glistening with sweat, even though the morning was cool.

"I told Betty Jean to call you, Sheriff. First thing."

"From the looks of it, she must have called everybody else in the county before she remembered my number." The sheriff pulled a white handkerchief out of his back pocket and mopped off his face.

"I'm sure she called you first. It's just that you had to walk down here, and the chief and Paul came down in their car."

"I don't guess that matters now." The sheriff pulled in a breath and blew it out. "What's this about a body on the steps? Whose body?"

"I don't think he's been identified yet."

The sheriff's eyes tightened a little. "What happened to him?"

"I can't be sure. I didn't think I should disturb the body until after Justin had a look. He's examining him now."

The sheriff glanced toward where the coroner was bent over the body. "Yeah, well, he'll probably be able to tell he's dead anyway." He took a sip of the coffee in his mug, made a face, and slung the rest of the brown liquid out on the ground. "What do you think, Mike? You're bound to have seen this kind of thing a lot up in the big town."

"Not that much, but looks like he was shot."

"Shot, huh?" The sheriff didn't wait for an answer. "He shoot himself?"

"No indication of that. No weapon nearby."

The sheriff muttered a few choice words before

he turned his attention to Paul and Buck. "What are those two going at each other about?"

"I think they're trying to work out whose jurisdiction this falls under."

The sheriff rolled his eyes heavenward and mopped his brow again. "I reckon I'd better go straighten them out and then see what Justin has to say." He shoved the empty cup at Michael. "Next time somebody gets shot on the courthouse steps, you make sure Betty Jean calls me first."

Michael didn't bother to answer as the sheriff stepped over the police line fairly easily, in spite of his considerable bulk. He looked back at Michael. "Good idea these police lines."

"Yeah, if we could just keep the people on this side of them." Michael looked around at the people leaning across the strips to get a better look.

"People want to see what happened. Natural as breathing. Find Lester and get him to help you keep the crowd back."

Crowd control. Michael couldn't keep an ironic smile off his face. But it didn't matter. The sheriff had already turned away to pat Paul's shoulder and punch Buck's arm. The sheriff knew how to handle people, and Michael supposed he knew how to handle crowds.

He'd pulled a lot of that kind of duty in the city. Kept the spectators out of the street during parades. Dragged protesters off to jail when they wouldn't clear an area. Worked the crowds at concerts to make sure the kids didn't trample each other in their fan frenzy. Held back reporters when some big shot got arrested. It wasn't something he enjoyed doing, and it wasn't something he ever expected to need to do in Hidden Springs.

Almost as if the sheriff had called him, Lester Stucker came out of the courthouse and stared in a kind of dazed wonder at all the people. When Michael motioned to him, the little deputy slowly made his way over. It took him awhile since he couldn't push anybody out of his way and no one paid him much mind. Lester was so thin that folks joked about him getting under a clothesline to get out of the rain. He always laughed with them, even though he must have heard the same joke or some version of it a thousand times.

Lester liked being a deputy sheriff, especially his duty as crossing guard at the elementary school. Lester had only missed being in his appointed spot twice in the three years he'd been working the street in front of the school. Once when he'd had pneumonia and once for his father's funeral. It was the first important job Lester had ever had in his forty-three years. While his mother had told him bagging groceries was important, even Lester knew wearing a uniform that included a gun, whether it was loaded or not, was miles ahead of that.

Now, when Michael told him they needed to

keep the people back, Lester's eyes lit up as he fingered his whistle. "Sure, Michael. Do you think I'll need to blow my whistle at them? You know, to get their attention like I do the kids out at school."

"I don't think so, Lester. Just tell them to step back if they're getting too close. They'll listen without the whistle."

"What about that Hank Leland?" Lester's eyes narrowed as Hank came toward them. "He won't listen to anybody."

"I'll take care of Hank," Michael promised.

Lester gave Hank a look as he headed over to tell Miss Stapleton from the bank to step back a bit.

"What's Lester looking so pleased about?" Hank asked.

"He's getting to tell people what to do. Grown-up people."

"I ought to take a picture of him and put it in the paper. That might make him decide I'm an okay guy and give me a tip sometime."

"A tip about what? Who's playing hooky at the grade school?"

"Yeah, well, it's a thought." Hank shrugged with a grin. "Sometimes news in Hidden Springs is slow."

"Not today."

"No siree," Hank agreed. "Not today. Did you hear Justin's pronouncement?"

Michael shook his head, not looking at Hank but watching Paul and Buck move apart and finally head over to look at the body. Sheriff Potter stood back and watched them like a satisfied father.

Hank followed his gaze. "They're a pair, aren't they?"

"No comment."

"Oh come on, Michael, don't give me that. Somebody around here has to comment on something." Hank fingered the little notebook in his shirt pocket. "If I quote you, I promise I'll say it was from an anonymous source."

"That's a promise you won't have any trouble keeping because I'm not saying anything to quote." Michael kept his eyes on Buck and Paul. Buck was groping through the dead man's pockets, and Paul was taking notes while he listened to the coroner. "What did Justin say?" he asked Hank.

"That the guy had been shot." Hank paused a little to give his next statement more emphasis. "In the back."

"He sure about that?" Michael wasn't surprised, just sorry.

"Yeah. *I* could be sure about that. Of course Justin said he'd have to send the body up to Eagleton for an autopsy, seeing as how it appears that there could be, and I quote, 'foul play involved.' "

Hank stared at Michael to gauge his response to

his words. Michael kept his mouth shut and his face expressionless.

"You're not helping me." Hank leaned a little closer to Michael. "You know, I could always put in the paper that Deputy Sheriff Michael Keane showed no sign of surprise upon learning that a man had been murdered on the courthouse steps."

Michael ignored the jibe. "Justin thinks he was shot out here then."

"What's Justin know? He's just an undertaker."

"He's had postmortem training." Michael took up for Justin.

"Yeah, whatever the state makes him take, but we both know he's coroner because he just happens to be the only man in Hidden Springs who doesn't mind looking at dead bodies."

"Him and you." People were always complaining about Hank publishing shots of accident scenes before the victims were carried away. There would be another sheet-covered body in tomorrow's edition.

"What can I say?" Hank threw out his hands in a gesture of helplessness. "Death sells newspapers. And I have a feeling murder will sell even more. Anyway, it's pretty obvious the poor guy was shot out here. Who would carry a body to the courthouse in the middle of town to dispose of it? Plus, he seemed to be sitting the way he fell. It'd be pretty hard to dump a body that way, don't you think? Who found him?" Hank sort of slipped in that last one as if he hoped Michael wouldn't notice it was a question.

Michael noticed, but answered anyway. "Miss Willadean. She thought he was drunk. 'Inebriated,' I think is the word she used. I'm sure she'd love to tell you all about it."

"Several hundred times over the next couple of years, and I might even enjoy the first ten or so times." Hank looked around. "Where is she?"

"Still in the courthouse, I suppose. She had a bit of a fainting spell when she found out the real reason the man wouldn't speak to her had nothing to do with his manners. I left her under Neville's care."

"This must be Miss Willadean's lucky day." Hank shook his head. "I guess me taking her picture and putting it in the paper will just about be the capper."

"She won't be able to tell you much. She saw him on the steps. She didn't know who he was, and he didn't speak to her. She went back to the sheriff's office, and in due course, the deputy came out to investigate, arrest the drunk, whatever needed to be done."

"Only the drunk wasn't drunk."

"Whether he was or not, that wasn't his major problem. Put it that way."

"Got to give it to you, Keane. You're observant." Hank let his gaze wander back over

35

the scene. "What else did you see that none of these others will think to look for?"

"Not a thing. I'll have to read the paper when it comes out to find out what happened."

"You and everybody else." Hank focused on Michael again. "So help me out with a few facts. Who is the victim?"

"Never saw him before. How about you?" Michael looked from where Buck was helping Justin load the body in the Hidden Springs Funeral Home hearse back to Hank. Sometimes the editor surprised him. This might be one of those times.

But Hank shook his head and pulled the little notebook out of his shirt pocket to scribble something in it. "If he's a *Gazette* subscriber, he's never been in the office. I remember faces."

"Even more telling, Miss Willadean didn't know him."

"A total stranger then for sure." Hank jotted down a few words.

Michael had seen the notebook pages once. They were covered with nothing but disjointed letters that could be deciphered by Hank and Hank alone.

"What else can you tell me, Michael?" Hank looked up.

"You know as much as I do."

"You came out to investigate. The man was deader than a doornail. So you called in the troops."

"That pretty much covers it. I'm sure Officer Osgood will be able to fill you in on more details." Michael nodded toward Paul Osgood making his way over to them.

❧ 4 ☙

The editor's demeanor changed as Osgood came up. No sign of a grin on his face now. He was all business, his eyes sharp on Paul's face. "What can you tell me about the murder, Officer Osgood?"

Paul pulled himself up to full height at the word "murder." Paul was always stretching up until he was almost on his tiptoes, like a kid hoping to look taller. Paul blamed not getting into the state police academy on his lack of inches. Whether it was true or not, he didn't make it and had to settle for a spot on the city police force. Some folks in Hidden Springs claimed he'd only married Caroline Sibley because her father was police chief. After all, Caroline was an inch taller than Paul. But if she slumped and Paul stretched, they were close to the same height and were always calling each other honey and darling.

So if it was a sacrifice Paul made, he didn't appear to regret it. His only complaints were about the job itself. "A man only has so many parking tickets in him," Paul told anybody who would listen. "Doesn't anything exciting ever happen around here?"

Something had happened now, and Paul seemed eager to take full advantage of it. "The case is under investigation." He used his most official voice.

Hank chewed his lip to hide a smile and scribbled in his notebook. Michael turned away from them, not wanting to hear any more.

"Wait, Michael." Paul put out a hand to stop him. "I need to talk to you."

"I'm not leaving the county." Michael stepped back from Paul's hand. "But Lester needs help with the crowd. It's time everybody went on about their business before somebody decides this might be a good time to clean out the bank up the street."

Paul's face was a mixture of worry and hope. A bank robbery would be almost as exciting as a murder.

Hank shot Michael a look without giving any sign of a wink, but the wink was there. He turned back to Paul. "Do you think this could all be a diversionary tactic, Officer Osgood?"

"You mean somebody may have planted the body here just so the bank would be unoccupied?" Paul glanced up the street nervously. The trees on the courthouse lawn hid the bank on the next block from view. "Maybe I should send some-body up that way."

At times, Michael wouldn't spoil the editor's fun, but today wasn't one of those times. A murder was no joking matter, whether they knew the victim or not. "Nobody's going to rob the bank, Paul."

Paul caught on then and glared at Hank. "I have more important things to do, Mr. Leland, than play games with you."

"You've got me all wrong, Officer Osgood. No game playing here." Hank widened his eyes and adopted an innocent look. "A good newspaperman has to be ready to follow up every potential lead in a story, no matter what the odds are of it amounting to anything. Some of our best stories are uncovered in that way. I'm sure it's the same with you. You can't afford to ignore even the smallest clue, right?"

Paul looked mollified. "If you have any questions about the case at hand, I'll be glad to answer them for you."

Michael left Paul at the mercy of the editor and began easing around the crowd, telling everybody to go on back to work or home since the show was over.

Buck Garrett fell into step beside Michael. "What's Osgood telling Leland?"

"Nothing but the facts, I'm sure."

"Facts." Buck spit on the ground. "Osgood wouldn't know a fact if it jumped up off the ground and smacked him full in the face."

"What are the facts, Buck?" Michael asked.

"The John Doe is Caucasian, about fifty years old. No ID on his body. No cell phone. A cheap department store watch. No rings or signs that he had been wearing rings. Small change in his jacket pocket, a roll of bills in his pants pocket. Two twenties on the outside, the rest ones. Clothes clean. Nice crease in his pants. Shoes shined. Colored his hair with that comb-in stuff. Shot at close range with a small caliber revolver. Maybe a Smith & Wesson or a Ruger. Probably by someone he knew. Shot in the back. Might have powder burns on his jacket. Must have staggered around a step or two and then landed against the pillar before he slid down there and stopped breathing. Three, four minutes maybe. Or not that long."

Michael was impressed by Buck's recital and a little embarrassed he hadn't noticed as much when he looked at the corpse.

Buck saw Michael's surprise. "I know what to look for, Mike. I've been a state trooper a long time. Going on twenty years now."

"But I wouldn't have thought you'd handled many murders."

"Not here in Hidden Springs, but something's always happening somewhere in the state. I keep up, and you know how we are. Always talking cases." Buck looked closely at Michael. "How about you? You see murders up there in Columbus?"

"Some, but I didn't have much to do with them. I was just a beat cop," Michael admitted. "Found a few bodies. That's all."

"And now you found another one. What'd you think when you came out on the steps and saw the stiff?"

"I don't know, Buck." Michael paused, considering the question seriously, even though Buck wasn't expecting a serious answer. "I was surprised, I guess. And sorry. Especially sorry."

"What'd you have to be sorry about? You didn't shoot him, did you?" One corner of Buck's mouth lifted up in a smile.

"I didn't shoot him, but somebody did."

"That's for sure." Buck's half smile disappeared. "And Little Osgood with some help from his friends will have to find out who." Buck glanced back at Paul Osgood still talking to Hank Leland and made a growling noise down in his throat. "I can't wait to read the paper tomorrow."

"Maybe Leland will go easy on him," Michael said.

"Fat chance of that. Leland enjoys making us all look like idiots. He'll have a field day with this."

Michael didn't bother to argue the point. He'd seen a few of his own quotes in the paper. Words that had sounded fine to his ears when he was speaking them often as not looked foolish in print. He steered the subject back to the murder. "You have any idea who might have shot the guy?"

"There are always suspects," Buck said.

"Then where are they?" Michael looked around at the thinning crowd. "I didn't see anybody conveniently hanging around with a smoking gun in hand. No witnesses have run up claiming to have seen it all. And the victim isn't talking." Michael frowned at Buck. "Looks to me like we don't have suspect one."

Buck shook his head. "You've been watching too many detective shows on television. Most murders are pretty simple affairs. I expect this one will be too."

"You do? In what way?"

"I don't know. We might go out to the campgrounds and find some wife who just got tired of looking at the bozo's face over breakfast, or it could be a jealous girlfriend, or the guy might have owed the wrong people money."

"That doesn't explain how he ended up getting shot on the courthouse steps," Michael said.

"Maybe he and the little woman were coming in to file for a divorce and they had one last doozy of an argument. Or he was running from somebody to get help and whoever he was running from caught up with him first. People get shot all the time."

"Not usually in the middle of a town like ours."

"That's so," Buck said cheerfully. "But you wait and see. It'll be something simple. We just have to find out what." Buck looked back toward Hank and Paul still talking. "I'm going to have to go break that up."

"Watch that you don't get knocked down yourself," Michael warned. "Hank is quick with his pencil."

"He won't get nothing out of me. Just you make sure he don't get nothing out of you either."

"He can't get anything out of me. I don't know anything to tell him."

"Don't worry, Mike. Somebody will have seen something." Buck glanced around, then grinned a little. "In this town you can't even scratch your backside on the courthouse steps without somebody seeing you, much less get shot."

Buck was right. Somebody had to have seen something. Michael looked past the people still clustered on the courthouse lawn to the other side of the street. Joe's Barbershop, Reece Sheridan's law office, and Jim Deatin's auto supply store. One of them might have seen something. He'd check that out. Right after he found Anthony Blake to put a little scare into him so he'd go on to school. He didn't want any throwaway kids in Hidden Springs.

Michael worked his way through the people still milling around, but Anthony was nowhere to be found.

✧ 5 ✧

After people drifted away to their jobs and errands, Michael went back to the sheriff's office to listen one more time to Miss Willadean's version of finding the body. With each retelling the story grew and changed a bit until what she had to say was next to useless.

The sheriff thanked her and told Lester to escort her home since she claimed to still be feeling faint. Miss Willadean touched a handkerchief edged in purple pansies to her nose as she slowly stood up, reluctant to give up the spotlight. She smoothed down her hair and started in again about how the man had just been sitting there and how peculiar he'd looked and how she'd suspected something must be dreadfully wrong with him right away.

"That's fine, Miss Willadean," the sheriff put in when she paused to get a breath. He tapped the recorder in front of him. "We have it all right here."

Miss Willadean glared at him and spluttered a few more words about what a sorry state the world had come to when a person could no longer feel safe on Main Street. At last she swept out the door Lester held open for her. She hadn't had much good to say about Sheriff Potter since she reported her purse stolen last year and he suggested she might have merely misplaced it. The fact that he retrieved her purse from under her regular booth at the Grill hadn't made her like him one bit better.

The sheriff kept an impassive smile on his face until the door closed behind the old lady and Lester. Then he gave his head a quick shake, as if clearing it of Miss Willadean's words, before he turned to Michael. "Okay, Mike. You tell us what you saw when you went outside."

So Michael went over everything he'd done from the minute Miss Willadean had come into his office. There wasn't much to tell, and it didn't take long.

While he talked, Paul took notes, Buck studied the coffee in his cup, and Chief Sibley slouched down in the only comfortable chair in the office with his eyes shut. Betty Jean made a fresh pot of coffee and answered the phone that started ringing again the second she hung up the receiver. Only the sheriff and Judge Campbell, who had followed them into the office, kept their eyes on Michael as he talked.

When Michael ran out of details, there was a little silence except for the phone ringing, the last drops of water gurgling through the coffeemaker, and Paul flipping over his notebook page.

"That doesn't tell us much," the sheriff said finally.

"You think he was shot out there then?" the judge asked.

"That's how it appears," Michael said. "I didn't see any blood leading up the steps, but by the time I looked, several people had already walked around out there."

"I sure am sorry about that." The judge hung his head a little. "I wanted to get a closer look at the man. See if maybe I knew him, you understand."

"Had you ever seen him before?" Michael looked over at Judge Campbell.

"Why are you asking me that, Michael?" The judge frowned. "Don't you think I'd have told somebody straight off if I'd ever seen him around Hidden Springs?"

"Nobody knew him." The sheriff gave Michael a look that said let him ask the questions. He turned to Buck. "What do you think, Buck?"

Buck had barely started on his theories about the murder when Paul interrupted to be sure they all understood he was in charge of the investigation. "Whatever you do find out when you check out those leads, Buck, you need to report directly to me immediately. Then I can decide how best to proceed on the findings. The same goes for you, Michael."

Michael managed a little nod, but Buck just glared at Paul while his knuckles turned white on his coffee cup until it looked as if he might crush the cup in his bare hand.

"Now, boys, we're all on the same team, and won't any of us forget that you're in charge, Paul. No need to make any speeches. We all want the same thing. To apprehend the responsible party as quickly as possible." Sheriff Potter smiled at Paul and then nodded toward Buck. "And I wouldn't be a bit surprised if Buck turns out to be right and this is just some kind of domestic dispute. It'll no doubt sort itself out quick enough once we get a positive ID on the victim."

"I'm working on establishing that." Paul glanced up from his notebook.

"Of course you are, Paul," the sheriff said. "And we'll help you every way we can. Mike here will let you know if anything comes in through this office."

Paul looked toward Michael without making eye contact. That was all right with Michael. They might have to work together at times, but they didn't have to like one another. Michael couldn't help it that he was a head taller than Paul or that Paul didn't get the jobs he wanted while Michael had been part of a big city police force. The fact that Michael gave up that job to come home to Hidden Springs and spend his time directing traffic and writing up fender-bender accident reports merely seemed to make Paul resent him more. And now Michael was the first officer on the scene of an actual serious crime here in Hidden Springs.

Paul studied his notebook again, then droned on about things they all already knew.

Judge Campbell stood up in the middle of Paul's monologue. "Well, I guess if that's all, I'll head back over to my office. Folks will be calling in about their potholes just to find out what's going on, but then they'll still want their potholes filled in. Nobody likes a bumpy ride into town."

When everybody except Paul laughed a little, the judge, who like the sheriff was a politician from way back and knew when to pat a shoulder or tell a joke, looked at Paul. "I'm sure you'll have our murderer behind bars in no time flat, son."

The phone rang for about the twentieth time, but this time Betty Jean didn't take on her "reassure the public" tone. She pointed the receiver at Michael. "Your Aunt Lindy."

Nobody dared suggest he not take the call until their meeting was over, especially Michael.

"Tell Malinda we've got things under control," the judge boomed as he went on out of the office.

Michael turned his back on the others and spoke into the phone. "Aunt Lindy? Is everything okay?" Aunt Lindy had been teaching algebra out at the high school since before Michael was born. Never once had she called him during school hours.

"You tell me. Are things under control the way Wilson says?" Aunt Lindy was one of the few people in Hidden Springs to call the judge by his first name. Even the judge's wife often did not.

"If the judge says it, it must be so. The sheriff and Paul have just been going over a few things to make sure we have everything covered."

Aunt Lindy's voice was crisp along the phone line. "What you're saying is that you are all sitting around Alvin's office drinking coffee while a murderer is on the loose in Hidden Springs."

"I guess that about covers it." Michael pressed the phone up closer to his ear so none of Aunt Lindy's words could leak out into the room.

"So there *was* a body on the courthouse steps. This isn't just a wild rumor circulating in the halls."

"No, it's true."

"You let someone get killed on the courthouse steps?"

"You could say that. It happened." Michael kept his voice level, conscious of the men behind him listening to his every word.

Aunt Lindy was silent for a minute, then almost as if it were an afterthought, she asked, "You are all right, aren't you?"

"Yes." Michael almost smiled. That question was the sole reason she'd called.

"Good." Her voice recaptured its briskness as she went on. "I need to get back to my classroom. The tardy bell will ring in three minutes, and there could be one child here still ready to learn something in spite of the uproar in the halls."

Aunt Lindy loved teaching. She said it was her calling. An honorable calling and every bit as important as being a preacher. Michael just wished she thought being a police officer was the same kind of honorable calling, but she didn't. At least not for Michael. She was certain the Lord had something special planned for Michael's life, and she wasn't sure that was being a police officer in Hidden Springs or anywhere else. She didn't know what it was, but she claimed if Michael listened a little harder to what the Lord might be telling him, he'd figure it out.

Michael hadn't exactly shut his ears. He went to church and tried to keep his eyes open through the sermons. Most every morning, he said a grateful prayer or two when he got up and looked out over the lake behind his log house. He aimed to live right. On the other hand, he hadn't ever asked the Lord to send him any career advice.

"You'll have them back on task in five minutes," Michael said into the phone.

"Wasted minutes," Aunt Lindy said curtly. "Students these days throw their minds away if they get the slightest chance."

"But you won't let that happen. By the way, have you seen Anthony Blake today?" He hurried the question out before she hung up.

"You know he's not in any of my classes."

"In the hall, I mean."

"I stay out of the halls as much as possible.

An old woman could get trampled out there."

"Come on, Aunt Lindy. You know none of the kids would so much as jostle you. But about Anthony. Could you check for me? See if he's there."

"I can check, but he'll be at the house tomorrow night for his lessons. I can ask him then."

Michael had talked Aunt Lindy into tutoring Anthony to keep him from flunking out of school and violating his parole agreement. "Does he ever skip those?" Michael asked.

"Of course not. He knows that's not allowed." With that, Aunt Lindy disconnected the call without so much as a goodbye.

That was Aunt Lindy. Decisive, determined, dedicated. As Michael handed the phone back to Betty Jean, he thought it was a good thing for him that she was. He owed his life to her. It was that simple. Or maybe there was nothing simple about any of it.

Seeing death always brought back the memory of the heavy blackness that had trapped him inside his head for months after the wreck when he was fifteen.

He was on the way home from church camp after three weeks as a junior counselor. His parents had been so happy to see him when they came to pick him up. His mother wanted to know all about the camp as they drove toward Hidden Springs, and Michael had tried to answer her questions even though his eyelids kept sliding shut.

The night had been cloudy, raining some, thunder rumbling in the distance. The windshield wipers swooshed back and forth, dragging against the glass whenever the rain let up a little. The road was nearly deserted, and their car lights punched holes in the dark until it almost looked as if they were in a tunnel riding through the night.

All at once lights flashed in front of them. His father had jammed on the brakes and jerked the car to the right, but the lights came straight at them. His mother's scream was the last thing he remembered.

The car crashed into a tree, killing his parents instantly, and the doctors held out little hope for Michael. It would take a miracle, they warned Aunt Lindy. Even if he kept breathing, he might never be a functioning person again.

Aunt Lindy listened and then quietly moved into his hospital room, refusing to leave. Weeks without a response hadn't discouraged her. She ignored the doctors, kept talking to him, reading to him, and exercising his arms and legs for the day when he'd regain consciousness. Her father had been a preacher. Her brother, Michael's father, had been a preacher. She not only believed in miracles, she expected them. She had no doubt the Lord would heal Michael. Long before the blackness parted, somehow Michael had been aware she was there and knew she was refusing to let him go.

❧ 6 ❧

Malinda Keane clicked off the phone in the teachers' lounge.

Thank the Lord Michael was all right. She shut her eyes and whispered a prayer for him. She'd prayed for him every day since the first time his newborn baby hand grabbed hold of her finger. Such a perfect baby. A good boy. A teenager spared death and given back for some special purpose. A fine man who would someday realize that purpose in the Lord's good time.

She shouldn't have given in to the impulse to call Michael. He wasn't a child. Hadn't been a child for many years. She'd managed to allow him to patrol the Columbus streets without calling him every hour, although sometimes worry for his safety had been like a live thing perched on her shoulder, digging its talons down all the way into her heart.

But for some reason when the rumors and stories began flying around the school about a man found shot on the courthouse steps, she hadn't been able to contain her uneasiness. Prayer hadn't helped. Telling herself not to be a meddling old lady hadn't helped. She had to know, to hear with her own ears, that Michael was not that man.

Not that she really thought he was. She told

herself he wasn't. Nobody had any reason to shoot Michael on the Hidden Springs Courthouse steps. But somebody had gotten shot there. Somebody whose family was going to hear how he died and say there wasn't any reason for it. What possible reason could there be for anybody to get shot on the courthouse steps?

When things were not lining up with cause and effect the way numbers in an algebra equation lined up, then anything could happen. Anything could have already happened. And so the uneasiness had spread inside her until she wondered if there was a reason for it. That was why she'd let her fingers punch in the sheriff's number. She could have called Michael's cell, but she hated those things. Left her own in the car during the school day. But she'd had to know.

Michael wasn't her son but near to it. After the accident that took his parents, she guided him through a kind of rebirth that made a special bond between the two of them.

Even now, more than ten years later, she still missed James and Eva. In ways, James had been her child too. He was barely eight when their mother died suddenly. Malinda had been fifteen going on thirty, or so her father always told people. He said she was born responsible. It had never felt like a compliment. Plenty of times Malinda hadn't wanted to be the responsible one. Times when she wanted to be flighty yet beloved like her mother. Or beautiful and treasured like some of her friends. Even carefree and happy the way James was then.

But a person was whoever they were. Perhaps the Lord looked ahead in her life and knew what she would need to be to do the tasks he had in mind for her. Knew that her mother would be hopeless at running a household, even when she wasn't crippled by those blinding headaches. Knew her father would lose heart for pounding pulpits and preaching repentance and would retreat from the world after her mother passed on. Knew that James would need a mother more than a sister to help him become the man the Lord wanted him to be.

Thank heaven for Eva. She was a special gift to James. Eva was as different from Malinda as two women could be, but they were alike in their devotion to the Lord and to James. From the first moment they met, they were sisters in their hearts. Malinda missed Eva every bit as much as she missed James. Maybe more. She'd known she couldn't step into Eva's place in Michael's life the way she'd stepped into her mother's place for James. She'd always been more mother to James than sister, even before their mother died.

At the same time, she hadn't been about to let Michael follow his parents into death. Not without an all-out battle. She'd prayed fervently with absolute faith the Lord would move the mountain of darkness that trapped Michael. She listened to the doctors but refused to believe them when they warned there was no hope. With the Lord, there was always hope. What medicine and doctors couldn't do, the Lord could. And the Lord had.

After weeks of no response, Michael had suddenly grasped Malinda's hand and held on as she led him slowly back through the tunnel of oblivion into life. It was longer still before he was back on his feet learning to walk again while she hovered behind him. In a sense, that's where she'd been ever since.

Not noticeably where he wouldn't be able to grow. Where he couldn't use his wings. But she'd been there putting prayers under his wings. Pushing the truth that the Lord had brought him back for a purpose. Second chances at life came with responsibilities, and in time, the Lord would show Michael the true purpose of his life.

Michael hadn't found that yet. There was nothing wrong with being a police officer. It was a respectable occupation. But Malinda was sure there was more in store for him. Their Keane ancestors had founded Hidden Springs. The Lord had led Michael back to their town. There was a reason for that. A purpose.

Malinda didn't know what that was. Michael didn't know what that was. But the Lord did.

Malinda went by the principal's office on the way to her classroom. Michael was right. No students pushed against her. Instead, an oasis of quiet followed her. That was all right with Malinda. She demanded respect. She didn't want to be her students' buddy. She was their teacher.

The secretary in the office confirmed what Michael had said. Anthony Blake was absent from school.

"Did you call his aunt?" Malinda asked.

"Why?" Angela Perry looked up at Malinda. "He's not in any of your classes, is he?"

"No, but he should be. He should have never been allowed to slide around taking algebra. He has a good mind. He should have been forced to use it."

"Right. And I did call. Anthony's name on the absentee list is always a red flag." Angela ruffled through some papers on her desk. "I took a message for Mr. Whitson. It's here somewhere."

Angela had been one of Malinda's students. Not one of her better students, but it didn't take a lot of mathematical ability to answer phones and take messages. She was cute, with a dimpled smile and curly brown hair. Cute made up for a lot when a person was sitting behind a desk greeting people.

The girl was capable, but it wasn't uncommon for Malinda's former students to become all thumbs when she was around. She waited a few seconds for Angela to find the note, but Malinda didn't have all day. "Don't you remember what the woman said?"

"Who?" Angela asked.

"Vera Arnold. Anthony's aunt." Malinda tried to keep the irritation out of her voice, but she didn't completely succeed. But who else would they be talking about?

"Oh, well, yes. But you have to remember that I've talked to dozens of people today and I thought maybe you wanted to know exactly what she said. It's been a crazy day in here with everybody asking questions about somebody getting killed at the courthouse this morning. Did that really happen?" Angela stopped shuffling through her papers and looked at Malinda again.

"So it seems." Angela's eyes widened, and Malinda could almost see the questions bubbling up to her head. She jumped in front of them. "But what about Anthony? What did Vera say?"

"You know she doesn't care where Anthony is as long as he's not bothering her. She said he left this morning the same as usual. She thought he went to school, but maybe he got sick and went to a friend's house or something. She promised to find out why he wasn't here when he came home. If he came home." Angela made a face. "It's a waste of time talking to her. She doesn't care if he comes to school or not."

"She may not, but we do. I do. If he shows up, send one of your office helpers down to let me know." Malinda tapped the counter beside Angela. "Don't forget."

"Yes, ma'am," Angela said.

As Malinda left the office, the bell was ringing. Her students were going to get a kick out of her being tardy to class. She might even let them laugh about it for one of those minutes Michael thought she'd need to get them back on task.

⇥ 7 ⇤

Back at the sheriff's office, Michael turned around to face the others with a shrug and a self-conscious grin. "Aunt Lindy heard we'd been letting people get killed on the courthouse steps, and she doesn't think that's exactly the sort of thing peace officers should allow to happen."

Sheriff Potter chuckled. "Malinda has drawn a bead on the truth there."

Paul stared straight at Michael. "I must insist we don't discuss our investigation with anybody outside the police departments."

"Sure, Paul, whatever you say." Michael took a deep breath and forced himself to unclench his fists. He walked past Paul to the door.

"Wait a minute. I'm not through," Paul started, but Michael went on out into the hall as though he didn't hear him.

Buck followed, right on Michael's heels. "I thought I was going to have to slug him before I got out of there." Buck smiled over at Michael.

"And I thought you were going to for sure. The little bozo. Who does he think he is?"

"You heard him. The officer in charge of this investigation." Michael looked over his shoulder, glad Buck had pulled the office door closed. "He must have been studying up at night on how to handle a murder just in case somebody got shot in Hidden Springs."

"Maybe he did it." Buck made a gun with his finger and thumb and pretended to shoot it.

Michael laughed. "I don't think he'd go quite that far to stir up excitement, but you never know. Anyway, the sheriff will smooth down Paul's ruffled feathers before he wakes up Chief Sibley and ushers them out the door."

"And Little Osgood won't even know what Al's doing."

"The sheriff has a knack for getting folks to do what he wants them to do."

They pushed through the front door, and Michael couldn't keep from looking over to where the body had been. A couple of men in overalls had crossed the yellow police tape, still zigzagged across the yard, to get a better look at the brownish-red smears on the post and the steps.

"Somebody needs to clean that up," Michael said.

"Oh, I don't know. It gives people something to gawk at and keeps them from pestering us for answers we don't have. At least not yet." Buck nodded toward the farmers, who didn't even look their way. "But what's this about Anthony Blake? You're talking about that kid we caught breaking into a car a couple of months back, right?"

"That's the one." Michael looked over at Buck. "Why?"

"I don't know. I just didn't expect to hear his name this morning." Buck's voice changed, became guarded. "You don't think he has anything to do with what happened back there, do you?"

"Anthony?" Michael was surprised. "No. But I saw him in the crowd this morning, and he's not supposed to skip school. Not if he wants to stay out of juvenile detention. That was one of the conditions handed down by the juvenile court judge, but you know how some kids are. There's no helping them."

"Yeah." Buck sounded relieved Michael hadn't spotted something he missed about the murder. "A hard-luck kid for sure."

"Sometimes luck has little to do with it. Anthony goes out hunting trouble."

"That's what hard-luck kids do best. I remember when his mother took off years ago. Told the kid she was going to the grocery store and left him watching television. He was there alone a couple of days before anybody knew she was gone. He was just a little fellow. Around five, I think."

"No wonder he's mad at the world." Michael

frowned. "Aunt Lindy says his mother left the same summer my folks were killed in the auto wreck."

"Yeah, that's right. Best I remember, you were hurt pretty bad in that wreck yourself. Everybody thought you might be out for the count." Buck turned and gave Michael's arm a light punch. "Glad you weren't, kid."

"Me too," Michael said. "But that summer is sort of a blank for me, so I don't remember anything about Anthony's mother leaving."

"You could ask your aunt. She could fill you in."

"I have, but she won't talk about it. Says what's in the past might as well stay there."

"Could be she's right. And I don't guess it matters all that much now. Most people figured Roxanne ran off with some man." Buck blew out a breath. "I had a hard time believing it at first. But she never did show up anywhere, so I guess she did. Still, she did act like she thought the sun rose and set on that kid. It didn't seem like something she'd do. Running off maybe, but not leaving the kid behind. That never seemed right."

"Did you know her?" Michael asked.

"Sure. What man in Hidden Springs didn't?" Buck shrugged. "She was a treat for the eyes."

"A prostitute?" Michael glanced over at Buck with raised eyebrows.

"Not as far as I know. She was a waitress, but rumor had it she made some money on the side. If she did, I never saw any proof of it, but you know how folks around here are. They pegged Roxanne back when she had that kid and wouldn't tell who the daddy was."

"You sound like you knew her pretty well." Michael stopped walking to look straight at Buck.

"Now don't be getting the wrong idea here." Buck swiped a hand across his face as if to rub away the surprising red that popped up there. "I was already married to Susan and had Billie Jo then. But sometimes when I stopped in at the Country Diner for coffee, Roxanne and me would swap kid stories, you know. She always got this different look on her face when she talked about the boy. I still can't figure her taking off without him."

"But she did," Michael said.

"That's what everybody decided."

"You didn't?"

"I don't know." Buck stared off across the street for a few seconds as though gathering his thoughts. "Somehow it struck me as odd at the time. I was new to the job then, not a detective yet, just a patrol cop. But I poked around a little. Talked to everybody who saw her that day. You know, that kind of thing. Nobody knew anything about where she'd gone. Or anything about any guy she'd been seeing. She didn't draw her money out of the bank. She didn't leave her sister any kind of note asking her to take care of the boy."

"Nothing ever turned up on her?"

"Not a thing." Buck gave his head a shake. "I figured she'd send for the boy when she got things worked out, but then she never did. Could be she got sick or something. Who knows? And then she might still show up again someday."

"I'm not sure Anthony would be glad to see her after all these years."

"Well, it's not likely to happen anyway. She's been gone too long." Buck shook his head again, slowly this time. "But that Roxanne was a looker. No matter what else anybody said about her, no one ever denied that. Long, wavy black hair, blue velvet eyes. She could have been a movie star. The boy takes after her."

Anthony's hair was black and wavy, and his eyes were a dark blue. A good-looking boy who never acted like he cared how he looked. "You know who his father is?"

"Nope, and stop looking at me that way. Roxanne and I talked. That's all. Besides, the kid was already a year old before I started working this territory. I was over in Wingate for a while."

"I didn't think it was you," Michael said. "I just thought maybe you knew who it was and that maybe whoever that was might help the boy out. Give him a little money for school or something."

"You're dreaming, Mike." Buck gave him a look. "Nobody's going to step forward and claim that kid after sixteen years. Besides, Roxanne didn't mess much with hometown folks. She latched on to the guys passing through. Said they were less trouble."

"Sounds as if she had it figured out. All except for Anthony." No wonder the kid was messed up. Deserted by his mother at five.

"Yeah. Who can figure people? Just like shooting a guy on the courthouse steps. There have to be a million better places."

"I don't know. We didn't catch him." Michael glanced back down the street toward the courthouse.

"Don't you worry about that. We will. If we can keep Little Osgood out of our way." Buck pulled his keys out of his pocket. "What are you going to do?"

"Routine stuff. Ask a few questions. Find out what people saw this morning. How about you?"

"I'll head out to the lake. See if any of the tourists came up missing today." Buck started away, then stopped. "By the way, best keep in mind this guy got shot. That means somebody shot him, so be sure your gun's loaded. Could be you might need it."

⊰⊱ 8 ⊰⊱

Michael guided his cruiser through the dusky shadows down the winding lane to his log house on the lake. He'd rather be driving his old Chevy pickup that he called Old Blue. Rust was spreading like cancer on the wheel wells and along the dent in the driver's side door where somebody had sideswiped it while it was parked up in the city. Old Blue didn't ride all that smooth, but it still got him where he needed to go when he wasn't working.

In ways, the truck had helped him fit in again when he came home to Hidden Springs. Folks saw the old truck he'd always driven and decided maybe he was the same old Michael too.

His city friends told him he was crazy to move back to the sticks. What was he going to do? Pull dandelions out of the sidewalk cracks for fun? Watch to see when the corn tasseled out? Arrest people for shooting groundhogs? They warned him his mind would dry up and blow away.

When he assured them intelligent people lived in Hidden Springs, they laughed. And they began to look at him as if he lacked some gray matter up top as well. It was easy to see they thought he lacked the courage or ambition to make it in the big world.

Michael didn't care what they thought. He was

glad to be back in Hidden Springs. He had gone to Columbus after he got out of school. A man needed to try new things, new places. At least that's what he thought then. Big towns had more opportunities. He could get more training. Be a detective on the force or even land a job with the FBI.

A man needed ambition. A man needed to amount to something. Especially if he wanted to impress certain women who moved through life to a fast tune of ambition. Women like Alexandria Sheridan. Alex's ambitions far outstripped Michael's. Right out of law school, she got a position with a high-powered law firm in Washington, DC. There wasn't any way she would ever be impressed with a guy walking a beat no matter what city he was in.

When they were teens, they used to talk about what they would do when they got out of school. But she never mentioned Hidden Springs, and Hidden Springs seemed right in the center of Michael's future. He hadn't felt that itchy, crawly feeling inside his skin that made other people jump the fences of their youth and find more exciting pastures.

Michael liked the grass fine in Hidden Springs. He especially liked the feeling he was taking care of his town, protecting people he knew and cared about, keeping the peace without having to pull out his gun.

That thought brought him up short and made him too aware of the gun on his belt. The gun had felt extra heavy ever since Buck's parting shot that morning.

It wasn't that Michael didn't like guns. He did. He liked the solid feel of a gun in his hand when he was target shooting. He enjoyed the challenge of keeping his eye true to the mark and figuring out the quirks of different firearms, especially the antique guns passed down from his Keane ancestors. Last summer he even put on the Confederate gray and carried Pascal Keane's Sharps rifle in the Civil War reenactment over at the state park in Buxley. Like Uncle Pascal, he'd been shot early on in the battle, but next year he'd been promised a longer-lived part, maybe as a Union captain like another of his ancestors, William Keane.

The only thing he didn't like about guns was actually using them in his job. Most of the time, even in the city, he was able to leave his gun in its holster and handle confrontations with his voice and confident posture. And with Pete right behind him, his gun ready in an instant, that strange gleam in his eyes warning perpetrators not to mess with him.

Then Michael found himself in that dim old warehouse looking down the barrel of his gun at that girl child. He wanted away from that. He wanted to save lives, not take lives.

He wanted to save that girl. After weeks of looking, he found her and a little brother living in the corner of another deserted warehouse. At least they'd been sleeping there. During the day, they stayed on the move. For almost a week he watched them, making sure not to let the girl spot him. He didn't want to spook her and give her a chance to disappear again. One evening he caught the little brother alone, and a sack of hamburgers and French fries were enough to win him over.

The girl wasn't as easy, but she wouldn't desert her little brother, whatever the cost. Michael did some fast talking and managed to convince her he wouldn't haul them off to social services. At least not until they talked. She stayed on her toes, ready to grab the boy's hand and take off, but then the boy handed her some fries and a cookie.

Michael wasn't sure if the chocolate chip cookie won her over or whether she was simply too tired to run. He didn't badger her with questions. Instead, he sat there with them and waited, as though he had all the time in the world. At last she started talking, and like a dam bursting, her whole story rushed out.

Her name was Hallie. The little brother was Erik. In a few months their mother was up for parole and she'd promised to get a real job when she got out and leave the drugs behind. All they had to do was hold on a little longer. Hallie scavenged food out of supermarket trash cans and stole an apple or jar of peanut butter now and again.

But then school started, and Erik cried when she said he couldn't go. He was six and wanted to learn to read, but you had to have money to go to school. For fees and lunches. That kind of stuff. Erik couldn't say he didn't have it, not without people finding out no adults were on the scene. Hallie had already lost a little sister to social services. She was determined not to lose Erik. She'd promised her mother.

That first day, Michael gave her every cent he had on him. If Pete knew, he'd tell him he was crazy, that the girl was feeding him a line. Street kids learned fast who was a prime sucker for a sob story. But some sob stories were true. So he and Preacher Dan found the two kids a place to wait out the months. Michael had financed it. The last time he heard from Preacher Dan, the mother was out and had kept her word about getting a job. Hallie was going to high school and Erik had learned to read.

Michael still sent money. Nobody knew about it but Preacher Dan. Maybe Michael couldn't make a difference in every street kid's life, but he had made a difference in Hallie's. The day she turned and looked at him in that warehouse, her life had been in his hands. Sometimes he felt as if it still was.

But he owed her something too. She was the reason he left the city before he got hardened like Pete. He was happy to be back in Hidden Springs where people didn't need a gun shoved in their faces to listen to reason. Where there was some real chance of keeping the peace.

Then what happened? Some John Doe got himself killed on the courthouse steps. A preliminary autopsy report had come in from Eagleton right before he left the office. The victim was shot in the back at close range with a Smith & Wesson .38 Special, a gun as common as fleas on a dog, even in Hidden Springs. There had to be four or five of them, confiscated for this or that reason, gathering dust in the sheriff's evidence room at the courthouse.

So knowing the type of weapon wasn't much help. They hadn't gotten an ID on the victim yet either. The man's fingerprints weren't on file in the computer system, and nobody matching his description had been reported missing.

Michael wondered again if maybe he should have stayed at the office in case something came in, but the sheriff had practically pushed him out the door. "Don't look so worried, boy. Nobody expects you to solve a murder in a day."

"I'm not so sure about that," Michael muttered. Everybody he talked to that afternoon not only wanted a suspect behind bars, they had their own theories about the murder. Some wild stories that made absolutely no sense were making the rounds, but then what kind of sense did finding a body on the courthouse steps make?

The sheriff acted like he didn't hear Michael as they headed for the back door. The other offices were already locked up, and the hall was empty except for Roy White. The janitor pushed his mop along the hallway so slowly the mop practically had time to dry out before he finished his swipe and dipped it in the bucket again.

In spite of being stooped from years of pushing a broom, Roy was still half a head taller than Michael and a full head taller than the sheriff. His long bones had so little padding that sometimes Michael expected to hear them clattering inside his skin when the old man moved, but if they did, the jangle of the huge ring of keys clipped to his belt drowned it out. Roy looked up from mopping to ask the sheriff if he was sure it was safe in the courthouse.

"Now, have you ever had anything to worry about in all the years you've been cleaning the place here, Roy?" The sheriff smiled at the man. "Just how many years is that now?"

The old man leaned on his mop handle and gave the question some thought, concentration increasing the wrinkles lining his eyes. "Well, let's see, Sheriff. How long is it you've been in office?"

"Going on twelve years," the sheriff answered.

"And you were here a good many years before that."

Michael tried not to fidget as they waited for the janitor to consider his answer. A phone rang in one of the offices, a muffled, somehow lonesome sound. Roy and the sheriff paid it no attention as they both stood there, one thinking of an answer, the other waiting for an answer he already knew.

Finally Roy said, "I reckon it was twenty-two years back in November, Alvin. It was dry that summer and the tobacco didn't bring in much that year. Me and the wife, we took this on to make a little extra money for Christmas. So we could get all the kids and grandkids something nice." The old man brushed his hand over his keys and smiled a little at the noise they made. "I'm thinking of turning in my keys come July."

"What? Retire? You can't do that, Roy," the sheriff said. "We need you."

The old man laughed with pleasure. "So do the fish, Alvin. So do the fish."

"I guess I can't fault a man for wanting to go fishing." The sheriff's laugh joined the old man's before he got serious again. "But don't you be worrying none about what happened this morning. Mike here is checking into it all for us, and he'll find us some answers." The sheriff grinned over at Michael. "Why, the boy went to school to learn to be a law officer."

Michael knew the sheriff was poking fun at him, but he just smiled and took the opportunity to ask Roy a question he should have asked him hours ago. "Did you notice anything out of the ordinary today while you were cleaning, Roy?"

"Like what, Michael?"

"I don't know. A stray cell phone. Bloodstains maybe. A gun in a trash can."

The old man chuckled. "I reckon that would be out of the ordinary all right, but no, son, I didn't see nothing like that. 'Cepting the blood on the post and porch out front and a few smudges the judge tracked in here. The only thing I might say was anywhere near to out of the ordinary was my keys. They weren't where they ought to have been when I got here this morning."

"Where were they?" Michael asked.

"Oh, they were in the supply closet but not on the hook I use. I always hang them up on the top hook. That's my hook 'cause it's higher than most folks can reach easy. Keeps them out of their way. And then I only have to carry the key to the back door and the one to the closet in my pocket when I go home."

"You think you might have hung the keys on a different hook last night by mistake?" Michael asked.

With a frown, the old man considered that. "It could've happened, I reckon, but it ain't likely. I always hang my keys on that high hook. Been doing that for years now. It'd feel funny putting them anywhere else."

"How do you think they got on the other hook then?" the sheriff asked.

"Oh, I figure somebody must have borrowed them and stuck them back on the wrong hook. Nothing to get worked up about though. Can't nobody get into that supply closet 'cept them that have a key."

"And who all is that?" the sheriff asked, more to show an interest in what the old man was saying than because he thought it was important.

"Why, you do, Alvin. And Neville and the judge and Josephine from up in the court and Wilma and Burton."

"Somebody from all the offices here in the courthouse then?" Michael said.

"That's right, son. We keep the extra toilet paper in there, and folks has got to be able to get at that." The old man laughed.

"But why would they bother your keys?" Michael said.

"They probably moved a broom or something and knocked them down. Not meaning to or anything, and then just stuck them back on a hook they could reach. Happens now and again."

It had taken another ten minutes to get away from Roy. He had to tell them why he thought some kind of extremist group was behind the murder.

"Burton says one of those bunch of crazies has been wanting to make a parade through town, and the mayor's been finding ways to put them off. So they dumped the body here as a kind of warning." The old man looked satisfied with his explanation and a little worried at the same time. Burton Fuller was the jailer, and he and Roy enjoyed figuring things out over coffee in the little kitchen above the jail behind the courthouse.

"Then how come they didn't dump the body on the city hall steps where the mayor's office is?" Michael couldn't keep from asking.

When the old man got a confused look on his face, the sheriff shot a hard look at Michael before he smoothed things over. "Now that's an idea, Roy. About the extremists. We'll be sure to check into that."

They left the old man looking satisfied with his theory again as they went on out the back door to the sound of the mop licking the floor.

Once outside, the sheriff said, "You're going to have to learn to humor folks, Mike. What might seem foolish to you makes perfect sense to them, and it's a comfort for them to think they've got things figured out."

"Sorry, Sheriff, but it's been a long afternoon and I've heard just about every wild idea you can think of, from it was escaped convicts we don't even know have escaped yet to the mob. The mob's probably the front-runner right now."

"Could be they're right, Mike. They know about as much as we do at this point. But it's better if we don't make a big mystery out of every little thing."

"What do you mean?"

"Like those keys. Roy's getting old. In all likelihood he hung those keys on a different hook himself. Not that it matters. Can't see how that could have the first thing to do with that stiff out on the steps, can you?"

"I guess not."

The sheriff clapped Michael on the shoulder. "Now go on home and get rested up so you can listen to a whole new bunch of theories tomorrow. Just think of the ideas folks'll be able to come up with after a whole night to ponder on it."

⋅⊰ 9 ⊱⋅

At the time, Michael had managed to pull out the smile the sheriff had expected, but now as his cruiser bounced around a chughole in his lane, he groaned at the thought of more half-baked theories. He had about used up all his patience that afternoon, talking to people on the street and in the stores.

As hard as it was to believe, nobody had seen or heard anything. Not even from the three businesses across from the courthouse. Jim Deatin had come in to his auto supply store about eight o'clock, but he never opened up till nine. So he'd spent the time in the back figuring out his new order and hadn't even looked out when he unlocked the front door.

The yellow lines were already flapping in the wind over on the courthouse lawn when Reece Sheridan got to his office. Reece had come in a little earlier than usual because his secretary's little boy had an ear infection, but that was still after nine. He claimed nobody ever needed a will or a deed drawn up before ten o'clock in the morning anyway, and that was about the only kind of legal work Reece did anymore. His main job these days was puttering around the lake in his boat, catching fish.

Joe Jamison got to work early, same as any other day. Since his wife died a couple of years back, Joe drank his coffee and read the paper at his shop in case someone showed up early for a trim. Joe's Barbershop had been across from the courthouse ever since Michael could remember. When he was a kid, he hated getting his hair cut there, because no matter what he told Joe, the barber invariably cut his hair the same way. Some of his friends had talked their parents into taking them to Eagleton for haircuts, but Michael's father wouldn't even consider that.

"How would we like it if Joe went to Eagleton to church?" he asked.

At thirteen, Michael hadn't cared where Joe

Jamison went to church. He just wanted a haircut that would make the girls notice him, and Joe's haircuts weren't doing the trick.

It had never happened. After the wreck, Michael had bigger worries than the right haircut. Such as his parents being gone, learning to walk when one of his legs didn't work right, and living up to Aunt Lindy's expectations. In fact, after the wreck, he had sort of liked going to Joe to get his hair cut, because at least that hadn't changed.

Joe still cut Michael's hair. However the haircut turned out, it was usually worth it in information, because a good portion of the men in Hidden Springs sat in Joe's chair one or two times a month.

Michael should have gotten his hair cut today. Joe always talked more when he was cutting hair. Instead Michael had gone in and sat in the waiting chair. Since he didn't have any customers, Joe had settled in the barber chair. His orange tabby cat that somebody had traded for a haircut several years back jumped up into his lap.

When Michael asked Joe whether he'd noticed anything unusual that morning, such as a man getting shot on the courthouse steps, Joe stroked the cat's ears and considered his answer for a long minute.

"Fact is, Mike, I was a little late this morning, and first thing, I cleaned out the litter box and put out some food for Two Bits. Then I made my coffee." Joe looked up at Michael and then back down at the cat. "That's the way I always do it. Two Bits first, then coffee."

Michael waited without prompting Joe with more questions. The little man sat ramrod straight in the chair and rubbed the cat's ears with the same precise strokes he used when he was working with his comb and scissors. Well into his sixties, he still had a full head of black hair that most folks figured he dyed, even though he wouldn't own up to it. But his customers forgave him almost anything because of the way he laughed at even the dumbest jokes.

There hadn't been any jokes or laughter that afternoon. Instead, the silence stretched out till the air in the shop was almost taut. Finally, Joe sighed. "It's a bad thing, Mike."

Suddenly the barber stood up, spilling the cat out of his lap onto the floor. Two Bits landed on his feet with an indignant yelp and haughtily stalked into the back room. Joe paid the cat no mind as he rearranged his combs and scissors on the counter in front of the mirror that covered the back wall.

Again Michael was patient, and after a while, Joe said, "I didn't really see anything though. Like I told you, I was busy with Two Bits, and by the time I turned over the open sign, the man was already there. I saw him when I pulled up the shade, but I figured he was just waiting for the courthouse to open up. You know, so he could buy his car license or something. I never gave a thought to him being dead."

Michael went over to stare out the front window. A couple of boys were working their way up the walkway to the spot where the body had been discovered. Michael ignored the boys shoving and pushing each other toward the steps and made himself think about what Joe might have seen that morning.

"I guess it would be hard to see from here that he'd been shot." Michael kept his eyes on the courthouse steps. "Miss Willadean passed right by him and thought he was drunk." Michael turned away from the window as the two boys broke and ran, as if a ghost had risen up off the steps to chase them.

Joe smiled for the first time since Michael had come in his door. "Well, you have to make allowances for Miss Willadean, and it wasn't as if she was expecting to meet up with a dead man on her morning rounds."

"That's for sure." Michael smiled too. "Had you ever seen him before?"

"Even if I had known him, I couldn't have told who he was from here. The old eyes aren't what they used to be." Joe glanced at Michael in the mirror and then turned his attention back to his combs. "I wish I could help you, Mike, but I just didn't see it happen."

Now as Michael guided his cruiser around the last and biggest chughole, something about his talk with Joe kept nagging at him. He didn't know whether it was the way Joe had avoided his eyes or something Joe had said, but Michael had the feeling Joe knew more than he was telling.

Of course, Joe never looked at you much. He mostly kept his eyes on your hair while he worked, peeking at your face in the mirror now and again as he let out any news he might have heard in tiny morsels to be considered carefully before the next morsel was offered. Michael would go get a haircut tomorrow even if he didn't need one.

He came around the curve and there, on the other side of the cedars, Aunt Lindy's car was parked in front of his house. Michael sighed. He'd have to put off the long shower and the solitude he'd looked forward to out on his back deck while he tried to make sense of everything. But it wasn't all bad. Aunt Lindy rarely came empty-handed.

He parked the cruiser next to the sporty red car she'd bought last fall and kept trying to lend him in case he wanted to use it for a date. When he reminded her that Karen didn't mind riding in his old truck, she told him somewhat pointedly that Karen Allison wasn't the only woman in the world.

Not that Aunt Lindy didn't like Karen. She did. Michael thought she even admired Karen for being the first female preacher Hidden Springs had ever had. The Presbyterian Church had called Karen straight out of seminary three years ago. Since the congregation was small, some of the less forward-thinking people in Hidden Springs said the church couldn't find a man willing to take on the pastorate. But Karen was sure the Lord had led her to Hidden Springs and had a purpose for her being there.

That might be what Aunt Lindy really couldn't stomach. That Karen Allison had paid attention to the Lord's calling when it was Michael she wanted to pay attention to the Lord's purpose in his life. She didn't think that purpose was to be a preacher's husband, even though she often said a woman had to be called to make a good preacher's wife.

Whatever the reason, she was dead set against Michael drifting into a serious relationship with Karen.

"Karen's very nice," she told Michael last week when he took her a plate of food after Karen's church had a potluck meal. The words were more condemnation than compliment. "I suppose that's not altogether bad when you have a congregation to keep happy."

"They all love her." Michael set the foil-wrapped Styrofoam plate overloaded with food on the counter. It was more than Aunt Lindy would eat in a week.

"As they should. She's the best pastor they've had for years. She's not much of a preacher, but she's always there if they call her. As I said, she's nice." Aunt Lindy made a face that didn't exactly fit with the word "nice." "Church people need nice, but you need somebody to strike sparks off you. Somebody to wake you up. Somebody who can mother town founders."

"I don't think there are any towns left to be founded." Michael hadn't bothered to hide his smile.

"Your children will be pioneers in other ways. It's the Keane family tradition."

"Not the Keane family I know," Michael teased her. "We just sort of hide out in Hidden Springs and live a lot like the guy next door."

"There are all sorts of ways to be pioneers." Aunt Lindy lifted her chin defiantly.

"You call Dad following in his father's footsteps preaching at the Hidden Springs First Baptist Church being a pioneer?"

"It was his calling. The Lord used him to make the town better. And now it's your turn. You have responsibilities to Hidden Springs and to the family name. The important thing is keeping the Keane line strong and vigorous."

"Karen's more of a pioneer than I'll ever be. A female preacher. Here in Hidden Springs."

"And who knows where the Lord might call her next? A preacher has to listen to the Lord's calling, whether that preacher is a he or she." Aunt Lindy poked Michael's chest with a bony finger. "The Lord, on the other hand, has brought you back to Hidden Springs for a reason."

"If that's true, he hasn't let me in on the secret." Michael stepped back before she could jab him with her finger again.

"He will. In his own time." Her eyes narrowed with determination. "You young people are always in such a hurry you forget to notice what the good Lord is doing in your life. The Lord wants you right here in Hidden Springs."

Michael knew when to give up arguing with her. Instead, he had smiled. "You should have gotten married and had kids of your own. They couldn't have helped being pioneers."

"There was a man once a long time ago." The sadness that had flashed across her face stopped Michael's teasing. "He got killed in the service, and I suppose I never really gave anyone else a chance after that. But make no mistake, I do know what love is supposed to be, Michael, and I don't want you settling for anything less, simply because it's convenient."

Now Michael got out of his cruiser and slammed his door. The noise brought Aunt Lindy to the front door. He wasn't really surprised to see her there. She'd want to know what was going on, but she would never stoop to listening to rumors. Michael thought about Paul Osgood ordering him

85

not to discuss the case with anyone, but Michael didn't know anything to tell her the rest of the town didn't already know anyway.

Michael's black Labrador appeared out of the night to bang into him. Every time he came home, Jasper greeted him as if he carried a dozen dog biscuits in his pockets, and every time it lifted Michael's spirits.

Tonight he rubbed Jasper's ears a couple of extra times just because he knew it would aggravate Aunt Lindy. Then with a grin, he went on up the three steps and across the wooden porch. He and Aunt Lindy were the ones who struck sparks off one another like steel on steel, and he wasn't sure which of them enjoyed it the most.

⋰ 10 ⋰

Aunt Lindy offered her cheek up to Michael for a kiss. "Dog got paw prints on your uniform again."

"What can I say? He likes me." Michael brushed at the dirt on his pants. "And his name's Jasper."

Aunt Lindy pretended not to hear. She failed to find it amusing that Michael had named his dog after their town-founding ancestor, Jasper Keane, so she simply refused to acknowledge the dog's name. Jasper didn't mind. He loved Aunt Lindy only second to Michael. Not that he piled into her the way he did Michael. The dog would slide to a stop several feet away from Aunt Lindy, then slowly approach her with his tail madly flapping back and forth and his whole body quivering in anticipation of a pat on the head or any word of greeting Aunt Lindy might care to give him.

Now, without saying anything more, Aunt Lindy watched Michael unbuckle his holster belt and hang it on the hook just inside the door. While he always shed his gun as soon as he got home, tonight he felt doubly relieved to have the weight of the weapon gone.

Some of that feeling must have shown on his face, because Aunt Lindy asked, "You are all right, aren't you, Michael?"

Michael smiled down at her. She was so small, only a couple of inches over five feet, and just as her manner was always contained, so was her appearance. Years ago she must have looked in her mirror and decided beauty was not within her grasp so she had given up any pursuit of it. Yet the passing years had stolen none of the intensity of her blue eyes and had given her a certain dignity that was perhaps better than the fleeting beauty of youth.

"I'm fine, Aunt Lindy." Michael touched her arm. "You didn't have to drive all the way out here to check on me."

"I'm not so old that I can't drive out in the country at night if I want to." She sounded cross, but he caught a glimpse of a smile lifting up the corners of her lips as she turned toward the kitchen. "I brought you some pot roast."

With her customary efficiency, she set the food on the table while he washed up. Then she sat across from him and watched him eat, as she had hundreds of times in the past. He could almost see the questions she wanted to ask about the murder circling in her head, but instead she pretended this was a night like any other. "Karen called. Said you didn't answer your cell."

"I'll call her back later." She would have questions too. Everybody had questions he couldn't answer. He buttered a roll and waited for Aunt Lindy to start asking hers.

She chatted about everything but the murder until he finished off the last bite of chocolate pie. Then she got down to business. "Have you identified the victim?"

"Not so far as I know. Paul's in charge of the case. He may have found out who the man was and not shared that information yet." Michael looked over at Aunt Lindy. "He gave us all strict orders not to discuss the case with anyone."

"That's sensible." Aunt Lindy leaned back and folded her arms across her chest. "The town's buzzing with rumors enough, without the police adding to them. By the time the last bell rang at school, some of the students were almost afraid to go outside. Why, I can't imagine. The killer wasn't likely to be hiding behind the bushes in front of the school."

"And you, Aunt Lindy? What do you think? Do you believe he might still be hiding out somewhere in Hidden Springs?"

"What makes you think the murderer is a he?" She raised her eyebrows at him.

"I don't know." Michael shrugged a little. "All I actually know for sure is that a man apparently got shot right in the middle of Hidden Springs without anybody seeing anything. As impossible as that seems."

"You'll uncover some leads in due time." She reached across the table to pat his hand. "Perhaps if you knew why the poor man was in Hidden Springs."

"We might have a better idea of that once we find out who he is." Michael pushed his empty plate away. "You're going to make me fat with these pies, Aunt Lindy. Did you make it?"

"Don't be silly." She frowned at him as she stood up and reached for his dirty plate and saucer. "I bought it from Evelyn Higby. She enjoys baking."

Michael blocked her hand with his. "I'll take care of these."

She gave the dishes a look, as though sure they'd sit where they were until they took root, but she didn't reach for them again. Instead she picked up her jacket.

Michael came around the table to hold the jacket while she shoved her arms into the sleeves.

"You'll need to come by the house tomorrow night to talk to Anthony." She looked around at Michael. "How did you know he wasn't at school?"

"I saw him in front of the courthouse this morning after the body was discovered."

Aunt Lindy drew in a quick breath. "You surely don't think he could have anything to do with that."

"No. Anthony does seem to chase after trouble, but I don't think he'd shoot anybody."

Aunt Lindy buttoned up her jacket. "He's going to find trouble with me. He knows he's not to skip school. After school, I called his aunt, but she didn't know where he was or seem to care very much."

"No surprise there. Anthony hasn't exactly been an easy kid to handle."

"I suppose that's true." Aunt Lindy sighed a little as she straightened her jacket collar. Then she reached over to touch Michael's cheek. "Not all aunts are so blessed with their nephews."

Tender remarks were rare for Aunt Lindy, so Michael seized the moment to grab her in a bear hug and lift her off her feet.

"For goodness' sake, Michael. Put me down. I'm not your teddy bear." Back on her feet, she smoothed down her hair and straightened her jacket. "Finding that body must have caused you to revert to adolescence."

"That could be," Michael admitted. "I guess I thought things like that wouldn't happen here the way they did in the city, and then some guy gets shot right on the courthouse steps. Why would anybody kill somebody there?"

"Why does anybody murder anybody any-where?" Aunt Lindy counted off the reasons on her fingers. "Fear, greed, jealousy, revenge, or perhaps simple meanness."

"But why chance shooting somebody right in the middle of town? Why not somewhere out of town where there wouldn't be so much chance of witnesses?"

"Good question, Michael." Aunt Lindy slipped into her teacher's voice. "Now find the answer."

"I told you Paul's handling the case."

Aunt Lindy raised her eyes toward the ceiling. "Pretend what you like, but we both know Paul Osgood couldn't catch a Peeping Tom if he saw one standing on a stepladder peering straight at someone's window, much less a murderer."

Michael didn't see any reason to dispute that as Aunt Lindy went out the door. Like always, she had the "straight of it," the way the judge had said earlier that day.

He watched her lights go out of sight up his lane and had to fight the urge to follow her to be sure she made it home safely. But if she spotted him behind her, he'd never hear the last of it. More than once, she'd told him, in no uncertain terms, that she had taken care of herself for years without his help and was capable of doing so for several more years to come.

He would have to content himself with calling her later. There was no real reason to worry about her. If anybody was safe in Keane County, it was Aunt Lindy. She'd taught almost everyone there at one time or another, and she generally remembered not only their names but the kind of student they'd been. No one would hurt her. No one who knew her, but there could be a stranger in town. One who was a murderer.

The thought barely slipped through his mind before he could almost hear Aunt Lindy's voice chasing after it. *What makes you think the murderer is a stranger?*

Michael shook the thought away, tired of thinking about any of it. He wanted to push aside the memory of the surprised look on the dead man's face as if his last thought was that this wasn't supposed to happen. That's how Michael felt. It wasn't supposed to happen. Not in Hidden Springs.

If only he could go back to yesterday when his biggest problem was figuring out who stole Bonnie Wireman's laptop. He really hoped it wasn't Anthony Blake.

He liked Anthony in spite of the boy's

determined effort to keep him from it. What was it Buck had said about him? A hard-luck kid. That was true enough. Anytime there was a report of vandalism or petty theft, Anthony was first on everybody's suspect list. But surely he had nothing to do with the man on the courthouse steps.

Yet something bothered Michael about the way Anthony ducked out of sight when Michael spotted him. It was more than getting caught skipping school. Anthony would have simply dared Michael to do something about that, but this morning the boy hadn't looked defiant. Rather he'd looked . . . Michael searched his mind for the right word and was surprised when it came to him. Confused. The boy looked confused.

Michael carried the dishes to the sink. As he dumped them in, he caught sight of his own reflection in the kitchen window. Maybe when he'd thought Anthony looked confused, it was just his own expression reflecting back to him. Maybe murder was supposed to be confusing. Surprising, confusing, and frightening.

Then again, could be the boy had seen something. If so, Michael would have to find out what. Tomorrow. Till then he'd put it out of his mind and call Karen.

Karen did have questions, but when he didn't have answers, she just said she'd pray for the victim's family whoever they were. Then she talked about the play they planned to go see on Thursday night and if he'd be able to help with the youth picnic on Sunday.

As they talked, he pictured her honey-brown hair hanging loosely over her shoulders. She'd have on her slightly ratty red warmups while she studied for her next sermon. Her Bible would be there beside her and she would be skimming Scripture verses or making notes as they talked. It was a talent of hers, being able to think about two things at once.

Michael sometimes wished he could get all her attention, but even when they were alone together, she seemed to have some other thoughts in reserve that she wasn't ready to share. He told her that once. She hadn't denied it, but simply smiled a little sadly and insisted it was a fault they shared.

Perhaps she was right. He was fond of Karen, but he shied away from any talk of love or marriage. She never spoke of anything more than friendship between them either. No strings. No demands. Just easy companionship for a dinner out or a movie. Yet it seemed possible they might eventually drift toward a more serious relationship the way the whole town seemed to think they should. All except Aunt Lindy.

Later as the water flowed over Michael in the shower, he wondered if he should try to take that next step with Karen. After all, hadn't he come back to Hidden Springs looking for the kind of settled happiness he remembered his mother and father having? Happiness had almost radiated from them. They were in love with each other. They were pleased with Michael for a son. They were content with their church and the church people who were the same as family to them. They were even happy with Aunt Lindy in spite of the way she tried to shake things up from time to time.

She accused them of being afraid to try new things. She claimed that simply wrapping oneself in happiness could be mind-numbing. Michael's father would smile at her and say there were worse things than being numb with happiness.

As the steam rose around him, Michael began to feel a little numb himself. He twisted the hot water faucet off and let cold water dash him awake.

His skin was still tingling when he went out on the deck, where the gentle sounds of the spring night surrounded him. With Jasper stretched out at his feet, Michael thought through what he knew about the murder, but nothing came one bit clearer. The victim was a John Doe. There were no suspects. No witnesses. No murder weapon. No leads.

All he had were two people who hadn't wanted to meet his eyes. By the time he and Jasper went inside, he was almost ready to believe the mob or maybe the CIA *had* done it. Never mind why they'd picked the Hidden Springs Courthouse steps to dump the body. That was one of those details regular folks ignored when they were working out their theories. Tonight he'd be a regular folk himself. Searching out answers that made sense could wait for morning.

The next day Michael went through the back door into the courthouse the same as every morning. But this time he paused in the hallway to listen.

In the sheriff's office, Betty Jean was making coffee. The container made a thud when she put it back in the cabinet. The clerks in Neville Gravitt's office were turning on their computers, electronic beeps signaling the beginning of the workday. A phone rang in the judge's office, but no one was there yet to answer it. Somewhere in the back of the building, Roy's keys jangled on his belt.

Normal sounds. The same sounds he heard the morning before when a dead man was on the steps out front. Michael glanced at his watch and wondered if Miss Willadean would appear at the courthouse at nine sharp as usual. Of course after yesterday, she had probably taken to her bed with the vapors or was still on the telephone. Maybe both. Sixteen minutes from now, he'd at least know the answer to that particular question.

Betty Jean looked up from her newspaper when Michael came through the door and nodded toward his desk. "Hank got the paper out early this morning, so I bought you a copy. It's in the

Eagleton News too, but just one paragraph, no pictures."

Michael unfolded the *Hidden Springs Gazette* and the black headline jumped out at him. BODY FOUND ON COURTHOUSE STEPS.

Betty Jean put her copy down long enough to get a cup of coffee. "The picture of you is nice." She peered at the paper as she sat back down. "Thank goodness I came back inside before Hank pointed that camera at me. I look like a cow in pictures." Betty Jean took a sip of coffee. "But you look good. The way an officer of the law should look. Concerned, serious, in control."

Michael scanned the pictures on the front page. The biggest one was of the body being loaded into the hearse. Hank would get complaints about that. A hometown weekly paper was supposed to be different from the big-town dailies that might print that kind of thing. Then again, maybe this would be different since nobody knew the deceased.

At the bottom of the page were a couple of smaller pictures. One showed Paul Osgood talking to Miss Willadean, and another caught Michael standing by the bloodstained post after the body had been taken away. The bloodstains looked like smudges of ink on the paper. The caption under the picture identified Michael as the first law officer on the scene. Michael studied his own face in the picture and tried to see the in-control look Betty Jean said he had, but all he could see was a baffled expression.

He looked up from the paper. "Any new developments this morning? No new bodies on the steps?"

"Nope. I peeked out there when I got here to be sure. Felt silly doing it, but I did it anyway."

"You probably weren't the only one who looked." Michael smiled a little, remembering his own urge to check out front. "Anything else?"

"Nothing except Paul Osgood called a few minutes ago. Something about being sick. I don't know. I never talk to him any longer than I have to."

"Paul's not that bad," Michael said.

"You talk to him then." Betty Jean turned back to her paper and coffee. "Boy, I sure could use a doughnut this morning."

"Go up to the Grill and get one. I'll watch the office till you get back," Michael offered innocently, as if he didn't know Betty Jean was on one of her periodic diets, this time a little more seriously than usual because she was sure that the new teacher at the middle school would ask her out if only she were a little slimmer.

Betty Jean glared at him. "Go soak your head in a bucket. Or better yet, call Paul Osgood up and find out his marching orders for you today." When she flipped open the newspaper, it crackled loudly. Then as quickly as she'd snapped at him, she was laughing. "Wait till you see the picture Hank put in here of Paul and Buck going at it. Sheriff Potter's got a hand on each guy's arm, and it looks like he's barely preventing the second homicide of the day."

"Hank likes to stir things up. I don't even want to read what he quotes us as saying. Worst thing about it, we probably said every word." Michael skimmed the article, glad he spotted his name only a couple of times.

"Oh, it's not too bad. He just keeps harping on how nobody knows who, what, or why about any of it."

"Truth in journalism." Michael turned over to the back page. "Great picture of Lester patrolling the police lines."

"I saw it. We won't be able to live with him," Betty Jean said.

"It'll make his day for sure." Michael put the paper down. "Any other calls?"

"Just Miss Willadean. She wants to know if it's safe for her to come to the courthouse."

"What did you tell her?"

"What do you think? That the brave and mighty Deputy Sheriff Keane would be in soon, and she had absolutely nothing to fear." Betty Jean lowered her paper and looked across at him, her eyes suddenly serious. "You don't think she does, do you?"

"Of course not," Michael said quickly. "It's

probably the way Buck says. Some kind of domestic quarrel that just happened to come to a head here in Hidden Springs."

"On the courthouse steps?"

"Maybe the wife decided on a more final separation. Who knows?"

"Not you obviously." Betty Jean turned her attention back to her paper.

Michael looked at his watch. It was almost nine. "Did Miss Willadean buy it? Is she coming?"

"I guess we'll know in a few minutes," Betty Jean answered without looking up.

Michael picked up the phone and pressed the speed-dial button for the city police station. Chief Sibley said Paul had some kind of stomach bug and wasn't able to come in to work. But if Michael had anything to report, he could call Paul at home.

"He said not to worry about catching him at a bad time, if you know what I mean." The chief laughed a little. "He'll have his phone with him in the john. You have his number, don't you?"

"I do." Just because he had the number didn't mean he'd use it, but no need telling the chief that. "Did Paul get an ID on the guy?"

"Not yet," the chief said slowly. "Look, Michael, I don't know how long Paul's going to be, well, out of commission, so why don't you just run things out of the sheriff's office there till he gets back."

"If you say so, Chief, but don't worry. We'll

keep Paul posted. You heard anything from Buck this morning?"

"Buck isn't gonna be reporting in to Paul." Chief Sibley snorted. "You know that. He has his own way of doing things."

The Christian Church clock started chiming down the street as Michael put the phone down. Before two chimes sounded, Miss Willadean's heels clicked through the front door. Betty Jean grinned over at Michael when Miss Willadean's yoo-hoo to Neville at the county clerk's office carried down the hall.

Then the little lady came on back to step into their office and glare at Michael. She had on a lavender suit with a deep purple pillbox hat that had to be fifty years old, perched a bit haphazardly on her tightly curled hair.

"Good morning, Miss Willadean," Michael said. "Is everything all right today?"

"No indeed, it's not all right." She pointed toward the front of the courthouse. "There are bloodstains on the post out front. It makes a person tremble to walk past it."

"Yes, ma'am. I'll see if Roy can take care of that today."

"I should think so. What about you?" She sniffed loudly and gave her head a little shake. Her hat slid to the side. "You do know a murderer is on the loose."

"Yes, ma'am. We are aware of that."

"Well, isn't it time you did something about it then?" She shoved her hat back in place, upsetting a few curls in the process. She turned her glare on Betty Jean. "Where is Sheriff Potter anyway?"

"He'll be in soon, Miss Willadean. Did you think of something else to tell him about what happened?" Betty Jean picked up a pen as though ready to take notes. Michael was impressed that she kept a smile off her face.

"I have something to tell him all right. We elected him to keep the citizens of this county safe and not let people get shot on the courthouse steps." She slid a purple-flowered handkerchief out of her pocket and touched her eyes. "Oh dear, I could hardly sleep last night thinking about that poor man."

She was still sniffling when Lester came in from his crossing guard duty and pushed in front of her to get to the supply cabinet. "Excuse me, Miss Willadean. I need to get some parking tickets."

"We don't write parking tickets, Lester," Michael said. "The city police do that."

"Well, I'm writing this one." Lester kept digging around in the cabinet until he came up with a ticket book. "That car's been there too long. And it's not even a local car."

While Lester lacked a little in a lot of departments, he did know his cars. He kept up with what the townsfolk drove from stopping and waving them past at the school crossing.

"What car?" Michael silently berated himself for not checking out the parking lot already. What did he think? The man had dropped out of the sky?

"A Buick. Blue. The big model," Lester said. "License number CDF-149."

"You're right, Lester. Go on out and ticket it." After Lester hurried back outside, Michael went around his desk to put an arm around Miss Willadean's shoulders. "Now, Miss Willadean, I know how upset you are and with reason. But as you said, it's time we got busy keeping the streets of Hidden Springs safe."

She blustered a little but allowed him to usher her out of the office. He watched her go up the hall, where she stopped to wave her hankie at poor Neville. Back in the office, Betty Jean ran the license plate number. It took only a few minutes to find out the car was registered to a Jay Rayburn of West Chester up in the northern part of the state.

Out at the parking lot, Lester was sticking the ticket under one of the windshield wipers when Michael got there. The paper flapped a little in the breeze, a useless piece of paper. Nobody would ever collect this ticket.

Michael tried the door and found it unlocked. Not only that, but the keys were pitched onto the floorboard. Obviously, the driver hadn't been worried about crime in Hidden Springs. A fatal error on his part. The car smelled of fast-food fries and coffee. A few shirts and pants hung on a rack across the backseat and a duffel bag held underwear, socks, and a shaving kit. A pair of brown shoes were on the back floorboard. Several bundles of rubber-banded slick brochures with pictures of office printers on the front were stacked in the passenger-side front seat.

The console had a supply of napkins, a couple of ink pens, and some CDs. Country music. No phone. If the man had a phone, and surely he did, the murderer must have taken it.

Michael ran his hand under the seat and touched the wallet he hadn't dared hope to find. He opened it and the dead man stared up at him from the driver's license, but there was no surprise on his face in this picture. Just an ordinary guy with a smile.

⊰ 11 ⊱

After that, everything was almost too easy, and before noon, Michael knew not only who the victim was but a little something about him, even if he still didn't know why he ended up dead on the courthouse steps.

Jay Rayburn was a printer salesman and technician for TEKCO, a company based in Louisville. When Michael called the number on the back of the brochures in Rayburn's car, the man's supervisor made all the expected sounds of surprise, but he couldn't really help Michael with much information. The supervisor had been with the company only a few months and hadn't actually talked to Rayburn face-to-face but twice. Rayburn was on the road most of the time. However, he could connect Michael with a secretary, Lisa Williams, who'd started with TEKCO about the same time as Jay Rayburn, some twenty years ago. He put Michael on hold while he broke the news about Jay's death to the woman.

At first the secretary was so shocked she only managed to squeak out the words that it couldn't possibly be true. But after a few minutes, she regained enough composure to answer Michael's questions.

The next of kin was a daughter, Amy. Lisa Williams said the girl was married to a man named Cartwright, just like on that old television show *Bonanza*. That's why she could remember the name. Jay himself was divorced. For ten years at least. Maybe longer. She couldn't say for sure. Time went by so fast. His ex-wife had remarried after their divorce. Her name was Alice. Alice Hancock . . . Hansford. Something like that.

The secretary didn't have any idea where the ex-wife lived now. Jay had an apartment in West Chester, but he wasn't there much. Always on the road. The daughter got married a few years ago, and Lisa Williams was pretty sure she lived in Cincinnati. There was also a son, Jimmy. The last time Jay mentioned him, the boy was out in California. Lisa Williams didn't think Jay heard from him very often since he didn't talk about him much.

No, as far as she knew, Jay hadn't been in a relationship with anybody. Of course, he was on the road practically all the time, but if he had a girlfriend, she didn't know about it. She laughed when Michael asked if there was any kind of romantic entanglement between her and Rayburn. She let Michael know she'd been happily married for thirty-five years. Her laugh was clean and honest, with nothing hidden behind it.

The laugh cut off abruptly as the woman remembered Jay Rayburn was dead. No, the company didn't supply cell phones for their people. Part of their cost-cutting efforts. But yes, Jay did have one. She could give Michael the number. She thought it was the kind you bought with airtime loaded on it instead of one with a contract.

When Michael asked if that was because the man didn't have good credit, her voice became a shade cooler as she admitted that might have been the case. In the last few weeks, a few creditors had called the office in an attempt to track Jay down, but she was sure it was nothing major. Some shaky investments probably. Jay was always talking about someday striking it rich, but she figured that meant he was playing the lottery in some of the states he went through.

No, she had no idea who would want to kill him, her voice sad again. Jay had been a nice guy, quick with a joke and a smile and always ready to admire a new picture of her kids or grandkids. He remembered their names too. He had a good head for details. He practically lived on the road, but he seemed to like it. Said it gave him a chance to make friends all over.

She didn't think their company had any clients in Hidden Springs, but she would be glad to email Michael a list of the companies they did business with in the Eagleton area. She could probably come up with most of the places Jay had stopped last week, but Jay kept his own schedule. So she might miss some. When Michael said he didn't find an appointment book in the car, Lisa Williams said Jay used a phone app for that. He wasn't the greatest with paperwork, but he got the job done. That was good enough for his bosses. Jay was one of their best technicians.

Of course she'd be more than willing to answer any other questions Michael might have later on. She took down his number in case she thought of something that might be of help. It was bad enough when somebody was killed in a car wreck or something like that, Lisa Williams said, but to think about somebody you know being murdered, well, that was just too hard to believe.

Michael set Betty Jean to tracking down an

address for the daughter before he called Chief Sibley to tell him they had an ID.

"I'll let Paul know when he gets to feeling better. I talked to Caroline awhile ago," the chief said. "She says Paul's suffering something awful. Thinks it might be food poisoning, and if he doesn't get better soon, she's going to make him go to the emergency room over in Eagleton."

Michael made some all-purpose sympathetic noises and tried not to be glad Paul was sick. But the truth was, he hadn't looked forward to playing follow the leader in this investigation with Paul Osgood, the leader. Aunt Lindy was right. The man couldn't catch a Peeping Tom.

After he told the chief goodbye, Michael stared at the phone and wondered if he should try Buck Garrett's cell number again. Surely Buck wasn't sick too, but sick or not, he wasn't bothering to check in.

Michael didn't like the feeling he was withholding information from Buck about the investigation. Besides, he wanted to hear what Buck had to say about it all. Nobody ever wondered if Buck knew what he was doing. He was every inch a law officer and good at his job.

Buck's eyes had taken on a special gleam the day before when they were talking about the murder. It was almost as if Buck considered the homicide some kind of challenge to see which man found the answer first. Michael smiled. Buck wouldn't be happy when he found out Michael—better yet, Lester Stucker—had come up with the first real breakthrough.

Michael's smile widened. Since Buck wasn't answering his cell, he'd send Lester out to the cluster of motels, gas stations, and restaurants around the interstate exit to see if he could find him. Lester had a few hours before his crossing guard duty that afternoon. Buck wouldn't be happy to be chased down by Lester, but it would serve him right for not keeping in contact.

At her desk, Betty Jean scrolled through pages on her computer. She was a wizard at tracking down information and had a way of finding out more than he even knew to ask.

He looked over her shoulder. "How long before you have something?"

She frowned up at him. "This kind of thing takes time. You can't expect to find what you need without having to search a little. Now quit watching over my shoulder. You know I hate that."

"Right." Michael nodded. "Then I'll be at Joe's. I'm going to get a haircut."

"Didn't you just get a haircut last Monday?" Before he could answer, a new screen flipped up on her computer and she waved Michael out the door.

When he passed the judge's office, Judge Campbell hurried out to walk with him toward the front door. "Alvin tells me you got a name on the poor soul who was shot out front yesterday," the judge boomed. If anybody in the courthouse hadn't heard the news, they knew it now.

"Thanks to Lester. He spotted his car in the parking lot."

"Was there anything in the car?" the judge asked as they went outside. "I mean anything that might help you figure out who shot the man."

"Nothing so far, Judge. But we're bound to come across some kind of lead sooner or later. Hidden Springs is a little town. Somebody will have seen something." Michael tried to sound confident. "We'll catch whoever did it."

"I have no doubt at all you'll have the perpetrator in jail in no time flat." Judge Campbell clapped him on the shoulder. "Of course, if this was the big city, we'd just think it was a street mugging that got out of hand. Could be this Rayburn fellow, that was his name, wasn't it?"

"Yes. Jay Rayburn." There was no reason to keep that a secret.

"Well, then it could be this Rayburn fellow was even trying to rob somebody else when he got shot. He could have been asking for it."

"Then where's the person who shot him?" Michael asked.

"I don't know. They might have run away. Scared maybe. It could have happened that way. Bad things don't just happen in the big towns, you know."

Michael shook his head a little. "I don't think that's what happened, Judge. Rayburn had a regular job as a printer technician and salesman. I don't think he'd have been trying to rob anybody here in Hidden Springs."

"Sometimes people aren't what they seem." The judge's voice dropped to an almost normal volume. That only happened when he was the most serious. "He was here for some reason."

"That's true. We just don't know what that reason was."

When they reached the Main Street sidewalk, the judge put his hand on Michael's arm. "Come on up to the Grill with me and grab a sandwich. My treat."

"Thanks anyway, Judge, but I'm going to see if Joe is busy. Thought I'd get a trim."

"I don't think he's there." The judge glanced across the street at Joe's Barbershop and then looked at Michael. "Besides, your hair looks fine. Plenty short."

"Oh, you know how it is. I've got a big date coming up and I want to look nice." Michael ran his hand through his hair.

"With that sweet little Karen Allison, I guess." The judge was smiling again. "When are the two of you going to quit this pussyfooting around and tie the knot?"

Michael smiled back at him. "I don't think we're ready for that."

"What are you waiting for? Lightning to strike?" The judge chuckled. "That's the way it always was with Malinda. There was a time, you know, when I had my cap set for her. But she said she had to have fireworks and I guess I never got her fuse lit."

"Really?" The idea of a long-ago romance between the judge and Aunt Lindy was something Michael had never considered.

The judge's smile stayed firmly in place. "I expect it's just as well. I'm not so sure Malinda would have made a very good politician's wife. Too ready to speak her mind."

"She does say what she thinks. But here in Hidden Springs, everybody might have voted for you because they would be afraid to go against her."

"That could be." The judge laughed easily. "But between you and me, and I wouldn't want this to get out yet, there's a good chance the party is going to ask me to run for state representative next term. You know Representative O'Neal is retiring."

"Well, that's great, Judge. You've got my vote."

The judge slapped Michael on the back. "I appreciate that, Mike, but remember mum's the word. And it might not be a good idea to mention what I said about Malinda to her either. Things with me and Malinda never really got much past the 'wondering if it might be a good idea' stage, if you know what I mean. And what with her and June being such good friends, we wouldn't want to muddy the waters at this late date, now would we?"

"Not me." Michael barely kept from smiling. He couldn't imagine the judge's wife being jealous of Aunt Lindy, but if the judge wanted to believe that might be possible, then he wouldn't spoil his fun.

The judge clapped him on the back again and went on up the street. Michael headed toward Joe's shop. The judge was right. Joe wasn't there. The blinds were shut, and a note was stuck to the door.

"Gone to visit my sister."

The note bothered Michael. Joe didn't often take a day off, and when he did, everybody in town knew all the details of where he was going and how long he'd be gone days before he left. But Joe hadn't said a thing about going out of town yesterday when Michael had been in his shop.

Michael went into Reece Sheridan's office beside the barbershop. From the way unopened mail was piled on the secretary's desk, it looked as if Janelle's little boy must still be sick. Michael went on back to Reece's office, where the lawyer was dozing in his chair with Two Bits curled in his lap. Michael rapped lightly on the door facing.

Reece opened his eyes, almost as though he'd just had them closed in deep thought rather than being asleep. "Michael, I'm afraid you caught me napping." He grinned sheepishly. "I miss Janelle out front. She wears those clickety high heels that always wake me up before she gets back to my office to tell me somebody's here."

Michael laughed. "Guess I should have stomped a little coming down the hall. I was coming over to get a haircut, but I see Joe's closed shop and left you holding the cat."

Reece stroked the sleeping cat lightly. "Joe's gone to see his sister, Elizabeth. The one down in Tennessee."

"Sort of a sudden trip, wasn't it? I mean, for Joe."

"She's been sick, and he said he got word she was some worse. Said he had to go check on her. Asked me to watch Two Bits for a few days. Joe told me to just leave him in the barbershop, but I didn't want the poor thing to get lonesome over there all by himself. So I brought him over here for the day."

"He looks content enough."

"Just like me, eh?" Reece laughed a little. Folks in Hidden Springs had been bringing their problems to Reece Sheridan for more than forty years, and in all that time, Michael doubted he'd made even one enemy. The worst anybody could say about him was that he kept his best fishing spots secret.

"You said it. Not me."

Reece's laugh settled in the deep creases around

his eyes to let his smile linger on his face. "Alex would say too content. Did I tell you she's coming down for a visit this week?"

Alex Sheridan was Reece's niece. Until she went away to college, she'd spent at least a month every summer in Hidden Springs at Reece's house across the street from Michael. On those long summer days, the two of them had been practically inseparable, solemnly vowing one day to be friends forever and the next day vowing with considerably more heat to never speak to one another again.

After the wreck, Alex had written him every day even before he came out of the coma because she thought somebody needed to keep him up on the important things happening in the world. Not just the headlines but more obscure news about endangered panda bears, what color fingernail polish was all the rage, how the rain forest was disappearing, and which songs were number one. Old-fashioned handwritten letters. They were still at Aunt Lindy's house somewhere.

"Is Alex keeping things under control up in Washington, DC?" Michael asked.

"She says she's giving it her best shot." Reece shook his head. "Don't tell her I said this, but I think all the politicking is getting to her. I told her to chuck it all and move down here. I'd hang out a new shingle. Sheridan and Sheridan."

Michael laughed. "She'd have us whipped into

shape in less than ten minutes. Then what would she do?"

Michael didn't say what he really thought. That Alex would never be happy in a small town like Hidden Springs. But then again, maybe people had said the same about him a couple of years back, and look at him now. Just about as content as Reece Sheridan.

"Sometimes things aren't all that quiet here in Hidden Springs." The smile leaked off Reece's face.

"I guess that's true enough this week," Michael admitted reluctantly.

Reece looked up at him from under bushy white eyebrows. "You think your little friend Karen would mind if you took Alex out one night while she's here? You know, just to show her a good time. I'm not much for the nightlife anymore, and I don't want Alex to get too bored."

"Sure. Karen can go with us."

"Well, that's an idea." Reece tried to sound enthusiastic, but he couldn't entirely hide a flicker of disappointment. Michael did his best not to smile at the thought of Reece matchmaking for him and Alex. He remembered Alex the last time he saw her. That was before he left Columbus to come back to Hidden Springs.

She told Michael in no uncertain terms he could do better than walk a beat as a police officer. It wasn't too late for him to study law himself. Then he could be a district attorney if he wanted to protect society. Her blue-gray eyes had flashed as she'd lectured him on his lack of ambition. After she was talked out, he simply smiled at her and told her she was going to be one fine trial lawyer. She surrendered the argument with the comment that she supposed he could work up through the ranks to police commissioner somewhere.

Michael's smile slipped out. There wasn't much to work up to in Hidden Springs. He was in for sore ears when he saw Alex. Maybe he really would take Karen along for a buffer.

Michael shook the thought of Alex away. He'd worry about that battle when she got to town. Right now he had other things to worry about.

"Did Joe tell you when he'd be back?" Michael asked.

"Said it'd be according to how his sister was doing."

"Did he seem particularly worried about anything when he talked to you?"

"Other than his sister?" Reece frowned a little as he thought about Michael's question, then shook his head. "Not that I noticed."

"Did he say anything about the man getting shot yesterday? I thought maybe he might be upset about that."

"I'd say we're all upset about that. Somebody getting murdered right across the street from you can bother a man's sleep for a while. But I didn't notice anything out of the ordinary about Joe, if that's what you mean. Why do you ask?" Slowly, as they talked, the lawyer's eyes had become thoughtful.

"I don't know. He just didn't seem to be his usual self yesterday when I talked to him. I wondered if maybe he'd told you what was bothering him. Everybody else in Hidden Springs does."

"I guess I do have good ears. Not a bad thing for a lawyer." Reece was quiet a minute as though replaying his conversation with Joe over in his head. "But no, Joe just talked about Two Bits and his sister. I can't recall him saying anything about the murder."

As Michael walked up the street toward the Grill, he decided maybe that was the oddest thing of all. That Joe hadn't said anything about the murder. If so, he was the only person in Hidden Springs who wasn't talking about it.

The more Michael thought about it, the more his uneasiness grew. Joe knew something. Something he didn't want to tell. Maybe Joe had known Jay Rayburn. The next thought was too unbelievable, but Michael let it surface in his mind anyway. Maybe Joe had shot the man.

Michael shook his head. No way could he picture the barber even holding a handgun, much less firing it at someone. Besides, what reason could Joe have for shooting Jay Rayburn? Then again, what reason did anyone have for shooting Jay Rayburn? Michael didn't know, but he couldn't believe the mild-mannered barber was a murderer. He didn't care what people said about how you could never know everything about a person no matter how long you'd known them.

Michael caught sight of his face in one of the store windows and almost laughed. It was ridiculous to think that Joe Jamison had shot someone and left the body on the courthouse steps. If Joe had shot the man, he'd have come straight into the courthouse to turn himself in and hand over the gun. He wouldn't have scurried back across the street, fed his cat, and started cutting hair as though nothing had happened.

Joe wasn't the murderer. While Michael was certain of that, the fact was, Rayburn was dead. Somebody had shot him, and it could be that whatever had happened wasn't going to make any more sense than some of the impossible ideas people in town were coming up with.

Michael wished he could pick the theory he liked best. If he could, he'd go with Duke Benson's. Duke stayed drunk more than sober, and yesterday he'd been well on his way to his favorite condition when he'd poked his finger into Michael's chest for emphasis and claimed aliens had done it. He'd seen it happen, and he'd be glad to testify.

⊰ 12 ⊱

The Hidden Springs Grill had been frozen in time for decades. The same dark green counter with matching stools where Michael's mother and father might have sipped sodas on their first date stretched down one side of the Grill. Booths the same green huddled against the other wall while tables covered with green checkered cloths filled the middle. It wasn't a pretty green, but folks who came there to eat were more worried about what pie was on special than what color the counter and tables were.

By the time Michael went through the door, the lunch crowd was clearing out. He only had to stop twice to let someone tell him who might have killed the John Doe on the courthouse steps yesterday morning. He didn't bother telling them the John Doe had a name now. He just acted like he was taking mental notes before he escaped to a back booth, where he hoped to eat in peace.

There was little chance of that. Michael had hardly settled in the booth before Hank Leland got off his stool at the counter and carried his coffee over.

"So you know who the John Doe is now." Hank didn't wait for an invitation to join him, just slid into the seat across from Michael without asking.

"You should have given me a call. I could have taken a shot of you and Lester breaking into the car."

"I planned to do that." Michael smiled a little. "It must have slipped my mind."

"No need for sarcasm." Hank stirred another packet of sugar into his coffee. "Lots of reporters and policemen get along famously. They share leads, get shot at together, things like that. Don't you ever watch television?"

"I guess not the same shows as you. I thought the policemen were always shoving the reporters out of the way, telling them to take a hike and smashing their cameras."

Hank took a loud sip of coffee and shook his head. "And after I put that nice picture of you right up on the front page when I could have used that other shot where you didn't look like you knew what two plus two makes."

"You're probably saving that one for the next issue."

"That's an idea. It's according to whether you catch the killer by then." Hank grinned. "If not, I might just use it. How about this headline? 'Bumfuzzled Deputy Doesn't Know Beans about Who Done What.' " He drew the headline out in the air with his hands.

"You won't catch me arguing with the truth."

Cindy Tilford stepped up to the booth and set a cup of coffee down in front of Michael. She gave

Hank a hard look and took up for Michael. "Now you quit picking on Michael, Hank. Go pester the sheriff with your questions and let Michael eat."

"The sheriff never has much to say when I'm around," Hank said.

"Wonder why." Cindy raised her eyebrows at him, then turned back to Michael. "You doing the special, honey? Meat loaf? Or something else." She hadn't bothered to bring him a menu.

Cindy, a big-boned redhead whose hair was beginning to show streaks of white, was the waitress, cook, and along with her husband, owner of the Grill. She didn't put up with the first bit of nonsense in her place, but at the same time she had a sympathetic ear for a hard-luck story. Michael had talked her into giving Anthony Blake a part-time job a couple of weeks ago.

When she slid the heaping plateful of meat loaf, mashed potatoes, and green beans under Michael's nose a few minutes later, Hank complained. "Hey, you gave him an extra slice."

Cindy laughed. "Get used to it, Hank. He's cuter than you. Besides, look at your waistline. I was doing you a favor."

Hank looked at her suspiciously. "You been talking to my wife?"

"Us girls have to stick together." Cindy shrugged as she moved away to fill another customer's coffee cup.

Her husband, Albert, popped halfway out of the kitchen door to call across the room at Michael. "That boy didn't show up yesterday afternoon. He's not supposed to come today, but you tell him he don't show up tomorrow, he's history."

"Now, Albert." Cindy looked over at him. "The boy's got troubles."

"So, who doesn't?" He scowled at Cindy and then Michael again. "The boy took the job. He's supposed to show up."

"I'll talk to him, Albert," Michael said. "Give him another chance."

"How many chances you want to give that boy, Michael?" Without waiting for an answer, Albert went back through the swinging doors into the kitchen.

"Don't pay him no mind." Cindy came back to their booth to freshen up their coffee. "Albert was just wanting to go fishing yesterday, and then when Anthony didn't show, he wouldn't go. I told him I could handle the dinner crowd without him. To get his pole and go fishing. But he wouldn't. Instead, he started banging pans around in the kitchen till the folks out here were almost afraid to stay and eat. They might not have, except they all wanted to compare stories about that guy getting shot on the courthouse steps." She glanced at Hank. "Nobody wants to wait for the paper around here."

"That's the trouble with a weekly paper." Hank

sighed and hung his head. "The news is old before it ever sees print."

"But people still want to read what's in the *Gazette*. We sell out your copies every week. Can't say the same for the *Eagleton News*." Cindy waved at the paper stand inside the door. "That paper is shrinking down to nothing."

"They should try to up circulation by printing pictures of their subscribers' grandkids playing ball and winning science fair ribbons. That's how I keep my readers." Hank grabbed another packet of sugar and tore it open. "Plus a murder now and again to spice things up."

"I like the kid pictures best." Cindy headed back to the kitchen.

Michael attacked the plate of food.

Hank watched him a minute, then said, "Are you going to give me the lowdown, or do I have to wait for a press release from Paul Osgood?"

"Paul's sick. Last I heard Caroline was thinking about taking him to the emergency room over at Eagleton."

"You don't say. Nobody told me." Hank fingered his coffee cup handle.

"You're the reporter. You're supposed to find out things on your own. Who told you about the car?"

"I have my sources," Hank said noncommittally.

"How much do you know?" Michael took

another bite of the meat loaf. The editor was about as good at evading answers as the politicians in town were at avoiding his questions.

"Not near enough, but I'm betting you can fill me in on the rest." Hank pulled his little notebook out and flipped through it. "Name Jay Rayburn. Salesman. From West Chester up near Louisville. Worked out of New Albany. Company named TEKCO."

Michael swallowed and stared at him. "Betty Jean's not on your payroll, is she?"

"Are you kidding?" Hank closed his notebook. "Betty Jean wouldn't give me the time of day if she was the only person in Hidden Springs who owned a watch." Hank sipped his coffee and studied the faded cowboy print hanging over the booth as though he'd never seen it before.

"You must have bought Lester lunch."

"That beanpole eats more than you'd think he could." Hank brought his eyes back to Michael's face and grinned. "I guess you might say Lester was more appreciative of his picture in the paper than you were."

Michael shook his head and went back to eating. "I'd have thought it would take more than his picture in the paper and a hamburger to break a dedicated deputy like Lester Stucker."

Hank twirled his coffee cup on the saucer. "Well, as a matter of fact, I'm working up a piece on how important the crossing guard is in protecting the children in our community. Something that needed doing anyway. Maybe a tie-in with school safety week, and I can print some more of those pictures of folks' grandkids."

"You have no scruples, Leland." Michael wasn't really upset. Lester had saved him the trouble of letting Hank pry all the same information out of him. Before the *Hidden Springs Gazette* was published again next week, everybody in town would know the dead man's name anyway. Could be they would have the killer in jail by then. Maybe Buck had run down some leads out at the campgrounds. He might even be bringing in a suspect. Buck liked to solo.

"I could pay for your lunch if Lester left anything out."

"Nope. Sounds like you have pretty much everything I do. Except he was a printer technician and salesman. Worked on those big company machines."

"Nobody in Hidden Springs has anything like that, do they?"

"Not that I know of, but his company is emailing a list. Once I've checked it out, I'll let you know."

"That's the trouble with you, Keane. You want to wait till it's not news anymore and then tell me."

"You'll have to keep a lid on what you've already found out until we get in touch with the next of kin. Betty Jean's tracking down a daughter now."

"No problem. I don't owe the *Eagleton News* any favors. Let them dig up their own news."

"I'd just as soon you told them." Michael pushed his empty plate away. "One reporter stirring around is plenty."

"Stirring a little sometimes brings things to the surface that you might never notice otherwise."

Michael leaned back in the booth and studied Hank. There was something just a tad too pleased about the editor's face. "Have you brought something to the surface that I need to know about, Leland?"

"Now, you know I'd share the info with the proper authorities first thing if I uncovered anything I thought might be helpful in the investigation." Hank opened his notebook again and leafed through it. "Nothing of interest to you here." He was silent a few seconds, then asked, "But what was it you said was wrong with Paul?"

"I didn't. But the chief said it might be food poisoning."

"Did Buck take him out to eat last night?" Hank asked innocently.

"You burnt your bridges behind you putting that picture of them in the paper, and if I were you, I'd be careful not to give either one of them an excuse to lock you up."

"Do you think they would?" Hank looked

genuinely excited. "Really? That would make a great story. Police harassment."

"You'd better worry more about waking up to write your story if it's Buck who arrests you. He's been known to bash a few heads when folks don't surrender meekly. Mind, all of this is off the record and just a friendly little warning."

Hank laughed. "Don't worry about me, Keane. I'm meek as can be when I need to be. Besides, I know how far to push them without going too far. They all hate me, but I get my stories." Hank slipped his notebook back into his shirt pocket and stood up.

"How come you don't push me?"

Hank laughed again before he yelled over at Cindy to bring Michael a piece of that fresh apple pie. On him. Then he looked back at Michael. "Don't you feel me pushing?" He smiled widely. "You will let me know when you've talked to the next of kin?"

"I'll let you know."

"Good. Maybe I should go talk to some people over at the hospital in Eagleton. Find out what Osgood ate last night. You never can tell what might turn out to be important."

After he left, Cindy brought over the pie and scooted into the booth across from Michael. Between them they took a poll of which stories going around about the murder were the most popular. The mob was still ahead about three to one, although the idea of a wife paying somebody to do the guy in was gaining and was her own personal favorite. Michael didn't spoil her fun by telling her there wasn't a current wife.

When Michael got back to the office, Betty Jean had Amy Cartwright's address and had already arranged to have someone from the local police department break the news to her. A little later when Michael got the daughter on the phone, he tried to keep it impersonal, but the girl sounded so small and sad he couldn't keep from asking if someone was there with her.

"My baby's here. He was a month old yesterday. Dad was supposed to come see him next week." The girl had to stop and swallow back tears before she could go on. "Said he wanted to wait till Jason got big enough for him to hold without worrying that he might break him."

"I'm sorry, Mrs. Cartwright. I know this has to be difficult for you."

"I can't believe it's true. Why would anybody want to kill my father?"

"We don't know yet, but we're doing our best to find out." He gave her a minute to compose herself, but he had to ask his questions. "Is there anything you might be able to tell us about your father that would help?"

There was a long silence. Too long, and Michael wished he could see the girl's face. He was planning out how to phrase his next question when a door slammed in the background and a voice called the girl's name. At the sound, the girl began to sob.

An angry, strident voice came on the line. "Who is this?"

After Michael quickly identified himself, he tried to defuse the woman's anger by first apologizing, then explaining his purpose, and last, asking, "Are you Amy's mother?"

"I am, and Amy can't talk to you now." No hint of grief or tears showed in the woman's voice.

"I understand, Mrs. Rayburn. She can answer any other questions we might have tomorrow. I've arranged to meet with her in Eagleton to confirm the identity of her father."

The mother fell silent as if surprised by his words. Finally she said, "Is that really necessary?"

"I'm afraid so, Mrs. Rayburn."

"Stop calling me Mrs. Rayburn." Irritation was plain in her voice. "My name's Hawfield now. And you don't need to be bothering Amy about all this right now. Jay may have been a skunk, but he was her father."

The muffled sobs grew louder and were joined by the sound of a baby crying. "I am sorry, ma'am, but Mrs. Cartwright is the victim's next of kin." A long silence stretched across the line between them.

At last the mother sighed slightly and gave in. "If it has to be done, it'll be done. Now leave us alone." She disconnected before Michael could say anything else.

Michael considered calling back to ask the mother to accompany her daughter the next day. The mother sounded as if she might have some answers, and Michael needed answers. Right now he'd even be glad to have a few questions. His hand hovered over the phone, but he didn't want to further antagonize the woman. If she didn't show up with the daughter, he'd get her number and contact her then.

After his crossing guard duty, Lester came in to report he'd tracked down Buck. Lester was still glowing from his big discovery that morning, holding his thin shoulders back, strutting through the office over to the coffeepot. He poured the last of the coffee into his cup, but didn't bother making a fresh pot. He left it for Betty Jean the way Sheriff Potter always did.

Betty Jean opened her mouth to blast him, but Michael caught her eye and winked. With a scowl that said plain as words Michael was going to owe her, she pushed up from her desk to fill the pot with water.

"Had Buck found out anything?" Michael asked.

"I don't know." Lester looked up from his coffee, his cocky grin changing into a worried frown. "Buck got sort of mad."

"Yeah? Because you found the car before he did?"

Lester shook his head. "Not that. He was out at the truck stop and I kind of bumped into his table and spilled his coffee in his lap. It must've been really hot, the way he yelled and jumped up and held his pants leg out away from him."

Michael bit his lip to keep from smiling. "So you just told him the news and got out of there while the getting was good."

"I wouldn't run away like that."

Michael noted Lester's sincere look and was almost afraid to ask. "What'd you do?"

"There was a glass of ice water right there on the table, and seeing as how it was cold and the coffee was hot, I thought it would cool him off to pour it on his pants."

"It's a wonder he didn't shoot you." This time he couldn't keep from smiling.

Lester looked scared. "He wouldn't do that, would he?"

Michael rubbed his hand across his face to wipe away his smile. "No, Lester, of course not. When he calms down, he'll realize you were just trying to help."

"Yeah." Lester cheered up a little. "So when he quit yelling, I told him what you said quick like, since I had to get back to the school. I have to be there before the bell rings, because some of those kids get out to the street really fast, and I wouldn't want them to cross that road without me there." Lester smiled all the way across his face. "Did you know Mr. Leland is going to write a piece about me and how much I help the kids?"

"So I heard."

"Mr. Leland told me I must have a nose for leads and that's how come I spotted that guy's car this morning."

"He could be right," Michael agreed.

Betty Jean snorted a little as she measured out the coffee behind them, but Lester didn't notice as he sat up a little straighter in his chair.

"I'll let you know, Michael, if I smell out any more leads."

Betty Jean had a coughing fit and had to go out into the hall.

"You okay, Betty Jean?" Lester started to get up to follow her, but Michael waved him back into his chair.

"She'll be okay. She just needs a drink of water." Michael waited till Lester sat back down. "I need all the help I can get with this, Lester, so if you see anything else out of the ordinary, anything at all, you tell me right away."

Lester's eyes widened and he looked around as if expecting a new lead to pop up in front of him right there in the office. "I'll be on the lookout, Michael. You can count on that."

"I know I can. Oh, and by the way, it might be best if you didn't tell Hank Leland anything about what we find out. We want to keep what we know under wraps for a while until we have a suspect in hand."

"Right. He won't get anything out of me."

Michael looked at Lester and knew he didn't even realize Hank had gotten him to spill his guts at lunchtime. Michael was almost relieved when the phone rang so that he could give up on the impossible.

It was Chief Sibley. There had been an accident at the intersection of North Main and Bell Street and could Michael go write it up, since he was headed over to Eagleton to the hospital to be with Caroline. It seemed Paul didn't have a bug or food poisoning after all. His appendix had ruptured, and they were rushing him into surgery. Paul was out of his head and Caroline about as bad.

Michael left Betty Jean with instructions to tell Buck where he was if he called in.

Michael didn't like working accidents. The fender benders were boringly routine, and the bad wrecks always pushed him too close to the strange pool of blackness that held the memories of that other accident years ago. Of course, he had to work wrecks all the time from fatalities on down to the bumper kissers.

When the smashup was bad, it took Michael days to get over seeing the crushed cars and broken bodies. He had to turn off all feeling and become almost a robot to perform his duties.

This wreck wasn't bad. Irma Bottoms in the

compact car had a bumped head, and Billy West in the pickup truck was ranting about how Irma must be senile to pull out in front of him like that. Michael wrote down their statements. Sam's wrecker was just towing away the car when Buck showed up.

"You through here, Mike?" Buck leaned out his window. When Michael nodded, he motioned toward the other door with his head. "Then get in. Could be, it wouldn't hurt if we compared notes. But first turn those roof flashers off. Folks will think you're giving me a ticket."

As soon as Michael got in Buck's car, the man started in on him. "I guess you think it was pretty funny sending Lester out to tell me he found the stiff's car when I'd been out there busting my butt all morning trying to get a line on the guy."

Michael kept all hint of a smile off his face. "I figured you'd already called in and Chief Sibley had filled you in on the details. I just sent Lester out to be sure."

"Sure you did. I can see that smirk, Keane."

"Okay, okay, you got me, Buck, but I didn't want to put it out on the radio. And since you were being Lone Ranger on this one, I didn't know how else to get you the info." Michael pointed to the phone in Buck's console. "I called your cell and you didn't answer."

"Ease off, kid. Those things drive me nuts. Ringing at the worst times." Buck's voice was down in the growling range. "Besides, Osgood has that number and I needed an excuse not to answer if he called. You know I can't work with Osgood. I'd end up having to kill him."

"Paul's sort of off the case for a few days."

Buck looked directly at Michael for the first time. "You're kidding? What happened? Chief Sibley get some backbone or what?"

"Not exactly. Paul's getting his appendix out as we speak."

Buck swore and rubbed his cheek to hide his smile, then gave it up and laughed out loud. "I don't call in for a couple of hours and look what happens. Lester finds the stiff's car. You ID him from his driver's license, forever more, and before Little Osgood gets to give order one, he busts his gut. Things are going crazy in this burg. What next?"

"I don't know, Buck." Michael's smile faded away. "But I figure we'd better be ready. So if you've got to be the Lone Ranger, then you'd better let me be Tonto."

❧ 13 ❧

Buck had been busy. While he hadn't found a girlfriend or wife sitting in one of the little trailers or a motel room with a gun in her hand ready to confess, he had found a couple of locals who recognized the man. T. R. Boggess, who ran the gas station out close to the interstate, said the guy filled up there sometimes and he'd fixed his brakes for him last year.

The other man, Billy Samuels, owned the one restaurant out by the interstate that hadn't been taken over by a chain. The Country Diner drew in a good mix of local folks, along with tourists and passers through. Billy said their victim had been stopping at his place now and again for years. That he was a backslapping, friendly sort of guy who liked to swap jokes with Billy or commiserate about the weather or traffic. Everyday sort of stuff. Billy hadn't known the guy's last name, but his first name was Jay. The guy always paid cash but got a receipt.

The two waitresses told Buck this Jay whoever liked to flirt with them, but since it was harmless enough and he was generous with his tips, they didn't mind. The younger one, Kathy, said he sometimes got her to pick a number when he was buying a lottery ticket. He promised to leave her a thousand-dollar tip when he struck it rich. He was always studying tip sheets on the horse races and talking on his cell phone.

Hilda, the other waitress, said he was in there maybe once or twice a month and that they sometimes talked about their kids. Nothing really important. Just what this one or that one was doing. He showed her pictures of his first grandkid on his cell phone the last time he'd been through. That had been about two weeks ago. They were all sure he wasn't there on Tuesday.

They didn't think he knew anybody in Hidden Springs, but he did sometimes glance through the *Gazette* while he ate. He was always asking what was going on in the town. Said Hidden Springs was the kind of place he'd like to retire to some-day if he ever made enough money to get off the road.

Hilda said when she first started working there and he came in, he'd ask after one of the waitresses who had quit, but it had been so long ago Hilda couldn't remember who that was. She was shocked to find out Jay had been shot and couldn't imagine who might have done it.

Neither could Kathy, who seemed more disappointed than sad to find out Jay was dead. She had wanted to believe he might hit on the lottery, and she just knew if that happened, he would have given her that thousand-dollar tip.

Hilda laughed at Kathy and said guys were always coming in there expecting to strike it rich somehow. It never happened. And poor Jay, anybody could tell he was down on his luck. The grandbaby being born was the only good thing that had happened to him for a long time.

When Buck asked her how she knew that, Hilda told him there were just signs a person who looked could read. His shirt collars were frayed, and he had this funny look in his eyes. Buck pushed her about what kind of look. Hilda had shrugged and said she didn't know exactly how to describe it. Sort of like he wanted to hope for something, but was afraid to. It wasn't something a person could exactly put into words. It was a look. The kind of look people had when they knew they were in trouble but thought they'd figured a way to get out of it without facing the music.

That's the kind of guy Jay was, Hilda said. The kind of guy who bought an extra lottery ticket when he was next to broke. She'd loaned him a twenty spot a couple of times herself. She figured he put it on a horse at some track, but she felt sorry for the guy.

What Buck found out matched what Michael already knew, but though Jay Rayburn was beginning to flesh out as a real person, they still hadn't come up with any reason for him to end up dead on the courthouse steps. Buck had scrapped the jealous wife/girlfriend idea and now was ready to explore the possibility that Rayburn was in too deep with the wrong people.

That could be how it happened, Michael thought after Buck drove off toward Eagleton to check with some sources in the city. But it didn't feel right to Michael. Too many things didn't add up. If people like that were making an example of Rayburn the way Buck suggested, Hidden Springs was not exactly a prime spot to ditch the body. It didn't make sense, but then what had since Miss Willadean rushed back to the sheriff's office yesterday morning to report a drunk out on the courthouse steps.

Michael turned his car around and headed out to Wilbur Binion's old barn on Crooked Ridge Road. He couldn't spend all his time chasing for some elusive lead on Jay Rayburn's killer. Other things needed to be investigated, and Wilbur Binion's barn was one of them.

After Wilbur developed heart trouble a few years ago, he moved to town, but he kept some cows down on his farm. On Monday, he spotted tire tracks going back to an old barn on his place. He hadn't used the barn for years. Not since he quit milking cows. Wilbur's wife had talked him into calling the sheriff's office instead of checking out the barn himself. She worried that somebody might be growing marijuana on the back of their place, and everybody knew marijuana growers carried guns nowadays.

Michael radioed Betty Jean where he was going and then headed out of town. He liked driving the country roads that twisted and turned back through farmland. Here and there tractors crawled across the fields as farmers worked up their ground for planting.

When at last he got to Wilbur's farm, the place looked deserted. Michael opened the gate and drove back through the field. The barn's weather-beaten planks flapped in the wind to reveal the old log structure underneath. The tin roof was rusted all the way through in places, and if not for the logs, the whole thing might have collapsed years ago. Inside the barn, ancient hay dust filtered down from the loft to catch in heavy gray cobwebs dripping from every corner. Stanchions still waited to trap cows' heads, but not even a whiff of cow manure lingered in the air.

A couple of shoe prints were clear in a patch of soft black dirt in the breezeway. Squatting down, Michael ran his fingers over the design. Sneakers. Ten and a half or eleven. He doubted Wilbur even owned a pair of sneakers.

After running his hands around a door opening to a storage room to be sure it wasn't booby-trapped, Michael gingerly pulled it open. Blinking to let his eyes adjust to the dimness of the log room, he pulled out his flashlight and flicked it on. Nothing looked out of the ordinary in the room. No sign of marijuana or the equipment used to grow it. Just a large wooden feed bin, a rusty old metal milk cooler, and narrow wooden steps to the loft. Swiping away the cobwebs, Michael climbed the stairs. A mouse scurried out of sight in the empty loft.

Back downstairs the feed bin was empty too, but the milk cooler was not. Michael's flashlight beam bounced off Bonnie Wireman's laptop.

There were also a couple of iPads and a shotgun that looked like the one Perry Masterson had reported missing some weeks back.

Michael slowly closed the cooler lid and went back out to stare down at the sneaker prints. He wished they didn't make him think of Anthony Blake.

By the time he got back to town, the courthouse offices were closing and Sheriff Potter was on the way out. He grumbled but helped Michael carry the recovered property inside to store on the cluttered shelves in the evidence room.

After they had it all stowed away, the sheriff looked around and said the same thing he always said whenever he went in the small room. "About time we sorted through this stuff and had an auction or something to get rid of the things nobody ever claimed."

"Betty Jean's cataloging it on the computer," Michael said.

"What good's that going to do?" The sheriff pointed toward a handgun on one of the shelves. "How many of these are back here?"

"I'm not sure. I'd have to check the inventory list."

The sheriff stretched up for a better look. "I see four." He shifted a wire basket to the side to look behind it. "That's probably all. I can't imagine why we have that many. Must have been here when I took office."

"That's been awhile." Michael glanced around at the crowded shelves. Betty Jean had been trying to sort through it with Michael's help, but it was slow going because she couldn't work in the little room over an hour at a time without getting claustrophobic.

The place sort of closed in around Michael too. He hoped the sheriff wouldn't decide to start counting everything as he leaned down to peer at another shelf that held a couple of shotguns and three outdated car radios.

"At least we know none of these guns shot that Rayburn fellow." The sheriff straightened up and led the way back into the office.

"That's about all we know." Michael followed the sheriff out, glad to be out of the cramped room.

"We know a lot more than we did yesterday. By this time tomorrow, we may have the murderer behind bars." Sheriff Potter dusted off his hands. "Things can go fast once you start learning what's what."

"What do you think happened, Sheriff?" The sheriff was one of the few people in Hidden Springs who hadn't shared with him any conjectures about the murder.

The sheriff pulled the evidence room door shut, locked it, and dropped the key back into Betty Jean's top desk drawer. For a minute, he watched the blue and purple bubble screen saver flowing across Betty Jean's computer screen as if he expected some answer to appear there. Finally he sighed a little. "It's hard to guess at things like that. And there's really not much use in doing that anyhow. Even educated guesses turn out to be wrong more times than not."

"You surely have some thoughts on what might have happened. Everybody else in Hidden Springs does."

"Do you?" The sheriff looked up at Michael.

Every hint of the sheriff's good ol' boy smile usually settled comfortably on his face was gone. His eyes were so direct and intense that Michael felt like a little boy who'd just challenged his math teacher's ability to multiply. Michael cleared his throat. "I guess not. Nothing that makes sense."

The sheriff's smile inched back. "It could well be we'll never know who did it."

Michael frowned, and the sheriff came around Betty Jean's desk to throw his arm around Michael's shoulder. "Don't look so bothered, boy. When you've been a law officer as long as I have, you learn you can't solve every crime. And even when we do figure things out, a goodly number of those never make it to court for one reason or another. It's just the way things are."

"But murder's different. I don't like to think about a murderer on the loose in Hidden Springs."

"Nobody does, Mike. Nobody does, but whoever did it is likely miles away by now. What reason would they have to hang around here?"

"We might know that if we knew why the killer shot Jay Rayburn in the first place."

"And we should try to find that out. I'm not saying we shouldn't, but you can't let it get you down if the killer isn't hanging around town waiting for us to catch him. You'll probably have better luck finding out who carried off that stuff we just brought in." The sheriff stepped away from him toward the door to the hallway. "You talked to Anthony Blake lately?"

"I'm going to tonight." Michael kept his voice neutral. "He's supposed to be at Aunt Lindy's for a tutoring session."

"You tell Malinda to be careful around that boy. I know a bad apple when I see one."

"You were already in office when his mother disappeared, weren't you?" Michael followed the sheriff out into the empty hallway. "Do you remember what happened?"

"Sure, I remember," the sheriff said. "We put out an APB on her, treated it like a regular missing person, but it was obvious she just took off with one of the men she was always getting chummy with out where she worked."

"Where was that?" Michael locked the office door.

"The Country Diner." The sheriff waited for him, staring off up the empty hallway. "Billy

Samuels was the one who reported her missing when she didn't show for work. He was that sure something had happened to her. Said she never failed to call in if she was going to be even a few minutes late. So we checked it out. When we went out to her apartment, the kid—he must have been about five—peeked out the window at us. I can still see that kid's face." The sheriff shook his head slowly. "I don't see how she could have done it. Just to take off and leave him there by himself like that."

"Did you know her?"

"Everybody knew Roxanne." The sheriff gave Michael a knowing smile.

"That's what Buck said."

"Yeah, as I recollect, Buck was pretty chummy with her himself. He kept saying she wouldn't have gone without the kid, but she did. The kid, he didn't cry, you know, that day we found him there alone. Not till we made him leave. Then he pitched an awful fit. Screamed and grabbed the door facings. We had to pry his fingers loose one at a time to get him out of the place. He kept screaming he had to wait for his mama. That she told him she was just going to the grocery. I figure she went to the grocery a lot, if you know what I mean."

"Buck said she didn't take any clothes or clean out her bank account."

"Yeah, that was sort of strange." Their footsteps

sounded loud in the quiet building. Roy must have left early. The sheriff didn't say anything else until they were almost to the rear exit. "People don't normally leave behind their money when they decide to disappear. That's for sure, but maybe whoever she ran off with was in a hurry. Told her now or never. Who knows? But I tell you I ain't never seen anything so pitiful as that kid that day. I guess it's little wonder he's turned out the way he has."

"Anybody ever get any kind of trace on Roxanne?"

"Once somebody reported seeing her up in Louisville and then somebody said they saw her dealing blackjack in Las Vegas, but I figured it wasn't nothing but talk. We checked it out just in case but never came up with anything."

"Do you know who Anthony's father is?" Michael asked.

Although the sheriff's smile didn't change, his eyes did as if Michael had asked one too many questions. Still he answered in his same easy tone. "That'd be hard to say. Of course, there were rumors, but none you could believe. Actually Roxanne didn't have much to do with folks around here. So I figure the kid's father was a passer through. Could be he never even knew about the kid."

Michael dared the sheriff's ill temper with another question. "What rumors?"

The sheriff waved his hand as if to dismiss the whole thing. "You know how folks are around here. Always ready to gossip about anything and everything. Roxanne gave them plenty to gossip about. Not so much that she was having a baby but that she wouldn't name the father. That made everybody talk that much more. Me, I always figured she didn't know herself, but anyway, folks around town gave credit to just about anybody in britches. I even heard a few rumors about Roxanne and me, and seeing as how I knew for certain those tales weren't true, I figured none of the others I heard were either. Best to ignore them all. Nothing to be done about it anyway. Not unless Roxanne decided to sue whoever it was for child support and she didn't. Some things are better left buried."

"I guess you're right."

"I am. Folks do like to talk, and especially about their elected officials. Anybody who had ever been seen eating out there at Billy's place got some kind of story told about them." The sheriff laughed a little. "Folks could hardly wait for Roxanne to have that baby so they could decide who it looked like. Then when the kid was born, he was the spitting image of Roxanne, and that was that. After a while the rumors died down. There's no need in stirring them up again after all these years."

"I just thought it might help Anthony if he knew."

148

"I can't see how. Not after all this time. The boy's just gonna have to quit thinking the world owes him something because he had a rough time as a kid. Lots of kids have rough times."

"Anthony may not have done this." Michael nodded back toward the office.

"Maybe not." The sheriff looked skeptical. "But you can't go soft on the job just because you feel sorry for the kid. If he did it, he'll have to face up to it, and so will you. Some kids you just can't help."

The sheriff's words kept circling through Michael's head as he drove to Aunt Lindy's house. *Some kids you just can't help.* Michael didn't want to believe that about Anthony. Or any kid. After Aunt Lindy prayed Michael out of the darkness that swallowed him after the wreck, she was always telling him the Lord had a reason to let him live. She wanted it to be something monumental, but Michael was okay with the idea the Lord might be using him one on one to help kids going through dark times. The way he'd helped Hallie. The way he was trying to help Anthony.

The dark times they knew weren't the same. Michael couldn't do a thing about the wreck that had nearly killed him. Hallie had been caught in a web of circumstances pushing her into a desperate situation. While Anthony had some of those unfortunate circumstances in his life too, at the same time, he seemed to gather the dark around him like a comfort blanket. The sheriff could be right. Michael might not find a way to jerk the kid off destruction road.

Michael blew out a sigh and remembered the sneaker tracks in Wilbur's barn. About Anthony's size. At the barn, Michael had fought the urge to brush the tracks away. He didn't want to have to arrest Anthony, but if the kid had done the crime, he needed to pay the price. The sheriff was definitely right about that.

The trouble was, sometimes Anthony wouldn't deny doing a thing even when he hadn't done it. He said nobody ever believed him anyway, so he might as well save everybody a lot of hassle and just say what they wanted to hear. That didn't make Michael's job any easier, but Anthony didn't care. He worked hard at not caring about anything or anybody.

But he had cared about his mother. That was plain enough from the stories. Michael wondered if there was yet a way to track her down after all these years. Maybe Michael would ask Alex about it when she came to town this weekend.

She always liked a challenge, and it would give them something to talk about other than Michael's lack of ambition. Of course, she'd probably tell him she was a lawyer, not a private detective. That he was the one whose job it was to find missing persons.

Maybe there were some things he could try. First, he needed to find out all he could about Roxanne Blake. The rumors the sheriff talked about regarding Anthony's father seemed as good a place to start as any. Michael's mind clicked through the people who might tell him something. Billy Samuels out at the diner. Aunt Lindy.

Michael shook his head there. She'd be like Sheriff Potter about the rumors, even if she did remember them. She would think he was making trouble for Anthony instead of helping him. Judge Campbell would remember the stories, but that didn't mean he'd repeat them. He wouldn't want to make any enemies with a possible state representative race in the offing.

Joe Jamison's name surfaced in Michael's mind. Joe never forgot anything. Every story, every bit of gossip or scandal he'd ever heard, was filed away somewhere in his head, and if you could figure out the right way to ask, sometimes he would pull out the file you wanted and let you leaf through it with questions while he cut your hair. Michael was sure Joe would remember the rumors about Anthony's father the same as he was sure there was something about yesterday morning and the body on the courthouse steps Joe hadn't told him.

Michael was going to have to come up with a lot of right questions when Joe got back from visiting his sister.

❧ 14 ☙

Aunt Lindy lived in what some townsfolk called the Keane mansion, but the house was far from mansion size. It did have about ten more rooms than Aunt Lindy needed, except at Christmas when she opened up the house to the community. A Keane family tradition. Michael helped her unpack and arrange the decorations, but the open-house parties were never the same after his parents died.

Michael could still remember the spicy delicious fragrance of his mother's Christmas cookies baking and the special feeling of expectation in the air as he helped his father trim the trees, set up the nativity scenes, and arrange the lighted village houses in the fake snow on the oak library table.

The first Christmas after the wreck, Michael couldn't believe Aunt Lindy would even consider having the open house. He was still having trouble walking and hadn't started back to school, and while he had begun to remember or relearn a lot that the wreck had robbed from his mind, he felt far from ready to face the entire town.

Aunt Lindy paid no attention to his protests. She claimed they owed it to the town to have the open house the same as always. The day of the event Michael did his best to disappear in shadowy corners, but people found him anyway, smiling and talking too loudly while their eyes leaked their unspoken words. *Poor Michael. Such a shame. They say he may never be right again.*

By the next year, his limp was almost gone, he was back in school, and people knew he hadn't lost his faculties. So that Christmas the open house, while not exactly enjoyable, was bearable. In the years since, Michael thought the house might actually be at its best filled with the lights and sounds of Christmas. The rest of the year the unused rooms seemed to be in limbo waiting for the next Christmas.

Aunt Lindy claimed it wasn't Christmas but him the house was waiting for. It was his house, his heritage. She had moved back into the house with him after the wreck, but when he married, she'd find an apartment. That way he and his bride could live there and continue the Keane family tradition. She didn't want to hear it when he told her the thought of moving back into the house was enough to make him a confirmed bachelor.

Michael paused now on the front walk and looked at the house in the reflection of the street-lamps. It sat at the end of the dead-end street, and he had to admit the house had a certain stately air about it, almost as if the very stones and windows were aware of their prominence in the town's history. It seemed to look down a bit on Judge Campbell's impressive brick house next door and to completely look over Reece Sheridan's comfortable two-story frame house across the street.

Michael headed across the yard toward the back of the house. He didn't like going in the front way. They'd always used the back door. He still remembered getting home from the hospital after the wreck and staring at the handicap ramp some men from the church had built up to the porch. That added to the strangeness of the day. Going in the wrong door. Seeing his parents' empty chairs in front of the fireplace. Catching the faint scent of his mother's perfume. Wanting to cry, but knowing tears would disappoint Aunt Lindy. She expected him to be happy to be home. To be strong.

Michael refused to go in and out of the front door after that. He found a way to negotiate the steps in the back, and without comment, Aunt Lindy had the platform removed.

Michael ran up those back steps now, the struggle it had once been long forgotten. The doctors at the hospital had told Aunt Lindy not to expect Michael to ever be like he was before the wreck, that even a partial recovery would be a miracle. But Aunt Lindy informed them the Lord wasn't in the partial-miracle business.

Dr. Winthrop used to laugh about it when he treated Michael after the accident. "Those doctors didn't know what hit them when Malinda Keane moved into the hospital room with you. I could have told them if they'd listened. The truth of it is, you didn't have any choice but to get better. Malinda wasn't going to accept any other out-come. The same as I'm thinking every last one of Malinda's students will know how to do fractions on the day they die."

Michael smiled at the memory as Aunt Lindy held up her cheek for his kiss when he went inside. "Good timing. Anthony and I just finished up our lesson."

She led the way back through the kitchen into the comfortably shabby den. Bright yellow and orange pillows littered a worn brown couch that invited sitters. Aunt Lindy's cat, Grimalkin, was curled up on the cushion in one of the wooden rockers that provided the rest of the seating in the room since Aunt Lindy believed rocking enhanced the thought process. A wall of shelves held well-worn books and a hodgepodge of knickknacks presented to her by students over the years. In this room, it was easy for Michael to forget about the rest of the house crouched out there, waiting for him.

Anthony Blake sat at a battered card table in the middle of the room. When he raised his eyes from his book, Michael studied the boy in an attempt to picture the mother the sheriff said he looked like.

She would have taken more care with the black wavy hair, using it to her favor, just as she would have highlighted the vivid blue eyes. Perhaps her features would have been softer and not pulled so taut with anger. Or maybe not, for Roxanne might have had reason to be angry too. Even so, she would have surely known the value of her looks and used it to her advantage.

Anthony gave no sign of caring how he looked. His black hair was shaggy, in need of both a cut and a comb. He obviously hadn't shaved for a week, and the frown that tightened the skin around his eyes stole some of the light from their remarkable blue.

"I'll get us some drinks." Aunt Lindy went back out to the kitchen, firmly shutting the door behind her.

Anthony stared at the closed door. "This feels like a setup. You planning to take me in or something?" His voice was carefully casual.

"Have you done something you need taking in for?" Michael sat down at the card table across from Anthony.

"When did that ever matter?"

"It always matters." If he could keep from liking the boy, it might make things easier.

The boy's lips turned up a fraction, but his eyes stayed the same hard blue. "What am I, Deputy? Your special charity case?" He didn't give Michael time to answer. "Well, give it up. You're wasting your time on me."

"It's my time to waste." Michael didn't smile.

Anthony lifted his eyebrows a bit. "I could make you sorry."

"You could." Michael stared straight at the boy.

Anthony dropped his gaze to the table and began tapping his pencil against his book. "Get on with it. Say whatever it is you've come to say."

"You know you're supposed to go to school, Anthony."

Anthony tapped his pencil faster against the book. "Yeah, yeah. I was sick, okay? Puking sick."

"On the courthouse lawn?"

"When you gotta puke, it don't much matter where you are."

"Your aunt Vera know you were sick?"

"Aunt Vera wouldn't notice if I dropped dead." Then Anthony laughed without humor. "Wait, I take that back. She'd have a party if I dropped dead. A big party."

"Did you go to school today?"

"Yeah. I wasn't puking today." Anthony looked up at Michael. "Is the third degree over now? Can I leave?"

Michael stabbed his next question at Anthony before he could look away again. "What do you know about that guy getting shot on the court-house steps yesterday?"

For a moment the pencil froze in Anthony's hands. Then he shifted his eyes away from Michael to stare across the room at the bookshelves. Casually he began to drum the pencil against the book again. "Why would I know anything about that? You cops don't even know anything about that."

Michael frowned as he tried to figure out the look that had flashed through Anthony's eyes. Not fear or guilt. Michael had seen both of those emotions on enough faces to recognize them instantly. Not anger. Anthony wore that all the time, but this was different. Raw. Real.

A memory stirred in Michael's head. It wasn't in Anthony's eyes he'd seen the look before, but in his own. It was despair. The same kind of despair he used to see in the mirror when he was Anthony's age and remembered the townsfolk's prediction that he would never be "right" again. But what about Jay Rayburn's murder would cause Anthony to feel that way?

Michael put his hand on the pencil to stop Anthony tapping it. He waited until Anthony looked at him. "I don't know why you would know anything about it, Anthony. You tell me. Did you know the guy?"

"I can't believe this." Anthony's eyes were hard, his emotions under control again. "Can't you cops find anybody better to pin that on? Me, I skip school, steal a few hubcaps. I don't shoot people." He yanked the pencil away.

"I didn't say you did. But you do know some-thing, don't you?"

"Not me. Don't know a thing. Nothing." The boy slouched in his chair, looking bored. "You leaning on everybody who was there or just picking on me?"

"It's you I'm talking to right now." Michael kept his face expressionless. He wanted to grab the boy and shake the truth out of him.

The curved-up lips were back again. "Okay, so here's how it is. I was there. I saw the crowd and came along for the ride same as everybody else."

Michael went for another deliberate jab. "What do you remember about your mother?"

This time there was no mistaking the look on Anthony's face as he jumped up so fast his chair crashed over backward. Pure, hot anger. Not just a shell to hide his other feelings. The table wobbled precariously between them as Anthony leaned on it to glare at Michael. His voice was tight. "I don't talk about my mother."

Michael met his glare without a flicker. "Why not? Are you afraid of what you might find out?"

Anthony shoved off the table, knocking it toward Michael and sending books and papers flying. Michael steadied the table, but didn't stand up.

"You don't know nothing, Deputy," Anthony yelled, balling up his hands into fists.

"Don't even think it, Anthony." Michael kept his eyes steady on Anthony's face. "Hitting me won't help anyway. You're the one who has to face the truth about your mother."

Anthony's face flushed even redder. "You don't know nothing about my mother either."

"Nope." Michael kept his voice steady. "Except that it's time you found out what happened to her."

"I know what happened." Anthony's voice lowered, but there was still anguish there. "Everybody knows what happened." He spun away from Michael and kicked the rocking chair where Grimalkin was napping. With a yowl, the cat scrambled to the top of the bookshelves.

15

Aunt Lindy opened the door and glowered at them. "What's going on in here?"

Without answering, Anthony slid around her.

Michael stood up and pushed his words after the boy. "Whatever you know about the murder could be dangerous, Anthony."

Anthony turned slowly to look at Michael, and though his face was still flushed, the mocking smile was back on his lips. "Then Aunt Vera can have her party, and you can dance with all the pretty girls."

He headed on toward the back door, but Aunt Lindy stopped him again with a hand on his arm. "You upset Grimalkin." She gestured toward the cat peering down from the bookshelf with an injured air. "She's not a cat who forgives easily."

"I'm sorry, Miss Keane, but it was his fault." Anthony flashed an angry look at Michael.

"Some fault may lie with Michael." Aunt Lindy's eyes didn't leave Anthony's face. "But I daresay Michael did nothing to disturb Grimalkin's nap."

"I told you I was sorry." Anthony stared down at his feet.

"And I accept your apology," Aunt Lindy said. "Wait right there while I get your books. You have assignments to do before our next session."

Michael picked up the books and papers and handed them to Aunt Lindy, all the time expecting the boy to bolt out the door without them. Instead, Anthony not only took the books from Aunt Lindy, but he waited while she wrapped up some brownies for him. Finally she told him to drive carefully, patted his arm, and released him. He shut the door firmly when he went out, but it wasn't quite a slam.

They stood where they were and listened to Anthony start up the old Chevy Aunt Lindy had helped him buy when he'd claimed to have no way to get to her tutoring sessions.

"One good thing," Aunt Lindy said as the motor caught roughly and the car limped away. "That old heap won't go over fifty, so maybe he won't have a wreck on the way home."

"He'll calm down."

"Will he?" Aunt Lindy turned her eyes from the window to skewer Michael. "I won't allow you to talk to him here anymore if you are going to upset him like that. He's fond of Grimalkin." She went over to coax the cat down from the shelves. She smoothed down the cat's gray and white fur and murmured a few words of nonsense to her.

"I'm sorry, Aunt Lindy, but sometimes if you jolt people a little, they'll tell you what they might not tell you otherwise."

"I don't think that will work on Anthony." She gently deposited the cat on the couch. She picked up Anthony's overturned chair, folded it, and leaned it against the wall. "What is it you think he knows? Surely nothing about that man getting shot?"

"I'm not sure. Yesterday morning when I spotted him at the courthouse, he looked different. Sort of scared, and that's not a look you catch on Anthony's face very often. He knew something about this Jay Rayburn, or he saw something. I don't know which, but I have to find out."

"You're not going to get him to tell you anything by making him angry." Aunt Lindy sat down in one of the rocking chairs, her eyes on Michael. "Or by tormenting him about his mother." She'd obviously been eavesdropping from the kitchen.

"He needs to accept whatever happened with his mother. He's almost a man. He can't go on playing pretend forever."

"I doubt Anthony has ever 'played pretend.' It might be better if he did." Aunt Lindy peered at

Michael. It was a look he was used to, but one that still made him want to squirm in his seat like a kid with a guilty conscience.

After a long moment, she smiled slightly and went on. "You see yourself in Anthony, and that's perhaps understandable. You felt deserted when James and Eva were killed in the accident. A quite normal reaction. Anthony feels deserted too, but other than that, there's little comparison in your situations."

When Michael opened his mouth, Aunt Lindy held up her hand. "Hear me out. First, you had parents who loved you and did not leave you by choice. Second, you were fifteen when this happened. Anthony was five. Third, you had me, a constant source of both love and support before the accident as well as after. Anthony was not that fortunate."

"I know that, Aunt Lindy. I don't know what would have happened to me without you."

"You very possibly would have died," she said matter-of-factly. "But I'm not telling you all this to make you feel gratitude to me, but you do need to realize how very different things are for Anthony." She paused a moment. "Do you remember Roxanne?"

"I've tried, but no, I don't. Is there some reason I should?" Michael used to hate it every time he stumbled across a memory he should have but didn't. Now he just shrugged it off since he could do nothing to change it.

"Not necessarily, although Eva did occasionally visit Roxanne to encourage her to bring Anthony to Sunday school."

"I remember Mama teaching the little kids at church, but I draw a blank with Roxanne. Tell me about her, Aunt Lindy, the way you used to tell me about other things I needed to know but couldn't remember."

"We haven't done this for a long time." Aunt Lindy smiled faintly. "Let's see. Where should I begin?" She leaned her head back in the rocking chair and shut her eyes to gather her memories of Roxanne.

Michael sat back down and waited.

"All right." After a moment, she opened her eyes. "Even though Roxanne was twenty-five when you were fifteen, you would have definitely noticed her. She wasn't only beautiful, she exuded sensuality."

"Everybody I've talked to said she didn't have any trouble attracting men."

"She didn't just attract them. She bedazzled them with those blue eyes of hers. They were midnight dark like Anthony's but somehow filled with light at the same time." Aunt Lindy gave Michael a knowing look. "I'm sure if she ever so much as glanced at you, your teenage hormones sent you into a tailspin."

"I still don't remember her." Michael frowned as he raked through his memories. "When did she disappear?"

"Oddly enough, the week before the accident. Everything was crazy that week. You may not remember, but your mother was nervous about you being away at camp for three weeks." Again Aunt Lindy smiled. "She thought you'd get hurt or homesick or who knows what. Dear Eva was a worrier. Then we heard about Roxanne leaving." All trace of Aunt Lindy's smile vanished. "While Eva was worried about you, she was nearly distraught over Anthony's situation. She kept saying Anthony's father should come forward and take responsibility for the child."

"Did she know who the father was?"

"I don't think so." Aunt Lindy frowned a little. "If she had, she'd have surely told somebody then. She was so upset about it all."

"Do you know who Anthony's father is?"

"No." Aunt Lindy's voice was so crisp the cat raised her head off the couch to look at her.

"But there were rumors," Michael persisted.

"There are always rumors in Hidden Springs," Aunt Lindy said. Then she relented a little. "But you know I never pay much attention to gossip."

"It might help Anthony to know."

"And it might not. You see, you need to know, to remember everything, but for Anthony, some things in his past might be better left unknown or forgotten."

Michael started to disagree, but again Aunt

165

Lindy held up her hand to stop him. "Try to understand how it was for Anthony when Roxanne left. She was his whole world. Roxanne had long been alienated from the rest of her family, and rumors or not, there was no father on the scene. So when Roxanne went away, Anthony had no one. I suppose Vera has done her duty by him, but she has made the boy pay for it every day of his life."

Aunt Lindy rocked forward in her chair toward Michael. "So you see, while there are similarities between what happened to the two of you, there are more differences. Anthony needs understanding and patience. He needs someone to care about what happens to him."

"I do care, Aunt Lindy. Why do you think I'm trying to keep him out of trouble?" Michael thought of the footprints in Wilbur Binion's barn. At least he'd gotten a good look at Anthony's sneakers and the soles were nothing like the prints in the dirt. Of course, the sheriff wouldn't think that was enough reason not to suspect Anthony. After all, a kid could have more than one pair of shoes.

Aunt Lindy leaned over even farther to pat his knee. "And you are helping him. He's doing well here in our sessions together. He sometimes even talks to me about other things. Not often, but sometimes."

"Maybe you could get him to tell you whatever

it is he knows about the man who got shot yesterday."

Aunt Lindy sat back in her rocking chair. "Perhaps, but I will not interrogate him." The cat, reassured at last by the normal tone of her voice, jumped off the couch and climbed into Aunt Lindy's lap. Aunt Lindy rubbed Grimalkin's ears absentmindedly. "And I will not ask him about his mother. Even if he decides to talk about her on his own, I might not tell you what he says."

Michael knew better than to argue with her. She'd tell him what she wanted to and nothing more. He ran his hand across the card table surface. He'd done homework under her watchful eye on this very table. "Why do you think she left like that?"

"I didn't know her that well. I did have her in class when she was in school, but she was always something of a loner. Her father had a problem with drink, and the family was often destitute. When Roxanne was a senior, she dropped out of school, got a job out at the Country Diner. She actually lived with Billy Samuels and his wife for a few months until she found her own place. Everybody figured she'd be on her way as soon as she saved up some money, but then she had Anthony and seemed to settle down to stay."

"But she did go eventually."

"Yes." Aunt Lindy pressed her lips together for a moment. "I can't say anybody was surprised except that she didn't take Anthony. She was bound to have a man lined up to help her, because that was how she got by, but she could have found a man who would take the child too. As I said, she bedazzled men." Aunt Lindy shook her head a little. "I've just never understood her leaving him."

"Buck said the same thing."

"Buck was one of the bedazzled ones. He was married, but bedazzled nonetheless."

"Buck claims they only talked about their kids." Michael traced one of the scratches on the table with his finger.

"I have no doubt that's true," Aunt Lindy said. "Just because he was bedazzled didn't mean Roxanne was. She never got bedazzled even in high school. She knew exactly what she wanted from any boy before she made eyes at them."

Something about her voice surprised Michael. "Didn't you like her?"

Aunt Lindy stroked Grimalkin head to tail. "I didn't not like her. She put in her time in class, learned what she had to and no more, even though she had a good mind. She just wouldn't believe education could be a way out for her." Aunt Lindy looked up at Michael. "But why the interest in Roxanne's disappearance? Do you think that could have something to do with the poor man on the courthouse steps?"

"Not really. Except for my feeling that Anthony knows something."

"What could that be?"

"Hard to guess, but there's something." Michael blew out a long breath. "Who knows? Jay Rayburn has been passing by here on the interstate for years. Maybe he was Anthony's father."

Aunt Lindy frowned. "Do you have reason to believe that?"

"Not really, but it's a possibility. Then again, maybe Anthony just thought the guy knew something about where his mother might be now. Maybe this guy had even talked to Anthony. I don't know. As Anthony said, I don't know anything."

"Could it really be dangerous for him?" Aunt Lindy asked quietly.

"There's no way to know for sure, especially since I don't know what he knows." Michael met her eyes. "It could be that whoever shot Jay Rayburn is long gone from Hidden Springs."

"And it could be that he's not," Aunt Lindy finished for him.

⊰ 16 ⊱

Malinda walked to the front of the house to watch Michael's taillights until he turned off Keane Street. She'd watched him leave that way ever since he was a new driver. And sent prayers after him.

Please, Lord, watch over him.

As if it wasn't enough that she had to worry about accidents, then Michael had chosen to be a police officer. No wonder her hair had gone gray years ago. Not that she worried about her hair. Clean and neat was good enough.

She had never given her looks much thought, although she'd always been pleased Michael did have her Keane broad forehead. A better facial characteristic on a man than a woman. It bespoke strength and intelligence. When he was a teen, he let his brown hair flop down on his forehead. He combed it back now, thank goodness, and it waved a bit the same as his father's had at Michael's age. While Michael's features showed his Keane heritage, his eyes were Eva's. Pure blue. Honest. Sincere.

Malinda breathed out a sigh and turned from the window. This room held so many memories. Here in front of a cheering fire she had sat reading with her parents and then visited with Eva and James. Malinda had moved out of the house when James married. Found an apartment just off Main Street. A nice place. Only three rooms. All she needed. But after the accident, she had no choice but to move back to make a home for Michael.

She ran her fingers over the spines of the old books that had been on the shelves ever since she could remember. The same chairs were grouped around the fireplace, but now the room felt so very empty. The ticks of the mantel clock the only sound.

On the first day of every month, she wound the clock. It seemed wrong to let it run down, even if the room's life seemed to have run down after James and Eva died. Michael and she had made a new life in the back rooms away from the sad memories. Someday she hoped these front rooms would be open and full of life and light again and not just at Christmastime.

But that depended on Michael. Dear Michael.

Malinda spoke into the darkness. "He's like you, Eva. He cares. Not to say you didn't, James. I know how you loved your church, always concerned about your members." Her words sounded too loud in the dark room, so she lowered her voice to a whisper. "But you, Eva, you were the one of us who could love without conditions. I want people to do right and so did you, James. There are standards, after all. But Michael. He has your tender heart, Eva."

She shook her head and went back down the hall to her sitting room. People would think she was a doddering old woman talking to ghosts like that. But tonight the memory of Eva's eyes seemed to be following her. Those honest, sincere eyes.

Perhaps that was why. The honest part. Malinda had never intentionally lied to Michael. She hadn't tonight, but she hadn't been completely candid either. The rumors about Roxanne still lurked in her memory, but none that could possibly be true. It was all no more than gossip. She wasn't about to turn into a gossipy old woman like Willadean Dearmon.

That woman was insufferable. Some idiot had once suggested she should befriend Willadean since they had so much in common. Malinda could think of very little. Both spinsters. Both living in big, rambling houses. But that was it. Malinda went to work every day to pry open the minds of the next generation of Hidden Springs citizens and force them to learn something useful. Willadean's father left her a sizable trust, which meant Willadean could dabble in work, clerking at this or that store through the years.

Not a thing wrong with being a clerk. A necessary job, but Willadean never lasted long in any place. Took too much time from her real calling of town gossip. No story was too sketchy for Willadean to repeat. She was quite capable of filling in whatever details she felt necessary.

That day after school, Malinda had the misfortune of encountering Willadean in the bank. A ridiculous pillbox hat like Jackie Kennedy wore ages ago perched a bit sideways on Willadean's head. But the hat was not nearly as ridiculous as the story she was telling poor Aileen at the teller's window. Malinda was at the next window, but she heard every word. Everybody in the bank heard every word.

"I almost witnessed the murder, you know," Willadean said. "In fact, I do think I may have seen someone running around the corner of the courthouse. I could have been shot myself." Willadean placed her hand flat on her chest.

"There, there, Miss Willadean." Aileen had patted the woman's arm. "You're all right now."

"I am now, but for how much longer? A killer is on the loose in Hidden Springs and nobody is doing anything about it. Not one thing!" Willadean had peered over at Malinda then. "The police in this town don't seem to care if we are all murdered in our beds."

May the Lord forgive her, Malinda wanted to smack Willadean. Twice. Let her turn the other cheek and she would smack it too. But she managed to simply smile and turn away. Three of her students were at the teller windows. What would they think if she let her temper get the best of her?

What would the Lord think of her?

She sank down in the rocking chair and picked up the old Bible from the table beside her. Eva's Bible. All through it, verses were underlined and notations made in the margins of when James preached from this or that passage. Malinda had carried this Bible with her to the hospital after the wreck. A way of taking Eva into the room with her beloved son.

The Bible fell open to the verse from Lamentations 3 that became Malinda's hope and prayer as she fought death for Michael anew each morning. She smoothed her hand across the page. *Great is thy faithfulness.*

She would continue to hope and pray each morning for Michael. And for Anthony and all her students. And yes, Lord, even for Willadean Dearmon.

⇥ 17 ⇤

Michael pulled his cruiser out of sight behind some trees on Wilbur Binion's farm and settled down to wait. He hoped he wouldn't have to stake out the place for too many nights. In fact, he hoped the thieves would be accommodating and show up tonight. Clouds blotted out the stars and moon, and the air was like a black cloth wrapping around him. Away to the west, lightning flickered faintly with no sound of thunder, while closer around him spring peepers celebrated the night. Down the road, a lone dog barked and made Michael think of Jasper. The dog would be curled up on the porch, waiting patiently for him to get home.

Michael tried to wait as patiently as the minutes crept past. He stared out at the night and shuffled through the events of the last two days, searching for a glimmer of something, anything he might be missing, about the homicide. Why was Rayburn at the courthouse? Did Anthony know him? Could Rayburn be Anthony's father? Most important of all, who killed the man? The questions circled in Michael's head, but no answers rose up to meet them.

Michael sighed and checked his phone. 12:14. But no signal this far out in the county. He'd wait a couple more hours, then give it up for the night. If the guilty parties were kids the way Michael suspected, they might not strike again until the weekend. Unless it was Anthony Blake. Then he might come any night in spite of his curfew on school nights.

But instead of Anthony's old car, a new Ford pickup popped over the hill and screeched to a halt at the farm gate. Noise and light spilled out of the truck when the passenger side door swung open. The radio was thumping, and the two kids' laughter sounded as if they'd found an elevator up to the penthouse floor of excitement. One of the kids climbed up on the metal gate and, with a loud yahoo, swung it open. The driver gunned the motor and threw up dirt and gravel as he sped through the gate.

Neither boy even glanced around for anything out of the ordinary. They didn't know enough to be worried about getting caught. After the truck bounced across the field toward the barn, Michael radioed Sally Jo, who manned the dispatch center at night, to round up Buck or the sheriff, even though he didn't expect to have any problems making this arrest. He knew the boys. Doug Peterson and Barry Woods. Both kids whose parents gave them everything they could want.

Michael eased his cruiser across the grass without lights. It was going to be a bad time at the jail when these two kids had to call their folks. He hated this kind of stuff. Stupid kids.

The scene at the courthouse was every bit as bad as Michael had expected, with plenty of tears, drawn faces, and stunned disbelief.

The Peterson boy's father pulled Michael aside and offered to pay any amount for the stolen property. Michael pretended not to recognize the bribe as he explained the charges against the two boys and how they would have to appear before the circuit judge the following week.

"But they're just boys," Darrell Peterson said. "Come on, Mike. Didn't you ever do anything crazy when you were a boy?"

"Nothing I could get arrested for." Michael leveled his gaze on the man's face.

Peterson turned away in disgust, muttering something under his breath that Michael pretended not to hear.

After they let the boys leave in the custody of their fathers, Buck and Michael walked out to their cars together.

"You might as well have cut a deal with Daddy Peterson," Buck said. "The sheriff will tomorrow anyway."

"I know. Nobody wants those two kids to go to jail."

"It might not hurt that Peterson kid. He's a real wiseacre." Buck made a face. "One more word from him out there at the barn, I'd have had to sock him for resisting arrest."

"His daddy would have had your badge and run you out of the state." Michael grinned over at Buck.

"It might have been worth it," Buck growled.

Michael laughed. "I know what you mean, and that's why I let them think there was no way out of this mess. At least they'll have to sweat it out till morning."

"Don't bet on it, Mikey." Buck spat on the sidewalk. "I'm guessing Daddy Peterson will ring up Al pronto, trying to have *your* badge for arresting his precious son. After all, the big shot does own a car dealership in Eagleton. He's probably asking Al if he's in the market for a new car as we speak."

"Maybe so, but trust me, Buck. The sheriff will back me up on this at least till morning. He doesn't take kindly to people waking him up in the middle of the night, which is why you're here instead of him."

"I wasn't too happy about coming out myself."

"Yeah, but Sally Jo doesn't pay any attention to you or me. She enjoys waking us up." Michael clapped Buck on the shoulder. "Anyway, thanks for the assist."

"Yeah, sure. You owe me one. Maybe two." Buck unlocked his patrol car but didn't get in. Instead, he leaned against the door. "By the way, I didn't find out anything up in Eagleton about our stiff that we hadn't already guessed. He liked to bet. Small-time stuff mostly. Sometimes a little more, but one thing about him that didn't ever change was his luck. He was a loser. Big time. Some jerks never learn."

"We can hope that's not true for these boys."

"Time will tell." Buck opened his door and slid in behind the wheel. He poked his head back out. "You need backup in the morning, call somebody else. Got it?"

"Got it."

Buck waved and was gone.

When Michael finally got home, Jasper ran out to greet him, tail flapping the same as any night. That was the thing about dogs. They didn't hold grudges no matter how late you showed up.

Michael straightened up from ruffling Jasper's ears to stare out toward the lake. It was a different dark than the rest of the night as the water caught a few glimmers of light from somewhere in spite of the cloud cover. Morning was just on the other side of the horizon, but he might catch a few hours of sleep before heading to Eagleton to meet Rayburn's family.

Jasper poked him with his nose. "All right, boy." Michael gave the dog's head another pat. "A dog biscuit for you. Then time to turn in."

After he swallowed the dog biscuit in one gulp, Jasper settled on his rug by the bed with a contented dog sigh. Michael wished he could do the same. The bed was comfortable, the night quiet, and he was tired. Sleep should have come easily, but he couldn't get those two kids out of his mind. It was fun, they'd said when their fathers demanded to know why. And easy. They hadn't thought about what might happen if they got caught.

Michael wondered if he had ever been like those boys, so spoiled and pampered he had to hunt ways to feel alive. He knew he wasn't like them when he was their age. The spring he was sixteen, he spent hours throwing a baseball at an old tire. Everybody told him he had a great fastball before the accident, but if so, he lost it to the blackness.

Still, that year, that first year back, Michael had been frantic to reclaim as much of his life as he could. Baseball was part of who he was. He hadn't gotten his speed back on the ball, but with the help of his coach, Michael had developed other ways of getting batters out. He had an uncanny knack for reading the stances of the players up to bat and fooling them with pitches they didn't expect. In the end, the coach said he was a better pitcher than he'd been before the accident, but he wasn't the same.

Everything had been like that. Before the accident he was one person, and after the accident, another. So at sixteen, instead of looking for trouble because he was bored with his life, he was trying to figure out not only who he was, but who he had been.

It was as though he'd gone to sleep one night and awakened the next morning unable to move. Only instead of one night, it was weeks. Everybody in Hidden Springs gave up on him. Except Aunt Lindy. She brought him back with the same determination she used to solve complicated math problems. Every problem had a solution. You just had to find it.

Maybe she'd be able to solve the problem of helping Anthony. She might even get him to tell her what he knew about Rayburn's death. Michael had ruined his chances of Anthony telling him anything for a long time to come.

He would have to be smarter with his questions tomorrow for the daughter and ex-wife if she came along. Rather, today, he thought as gray light sneaked in the window. He would have plenty of time to think about what questions to ask on the drive to Eagleton, so he punched his pillow and finally went to sleep as the sky turned pink in the east.

⤳ 18 ⤵

Not enough hours later, Michael introduced himself to Jay Rayburn's daughter. She looked very young, with red, swollen eyes and an abundance of curly blonde hair. When he told her how sorry he was about her father, more tears gushed out.

The girl's mother was with her, and she, on the other hand, showed no sign of tears as she pushed a handful of tissues at the girl. "You'll have to forgive my daughter, Officer Keane. This has been a terrible shock for her."

"Of course. I understand," Michael said.

Everything about the mother was as controlled as the daughter was uncontrolled. Her well-maintained figure, her careful makeup, her color-coordinated shirt and creased cotton trousers —even her age, since she looked more like the girl's older sister than her mother. Her dark hair was short in that kind of wedge cut working women seemed to favor, and her face wore a practiced, polite receptionist mask.

Now she gave Michael an appraising look. "Do you?"

Michael met her eyes. "Yes."

She must have believed him because the polite expression became a bit more real. "I'll go with you to do whatever needs to be done. Amy can wait here."

The mother ignored Michael then as she settled the daughter on one of the plastic chairs. She gave her extra tissues, handed her a magazine, and gently pushed the girl's hair back from her face before she followed Michael down the hallway.

Once they were out of earshot of the girl, the mother said, "My son-in-law wanted to come with her and let me stay with the baby, but I knew it would be better if I came. I've helped Amy cope every other time her father let her down."

The woman's words surprised Michael. "I'm sure your ex-husband didn't intend to get shot."

She looked over at him, and her polite look vanished. Disgust, anger, and bitterness mixed and made her suddenly look years older. Then as quickly, she had her face under control again. "You didn't know Jay."

"No," Michael said. "But it might help if I did know more about him."

Again the assessing look. Again she decided to speak her mind. "If somebody shot Jay, he pushed them to it."

"What do you mean?" Michael slowed his step to look over at her.

"I mean, I doubt Jay was an innocent bystander." She turned her head to stare straight down the hallway. "He had a way of finding trouble. Trouble he brought home to me and the kids before I finally had the sense to leave."

"What kind of trouble?" When the woman didn't answer immediately, Michael slipped in another question. "Was he abusive?"

"Oh no." Her voice softened the barest bit. "Not in a physical way. Actually Jay was a very nice man. He loved us, especially the kids. His trouble was, he liked gambling more. He'd bet on anything. Sometimes before we got up in the morning, he'd want to bet with me whether or not the sun was going to shine."

She shook her head at the memory. "I begged him to go for help. I even tried betting with him a few times, and that if I won, he had to promise to change. He always backed out on those bets. He did that a lot. Didn't pay up on his bets and not just to me."

Michael kept quiet. He made a wrong turn and had to backtrack to the elevators. The woman didn't seem to notice. She was too busy trying to explain to him what had made Jay Rayburn the way he was, or maybe she was still trying to explain it to herself.

"He always claimed he did it for us. So we'd have more." Sadness pushed the other expressions off her face. "Jay was so sure he was going to hit the jackpot with one of his bets. He used to have me almost believing it myself. Then I realized that even if he did win big, he'd just lose bigger the next day." Her eyes came back to Michael.

"Do you know any compulsive gamblers?"

"I've come across a few in my line of work." Michael finally found the elevator and punched the button.

She smiled wryly. "I suppose you have. Men like Jay will do anything to get enough money to try again tomorrow. I'm still paying on some of the debts he made while we were married."

The elevator door slid open and they stepped inside. No one else was aboard.

"Do you know if he was in some kind of trouble at the present time?" The elevator doors closed and they began descending to the morgue.

"I wouldn't know. We didn't keep in touch. There was no reason to." She stared at the numbers of the floors lighting up.

"Do you think his death could be connected to his gambling?" The elevator lurched to a stop. He followed her out into the hallway.

"I'd be surprised if it wasn't. Jay must have been in deep to somebody because he hit Amy up for a loan a few weeks ago." The mother's eyes flashed with anger. "She didn't tell me until today."

"Did she give him the money?"

"Yes."

"How much?"

"Five hundred dollars." Her eyes narrowed and her hands tightened into fists. If Jay Rayburn hadn't been dead already, he'd have been in for some trouble from his ex-wife.

Michael wanted to throw out a few more questions before she regained her composure, but the guy at the desk was ready for them. She looked at the dead man's driver's license and confirmed he really was Jay Rayburn. Then she filled out the paperwork.

The identification process was grim even without having to actually physically identify the corpse, and the woman's polite receptionist look was back, along with a pale tightness about her mouth and eyes that hadn't been there earlier.

The guy at the desk was young with long, lank hair pulled back in a ponytail. Dead bodies were just so many file folders to him, but he seemed to enjoy the woman's discomfort as he slid his eyes over her. He smiled a little and asked, "You want a peek at the guy?"

The ex-wife's face went a shade paler.

"That won't be necessary," Michael said.

"If you're sure, that's good enough for us." He scanned the paperwork, then yelled at a man in the hallway leading back to the morgue. "Looks like we've got a name for number 47. That's the second ID today. We're on a roll, huh, Charlie?" Without waiting for the man to answer, he turned his attention back to the woman. "Where do you want us to ship him out to?"

Alice Hawfield coldly informed the man that arrangements would be made to have the body picked up as soon as the police released it.

As they got on the elevator, she muttered, "Creep."

"Creepy job, I guess."

She flashed him a look but didn't say anything.

As the elevator made grinding noises and started up, Michael asked, "Would you mind answering a few more questions before we rejoin your daughter?"

"That's all I've been doing ever since we left her." She didn't sound upset. Instead she smiled a little and her tone was almost friendly. "I don't usually talk so much." Her smile disappeared as the assessing look came back.

"I realize this has to be hard for you." Michael kept a few stock phrases ready to ease over awkward minutes, and somehow this had become one. "But anything you can tell me could prove helpful."

"You mean in solving the case?" she asked.

"Yes. Someone shot your former husband, Mrs. Hawfield. Even if you haven't kept in contact with him, you still surely want to see the responsible party apprehended and punished."

"Or rewarded." She appeared to be sorry as soon as she said it, but she didn't try to take the words back. Instead she lifted her chin and looked straight at Michael. "I guess that sounded terrible, maybe even incriminating, but there's no need in me saying I didn't mean it. I'm glad he's where he can't hurt Amy anymore."

Michael kept quiet.

After a moment, she breathed out a sigh and went on. "But I didn't really hate Jay enough to wish him dead. So ask your questions, Deputy Keane. I've nothing to hide."

The elevator stopped at their floor. They stepped out and moved over against the wall instead of heading back toward the lobby and the girl.

"You said Jay borrowed money from your daughter. Did he give her a reason for needing the money?" Michael was glad the corridor was deserted.

"He did, but of course, it was a lie. He told her he had to have some work done on his car and he was a little short on cash. He promised to have the money back to her within the month." Again the anger flashed across her face.

"Why are you so sure it was a lie?"

"Jay always lied. Worst of all, he lied to himself. I'm sure he really believed he'd be able to give Amy the money back when he said he would. That was always his problem. He wouldn't face the truth."

"What was the truth?" Michael considered pulling his phone out to record their conversation, but he worried that might stop her talking.

"That he'd always be a loser and one day his gambling would get him into trouble he couldn't get out of. I guess it finally did."

"How do you mean?"

"That seems obvious." She frowned. "Somebody shot him. He must have gotten in too deep with the wrong people."

"What people?" Michael asked.

"Those people who loan you money when you can't get it anywhere else. Loan sharks." She stared at the wall across from them. "He was already mixed up with people like that before we divorced. Some men followed him to the house once and pushed Jay around a little. Jay said it wasn't anything to worry about, that they'd wait for their money. He claimed to have some kind of deal going that would take care of everything."

"What deal was that?"

"Who knows?" She pushed aside his question quickly and went back to the past again as if it were playing out on the wall in front of her eyes. "I went to the mall the next day with the kids. Jimmy was thirteen, old enough that I didn't think I had to watch him all the time. Certainly old enough to go to the men's room alone." Her face became very still as the fear the memory brought back was still all too real to her. "They must have been following us, waiting. They painted red streaks on Jimmy's face and told him to tell his father next time it wouldn't be paint."

When she stopped talking, Michael asked, "Did you file a report with the police?"

The woman laughed without humor. "The police don't worry much about protecting families of men who play around with that kind of people."

Michael didn't argue the point, just let her keep talking.

"Jimmy had nightmares for months. He wouldn't go anywhere except to school. Was almost afraid to come out of his room."

"What did you do?"

"The only thing I could do." Her eyes, hard and cold, came back to Michael. "I begged the money from my parents and went with Jay to pay the men off. I didn't dare let him go alone because I knew he might stop and gamble away the money on the way. When we got home, I packed some clothes, and the kids and I moved back in with my parents."

"I don't think anybody could blame you for that." Michael pulled out another stock phrase.

"Amy cried, but Jimmy didn't. I should have left Jay long before I did."

⊰ 19 ⊱

When the daughter saw the mother again, new tears gushed out. Michael went in search of coffee to give them a few minutes alone. By the time he got back with the tepid, too-strong coffee, the girl's tears had slowed. She took the Styrofoam cup gratefully and, after a few sips, claimed to be ready to answer whatever questions he had.

The daughter couldn't tell him much more than

he'd already heard from the mother. Yes, her father had borrowed some money from her a few weeks ago. No, she hadn't seen him. She wired the money to him. He needed to fix his car so that he could make his service rounds and come up to see her baby. Here, she almost started to cry again, but she tightened her lips and blinked back any new tears.

No, she didn't know how he planned to pay her back. Out of his next paycheck, she supposed. As she said it, she looked down, a guilty flush spreading across her cheeks. The daughter, the same as the mother, had known she'd never get her five hundred dollars back.

Then, as if she felt disloyal, she lifted her head and stared straight at Michael. "But Dad said he had something going, and that when he paid me back, he'd pay me double so I could start a college fund for Jason." She jutted her chin out. "And he would have too."

At this, Michael half expected the mother to say it would have never happened, but instead she simply touched the girl's hand and said softly, "Your father would have thought Jason was something special."

Michael was afraid that would start the girl's tears again, but on the contrary, the words seemed to give her new strength. So he went on with his questions. No, she didn't know what her father might have been talking about.

She couldn't say whether or not he knew anybody in Hidden Springs. She'd never heard of Hidden Springs. She really didn't see her father that often. They talked on the phone maybe once every other week. She hadn't seen him since January. He just dropped by to see her whenever he was close to Cincinnati. He had planned to come next week to see the baby.

No, no one had ever called her or anything, looking for her father. When Michael glanced over at the mother, she said the same. They neither one had any idea who might have shot him.

When Michael asked whether Jay Rayburn had a girlfriend, the daughter said her father never mentioned any friends at all. That brought on a new stricken look as she said, "I never thought of that before. He must have been so lonesome."

The mother reached over to take the girl's hand. "Just because he didn't tell you about friends doesn't mean he didn't have them. Jay was always very outgoing. I'm sure he had friends, maybe even women friends." She didn't seem bothered at all by that thought.

"But if he did, you don't know who they are?" Michael looked straight at the mother.

She didn't shy away from his stare. "It's like I told you earlier. We didn't stay in contact. There was no reason to after the children grew up."

Michael hesitated, kicking himself for not asking this question before they rejoined the daughter, but he went ahead and threw out the question he wanted answered. "Did your husband have affairs while you were married?"

Alice Hawfield narrowed her eyes on Michael. "What could old history like that possibly have to do with Jay getting shot now?"

"Probably nothing," Michael admitted. "But for years, your ex-husband has been stopping at a restaurant near Hidden Springs. Maybe he made some friends there."

"You're not asking about other friends. You're asking about another woman," the mother said flatly.

"Yes." Michael didn't hesitate this time. He had to know.

When the mother glanced at the daughter, the girl said, "Mother, I'm not a child anymore. If you know anything that might help, tell him."

"I don't see how it could help." Alice Hawfield took another look at her daughter. "It wasn't another woman who took him from us, but there was once when I wondered."

She paused, looking more uncomfortable than she had at any time since Michael had asked his first question.

"When was that?" Michael prodded her.

"Not long before we split up. Eleven, twelve years ago." She shifted in the lobby chair, making the seat squeak. "I haven't thought about this for years. I'm surprised I even remember it with everything else that was going on. That could be why I do remember. We were having all these problems of our own, and Jay was obsessed with something that had happened to this woman he knew from the road."

Michael interrupted. "Do you remember her name?"

She thought a moment. "If he ever said her name, I don't remember it. He talked about people he met on the road that way. Without names. He knew I wouldn't know them anyway, so he'd say something like West End Bill or Louisville Lady."

"Did he do that this time?" Michael wanted to push Roxanne's name at the woman, but he waited.

"I don't think he ever said Hidden Springs anything, but then it's all been so long ago."

"But you remember him talking about a woman," Michael prompted.

"Only because when Jay talked about her I realized how attracted he was to her, whether he'd done anything about it or not. As I said, she was in some kind of trouble, and he wanted us to help her. I remember wondering if he was in love with her, and that's when I discovered I didn't care. Maybe that's why I remember it. Because I didn't care."

She sent a look of silent apology toward the daughter. "Jay talked on and on about this woman.

The hard time she was having. He even wanted to loan her money as if we had any money to loan. I remember thinking I should be jealous, but I just didn't care."

Michael pushed a few more questions at her, but that was all Alice Hawfield could recall. The woman Rayburn wanted to help might have been a waitress, but she could also have been a motel clerk or somebody in one of the offices Jay visited. She didn't think Jay mentioned a child or children, but he could have. It was so long ago.

At last, Michael threw out the name Roxanne.

"Roxanne?" The woman echoed the name, then shook her head. "I don't remember anything about a Roxanne. I'm sorry, but I can't see how any of this could help you in your investigation."

Michael took a drink of the stone cold coffee to give him a moment to think, but he couldn't come up with any more questions. He printed his name and phone number on a couple of Sheriff Potter's old campaign cards and asked them to call if they thought of anything else that might help.

When Michael trotted out a couple more of his stock phrases, the daughter gave him a trembling smile. The mother didn't smile, but her assessing look was friendlier.

Before going out the door, Michael glanced back at them. The girl stood forlornly watching the mother straighten the magazines on the table and pick up tissues and coffee cups.

On the drive back to Hidden Springs, Michael considered the mother. Her bitter anger toward her ex-husband could be counted motive. Marital complications often figured in homicides. The woman hadn't shown an inkling of sorrow that Jay Rayburn was dead, only relief that he wouldn't be able to hurt her daughter anymore.

Not that death always stopped those kinds of hurts. Especially a death like this, but if she thought it could, that might strengthen her motive. Even if she was at work miles from Hidden Springs on Tuesday, she could have hired someone to kill Rayburn. In that scenario, why not in Hidden Springs?

Michael let the idea circle in his mind as he pulled out and around a slow-moving tractor-trailer truck, but it just wouldn't fit the woman. If Alice Hawfield had shot Jay Rayburn, she'd have shot him point-blank, covered his dead body with an old blanket, and then washed her hands before she called the police. Simple, straight-forward, to the point.

As he stared at the road, Michael just couldn't make her a suspect. He was almost to the exit for Hidden Springs, the town's name little more than an afterthought to the real reason for the exit, Eagle Lake. Maybe he should have asked the mother about that. Rayburn might have linked the woman from his past to Eagle Lake. Eagle Lake waitress or something like that.

That morning, Michael had headed to Eagleton thinking Rayburn might be Anthony's father. Now he was driving home, somehow sure he wasn't. He didn't have any proof one way or the other. At the same time, Michael had a gut feeling the woman Rayburn had wanted to help was Roxanne. He could be reaching for straws in his search for a reason for Rayburn to be in Hidden Springs. Plus, even if the man had known Roxanne, what possible connection could that have to his murder? Roxanne left Hidden Springs years ago.

At the office, Sheriff Potter listened to Michael run through what the women had told him and then said, "So they weren't much help other than his gambling, and Buck had already found out about that."

Michael sat down at his desk. "I'll write up a report on what they said anyway."

"Good." The sheriff leaned forward in his chair. "We'd better go by the book on this one in case the higher-ups get involved. It might turn out to be more than we suspect, but right now it's looking like those men his ex-wife talked about finally got tired of waiting for their money."

"Could be." Michael gave the computer on his desk a look, but grabbed a notepad instead. He could think better with a pen in his hand.

"Oh, by the way." The sheriff's voice was casual, as though talking about somebody bringing in doughnuts. "Darrell Peterson came in this morning, and we got that mess all squared away."

Michael looked up. "Did you?"

"Sure. First offense. Juveniles like that. I don't think it'll happen again. They're basically good boys who just got carried away. You remember how it was, don't you?"

"No." Michael kept his eyes on the sheriff's face. He'd known the sheriff would let the boys off, and he did hope the boys would straighten up after their little scare last night. But he wasn't going to pretend he thought the sheriff had done the right thing.

Sheriff Potter gave a wave of his hand like he was flicking away a pesky fly. "No sense making criminals out of kids if you don't have to."

"What if it had been Anthony Blake who'd stolen the stuff? Would you have given him another chance?"

The sheriff's eyebrows almost met as he frowned over at Michael. "Good granny gravy, Mike, we've bent over backwards for that boy a dozen times, and what good has it done so far?"

Michael looked down at his desk. "I guess you're right, Sheriff. Sorry."

"That's okay. I know you've made a personal case of straightening up that boy, but sometimes in our business we have to face facts. And the fact is, the Blake kid doesn't want to straighten up."

"Aunt Lindy thinks he does. She has him doing his homework."

"Well, Malinda has worked miracles before." The sheriff leaned back, wincing when his chair creaked loudly. He looked over at Betty Jean. "Did you buy the oil for this chair yet, Betty Jean?"

"No, Uncle Al. You said you'd take care of that." Betty Jean answered without shifting her attention away from her computer screen.

"I did? Huh." The sheriff turned back to Michael. "But if I was you, Mike, I'd keep a close eye on that boy and think twice about letting him be alone with Malinda." Sheriff Potter picked up a pencil and twirled it between his fingers.

"Come on, Sheriff. Anthony's never done anything that bad. Minor stuff mostly."

"Maybe so, but the boy's got an attitude." The sheriff leaned forward, his chair popping and creaking again. This time he didn't appear to notice as he stared over at Michael. "I saw him the morning we found the body out front, and he looked guilty as all get-out. I'm thinking he knew something he wasn't telling."

"I know. I saw him too. I asked him about it, but he says he just happened by and stopped to gawk like everybody else."

"And you believed him?" The sheriff's eyes narrowed a little.

"No."

"That's what I mean. You've got to watch the boy. He's a hard one to peg, and it's no telling what he might do next."

"I can't believe he had anything to do with the shooting." Michael couldn't keep from coming to Anthony's defense.

"I'm not saying he did, but you best keep an eye on him, like I said."

"I plan to do that."

Sheriff Potter stood up and put on his hat. "I'm going up the street." He glanced at Betty Jean. "Got to get that oil. I'll be at the Grill if anybody needs me."

Betty Jean looked up from her computer. "You haven't told Michael about Paul calling."

"Oh yeah, I nearly forgot that." The sheriff turned back to Michael. "Paul's back to knowing where he is, and he wants you to call him over at the hospital and give him a report."

"Great." Michael didn't hide his lack of enthusiasm. "How about if I just take a copy of my report over to the chief?"

"Nope, you call Paul. He says they're letting him go home on Monday, and he's thinking he can run the investigation from his house for a while. Just till he gets back to the office." The sheriff grinned. "I told him we'd be glad to work with him any way we could."

"Thanks for nothing." Michael didn't crack a

smile as he added, "Actually Buck and I have been talking about taking a couple of weeks off to go fishing now that the weather's warming up. This might be the perfect time."

"Now, none of that kind of talk." The sheriff laughed. "You boys are going to have to learn to work together."

"You tell that to Buck."

"I expect I'll have to. Several times. But the fact is, it don't matter much anyhow. Like I already told you, I don't figure whoever did Rayburn in stayed around town."

"I wish I could believe that," Michael said.

"I don't know why you can't. Nobody in Hidden Springs even knew this guy, much less had any reason to shoot him. Now, I don't think we've got anybody in this town that would just walk up and shoot somebody without some kind of reason, do you?" He didn't expect Michael to answer as he went on. "That kind of meanness may go on in the cities where folks are pushed in too close on one another, but not out here. Not in Hidden Springs."

Judge Campbell spotted the sheriff in the doorway and came across the hall. "What's this that's not in Hidden Springs?" His voice was at normal boom level.

"I was just telling Mike here that if folks shoot one another in Hidden Springs, they generally have a pretty darn good reason, and I'm thinking we can be pretty sure whoever shot this Rayburn fellow is long gone from here."

"You haven't found out anything then about who did it?" The judge peeked around the sheriff at Michael. "I heard you went to Eagleton today to meet with the victim's family. Did they know why the man was here in Hidden Springs?"

Michael shook his head, and the sheriff answered for him. "They neither one ever heard of Hidden Springs."

"Neither one?" the judge said.

"The daughter and ex-wife," Sheriff Potter explained. "But the ex-wife backed up what we already knew about Rayburn. He was up to his eyeballs in debt to folks what don't mess around if you don't pay up."

"Then you think that's what happened." The judge looked from the sheriff to Michael again.

"It's a possibility." Michael shrugged a little. "But we're low on proof."

"Well, proof is good if you're taking something to trial, but proof in black and white isn't all that necessary if you're just deciding what actually happened." The judge looked back at the sheriff. "You've seen a lot of those kind of cases in your days, haven't you, Al? Ones where you knew who did it, but there wasn't any way you could get them convicted in a court of law."

"Not so many." Sheriff Potter's voice rose to match the judge's just in case some voters might be loitering out in the hall hearing their conversation. "We take care of our people."

"Of course you do," Judge Campbell said. "I wasn't suggesting that you didn't. I'm confident you'll get this cleared up in no time at all."

"Michael's working on it." Sheriff Potter's smile was back. "And the deputy always gets his man."

When both the men at the door laughed, Michael managed a smile, but he wasn't sorry when the two men drifted on up the hall and out the door. The judge's every word was clear till the front door swung shut behind them.

"Thank goodness they're gone," Betty Jean muttered. "The judge could wake the dead."

"He does have a way of broadcasting anything we tell him to the rest of the town." Michael got up and poured himself a cup of coffee.

"I don't guess any of it's a secret." Betty Jean looked up from her computer screen. "The investigation, I mean."

"No, I don't suppose so."

"Good." She looked relieved. "I mean, you didn't tell me not to say anything, and the judge was over here earlier asking how things were going with the case."

"Nothing unusual about that. The judge doesn't like anything going on in Hidden Springs that he doesn't know about." Michael sat back down at his desk and looked at the phone. He'd have to call Paul whether he wanted to or not.

"I guess so," Betty Jean said slowly. "But he seems extra interested in this."

"So's everybody else." Michael looked down at the little stack of messages on his desk. Paul's number was on the top. He tried to ignore it. "Wouldn't you feel better if we knew who the murderer was?"

"I think it's like Uncle Al says. Whoever did it is long gone now. Besides, it had to be the mob. Everybody says so." Betty Jean stared back at her screen. "But all this commotion doesn't help me get my work done. First Miss Willadean came in to see if it was safe for crazy old ladies to be out on the street. Then Hank Leland shows up, acting like I'm his favorite person in the world."

"Poor Hank. I guess you didn't give him the time of day."

"He's got a watch." Betty Jean gave a little sniff and went on with her recital. "He was still hanging around, trying to overhear me saying something on the phone, when Stella Pinkston saunters on back here. Of course, it doesn't take a genius to know she's more interested in the investigator than the investigation. She didn't tarry long when she saw you weren't here. And all the time the phone's ringing. Folks must think I'm Hidden Springs's own information bureau."

"You usually know what's going on."

"Knowing and telling are two different things," Betty Jean pointed out. "Anyway, then when the judge came in here acting like he's a real judge or something with all his questions, that was the last straw. I called Uncle Al and told him he'd have to come stay down here till you or Lester came in."

"Sounds like a traumatic morning all the way around." Michael grinned over at her. "Tell you what. If it'll help, I won't talk to you the rest of the day."

"Promises, promises." Betty Jean made a face at him. "Of course, when Lester gets here, he'll have to tell me all the cute things every kid did or said today."

"Quit pretending to be cross about that. You wish at least a dozen of those kids were yours."

"Only a half dozen," Betty Jean said without smiling. "Now keep your promise, call Paul Osgood, and let me get my work done."

Michael picked up the note with Paul's cell number, but didn't pick up the phone. When he felt Betty Jean watching him, he said, "I'll call him later. He might be resting just now."

"Whatever." Betty Jean shrugged. "Just don't try leaving this office without calling him. I've already talked to him once today, and once is my limit."

"Okay." Michael breathed out a sigh. "I promise

I'll call before I leave. Any of these other calls anything I need to know about?" He waved the pink notes at her.

"You could try reading them yourself, you know. But Karen called. Said she couldn't get you on your cell. She would have texted you, but she was afraid you'd left your phone at home or forgotten to charge it up. Does she know you or what?" Betty Jean shot him a look. "Anyway, she says tonight is sort of dress-up, and she was worried you might show up in your uniform." Betty Jean's fingers fell idle on the keyboard, and her eyes got dreamy. "It must be heaven to have a guy at your beck and call."

"I thought you were working on a new boy-friend."

"I'm not ready to let him know I'm interested yet and don't you dare say anything to anybody about it." She gave Michael a warning look. "I figure I'd better lose another twenty pounds first. That'll shorten the odds of him saying no."

"You're adorable the way you are, Betty Jean."

"Then how come you're going out with Karen instead of me?" She began typing again. "Oh yeah, and Reece Sheridan called. Said his niece would be in town tonight or tomorrow, and he really appreciates you taking her out to dinner while she's here." Betty Jean glanced over at him with raised eyebrows. "Maybe while you're up there at that show in Eagleton with Karen tonight, you can get another set of tickets for tomorrow night."

"Alex Sheridan is an old friend, Betty Jean. We used to play together when we were kids."

"What'd you play? Doctor?"

Michael shook his head at Betty Jean and changed the subject. "I guess I might as well go ahead and call Paul."

"Good." Betty Jean laughed as he punched in Paul's number. Then in her best Sheriff Potter voice, she said, "Because you boys are just going to have to learn to work together."

⊰ 20 ⊱

Paul Osgood had to hear it all slowly, and most of it twice. Michael could almost see him cranked up in the hospital bed, meticulously writing down Michael's every word on a yellow notepad.

Michael drew squares on his desk calendar and tried to be patient as he repeated the information. But there were limits, and his patience was wearing thin even before Paul started harping on how Michael had to find the murder weapon.

"It's all very well to know who the victim is," Paul said. "But finding the murder weapon is vital to solving the case. You did search the grounds there at the courthouse, didn't you?"

"You know we did." Michael drew a new square, darker than the others. "You were here."

"Could be you missed something. Make another search right away."

Michael pressed down so hard with his pen that as he drew a new line, the nib broke, but he kept his voice level. "Okay. Anything else?"

Betty Jean looked up from her computer, started to smile, thought better of it, and studied her screen again.

On the other end of the phone, Paul was speaking slowly. "I don't think so. It appears as if you've been handling things fairly well while I've been incapacitated, but I insist you make finding the murder weapon a number one priority."

"Whatever you say." Michael took a deep breath and relaxed his grip on the receiver. "But I sort of doubt it's just lying around waiting for us to find it. Whoever shot Rayburn probably carried it away with him."

"Then he may have disposed of it somewhere else. What do you think are the possibilities?"

"Well, let's see." Michael found another pen and began doodling again. This time he drew guns. "He could have put it in a trash Dumpster or maybe just stuck it under his car seat to use on the first policeman to pull him over. Who knows? Could be he pitched it in the lake."

"That's an idea." Paul sounded excited. "I'll bet that's what he did. The lake would make a perfect disposal place. He'd think we'd never find it there."

"And he'd be right."

"Not necessarily. We could get divers."

"Paul, what kind of medication are you on?" Michael's patience was ready to snap the way the pen's point had moments ago. "We can't search the lake for a gun we aren't even sure is in there, and even if we were sure, we'd still never find it. It's a big lake."

"We'll have to pinpoint the most likely disposal spot." Paul was obviously not bothered at all by Michael's arguments.

"If the killer tells us where he pitched the gun in the lake, we won't need the gun. We'll have the killer."

"That wouldn't negate the need for physical evidence."

"Maybe you'd better talk to the chief. See what he has to say." Michael gave up the fight. Then before Paul had time to come up with any other insane ideas, Michael said a quick "hope you feel better soon" and hung up.

Michael stared at the phone and wondered what the chances were of Paul needing some other kind of emergency surgery before next week. Slim to none, unfortunately. Instead, it looked like they'd have to figure out the easiest place to search the lake for a gun and make a show of it.

It would have to be done, crazy or not. Paul was like a pit bull when he got hold of an idea. He wouldn't turn it loose.

Michael stood up and told Betty Jean, "I think I'll go get a haircut."

"Joe's not back." Betty Jean kept her eyes on her computer screen. "I looked when I went out at lunch. They say his sister has cancer. I forget what kind, but it's bad."

"Well, then maybe I'll get something to eat. I forgot about lunch."

"I wish I could forget things like that." Betty Jean sighed.

Out on the street, Michael looked over toward Joe's Barbershop. The handwritten note was still taped to the door. Maybe it was just because of his sister that Joe had gone to Tennessee. Maybe being worried about her was what was bothering Joe when Michael talked to him after Rayburn's body was found. Michael's need for some kind of lead might have him imagining something when nothing was there.

Michael didn't know why he needed a definite answer as to who shot the man. He needed to accept the obvious. Jay Rayburn had not paid his debts to the wrong people one time too many. They'd cut their losses, shot him, and got out of town fast. Was Michael being like Paul, unable to let go of his own idea of what happened?

Michael smiled at that thought. He didn't have any absolute ideas of what happened to let go of. So why not let it be loan sharks?

As Michael passed the newspaper office, Hank

Leland almost tore off the door getting outside. "Hey, Mike, wait up."

Michael didn't stop walking but slowed down a little. "How's it going, Hank? Got enough news for next week's issue yet?"

"I think we're going to have to print three sections. A lot of stuff going on at the schools with just two weeks left in the school year." Hank was panting from rushing to catch Michael. "Where you headed?"

"To the Grill to grab a bite."

"Sort of late for lunch, isn't it?" Hank looked at his watch. "But what the heck? A piece of pie sounds good. Mind if I join you?"

At the Grill, the big round community table was practically full as the judge held forth about the latest happenings in the homicide investigation. The sheriff sipped his coffee and inserted a word here and there when the judge looked his way. Between them, the two men could get just about anything done in Keane County they thought needed doing.

"Here's the man now," the judge boomed when Michael came in the door. "Pull up a chair." He didn't notice Hank behind Michael.

"Got room for two?" Hank peeked around Michael to ask.

"Oh, hello there, Hank." The judge's smile stayed firmly in place. "Sure, we can always make room for one more."

"Never mind, Judge. We wouldn't want to crowd you." Michael got the judge off the hook. "Besides, I'm planning on ordering some of Cindy's special onion rings, and if I sit up here, every one of you would be wanting me to share."

Sheriff Potter smiled with a little nod at Michael. While the sheriff claimed not to have anything personal against Hank, that didn't mean he was ready to talk to the editor unless he had to.

Just having Hank in the room put a damper on the conversation at the middle table, and before long a couple of the men headed back to their stores. A Realtor had some houses to show, and one of the insurance agents needed to make some calls.

By the time Michael was finishing up the last of his onion rings, even the judge and the sheriff had left and the only other customer in the Grill besides Hank and him was a retired magistrate up in one of the front booths, leafing through the Grill's copy of the *Eagleton News*.

When Cindy came out of the kitchen to fill up their coffee cups and offer Michael a piece of pecan pie, Michael apologized. "Sorry, Cindy. Looks like we ran off your business."

"It wasn't you. It was old big ears here," Cindy said, but she was smiling. "Actually I might give you coffee on the house if you want to come in every afternoon about this time, Hank. Those guys come in here and drink enough coffee to float a boat. They've got so they don't even order pie most of the time. All on low cholesterol diets or something. I don't know how they expect us to make a living."

"But you're always trying to talk me out of pie," Hank said.

"That's because the more I say it's bad for you, the more you want it." She picked up Michael's empty dinner plate.

"Then tell me how bad ice cream is for me so you can plop a big scoop on top before you bring a piece of that pecan pie on over."

After she brought their pie and left a fresh pot of coffee on the table, she disappeared into the kitchen to start on the dinner offerings before the after-school crowd stormed in for fries and sodas.

Hank attacked his pie and finished it off in record time, saying it wasn't as good if the ice cream melted. Then he sat back and fingered his notebook as he watched Michael eat more slowly. He'd already third-degreed Michael about Rayburn's family, and Michael had told him the basic facts without going into detail.

But Hank had obviously been doing some checking on his own. "I hear our guy was a big-time gambler."

"I wouldn't say big-time exactly," Michael said.

"What would you say?"

"That he liked to bet, but he wasn't very good at it."

"You think he made one bet too many?" Hank asked.

"I think he may have had some financial problems, but I don't think that was anything new for him."

"Nope. According to my sources . . ." Hank apparently enjoyed the sound of that so much he repeated it. "According to my sources, Rayburn was over his limit on his credit cards, and his bank laughed and hung up on him if he asked about loans."

"You talk to somebody at his bank?"

"My source didn't want to be identified," Hank said importantly.

"Come on, Hank. Get down off your source horse."

The editor shook his head. "I can't tell you. Really. A newspaperman has to protect his confidential sources. It's a matter of honor." Hank looked almost sorry to hold out on Michael. "But I've already told you everything the person told me. You couldn't find out anything more by talking to him yourself."

"I might know better questions to ask."

Hank studied Michael's face. "Do you?"

Michael pushed away his pie plate and refilled his coffee cup before he admitted, "No."

"So." The editor sat up straighter and leaned a little toward Michael. "What do you think about it all? Why did this loser get dispatched on the courthouse steps?"

Michael's eyes went to the editor's notebook on the table.

"Okay. Off the record." The editor picked up the notebook and slipped it back into his pocket. "You know I wouldn't do anything to antagonize the only person left in Hidden Springs who will drink coffee and eat pie with me."

"Not unless you thought it would make a good story in the next issue of the *Gazette*."

Hank clapped his hand over his heart. "You injure me."

"Right."

Hank grinned at him. "Okay. So you don't injure me, but give me a break, Mike. If I wanted to be a low-down, dirt-grubbing reporter, I wouldn't be here in Hidden Springs. I'd be writing for the supermarket tabloids and making enough money to pay for my kid's braces."

"Why are you here in Hidden Springs, Hank?"

"Sometimes I wonder." Hank laughed and brushed a crumb off the table.

"I'm serious." Michael pushed him for a real answer. "You're good at what you do. Why not go where the money is?"

Hank's smile faded as he got a different look on his face. "I don't know. Maybe I like not having to answer to anybody but the folks who buy my paper. And maybe it's just because once a small-town kid, always a small-town kid. Hidden Springs is a lot like the little town where I grew up. I don't know why the courthouse crew has taken such a dislike to me. I don't aim to make anybody look bad."

"Sure." Michael shook his head. "I was swallowing your story up till that last line."

"Okay, so not too bad. I just aim to keep them straight. We've got people here who have been in office so long they think they were born to it or something instead of being voted in."

"Sometimes it almost seems that way." Michael couldn't argue with that. "Take the judge. He's been judge executive ever since they had such a thing in Keane County. I can't remember when he wasn't calling the shots about whose potholes got filled. The sheriff's been in office almost as long, but they do their best for the people."

"Sometimes they only do average. That's when I goad them up to a little higher level of public service by reminding them they are accountable even if they could win the next election without ever kissing another baby."

"It would be a waste of time and money to run against them." Michael took a sip of his coffee. "I don't think the judge has had any competition the last three terms."

"Yeah. I thought about running once just to make it interesting, but I figured folks would take it wrong and cancel their subscriptions." Hank grinned again before his face turned thoughtful. "Now it's my turn. How about you? What made you come back to Hidden Springs? You hanging around hoping to run for sheriff when and if Potter ever decides he's tired of catching the bad guys?"

"Me? Sheriff? I don't think so." Michael ran his finger around the rim of his cup.

"Why not?" Hank leaned on his elbows and studied Michael. "You'd make a good sheriff, or even better, you could take over for the judge if the rumor going around about him running for state representative is true. After all, you are a Keane. It would be like carrying on where your great—however many greats—grandfather left off."

"It's Aunt Lindy who worries about that sort of thing. Not me."

"You're here, aren't you?" Hank sat back and twirled his coffee cup around on the table a couple of times. "We both know it's not for the money a deputy draws down any more than I'm putting out the *Gazette* to get rich."

Michael looked away from Hank out toward the front window. The sun glanced off the dirty window glass and hid the view outside, but Michael knew what was there. People in their stores and businesses going about their quiet, everyday lives.

"What's the matter, Mike?" Hank asked after a minute. "The question too hard?"

"Maybe it is." Michael looked back at him. "I'm

not sure why I came back except that this is where I belong. My roots are here. I want to raise my children here."

"What children?"

"Someday, Hank. Someday."

"Have you told Karen?" Hank raised his eyebrows at Michael.

"Someday doesn't have to be tomorrow. It's better to take things like this slow."

"Nah, it's better to jump in with both feet." With a laugh, Hank reached over and poked Michael's hand. Then he turned thoughtful again. "Sometimes I think that's why you're here, Deputy, because you like having all the answers before you start. And you think you can have the handle on those answers here."

Michael frowned. "You don't know what you're talking about. I've had times when I didn't have any of the answers." A familiar flash of uneasiness shot through Michael as he thought of all the answers lost forever in the quicksand of his mind. Sometimes he had the weirdest feeling that something important, vital even, was trying to struggle to the surface, but it never made it out.

"Maybe that's the reason you like having the answers now," Hank was saying.

"It's my job to find the answers." Michael smoothed out his napkin and began folding it into accordion pleats. "But could be you're right. I didn't like it much in Columbus where I didn't even know what questions needed answers. It feels better here. Safer."

"At least it did before Tuesday, right? That guy getting shot within shouting distance of the sheriff's office had to put a chink in your armor, I'd say. In all our armors." Hank peered at him over the rim of his cup. He took a slurp of the coffee and put his cup down. "I hear Clay Turner sold completely out of locks yesterday. 'Course he probably only had two in stock."

"Folks can get in a panic easy. It's probably like the sheriff says. The murderer is probably long gone from Hidden Springs."

"Do you believe that?"

Michael looked straight at Hank and turned the question back at him. "Do you?"

Hank thought a minute, then sighed. "I wish I could, but I don't know. There's just a bad feel to it somehow, if you know what I mean."

"Come clean, Hank. Do you know something about all this I don't?"

"Me? I was practically the last person in town to even know the guy got shot. I'm always two steps behind." Hank shook his head. "No, this is just a hunch. A reporter's hunch. My granddaddy was a newspaperman back in Hampstead when I was a boy. The paper was going busted even then, but my granddaddy liked to dream I'd take it over someday, and I guess so did I. Anyway, he used to say a hunch to a reporter is like a fleck of gold to a prospector. Once he sees that first little sparkle no matter how tiny it might be, he wants to keep digging to turn up some real nuggets."

"Where are you digging?" Michael asked.

"That's the trouble with this particular hunch." Hank kept his eyes on his cup. "Nobody left behind a map, and it's sort of like the fleck of gold floated down out of thin air. I don't have any idea where it came from, so there's no way to know where to dig."

"So what do you do?"

"Go around dipping in my shovel here and there to see what I might turn up while I keep a real close watch on where other folks are digging." He looked up at Michael. "You for one."

"I haven't turned up much."

"I figure more than you're letting on. Cops can have hunches too." Hank fingered the notebook in his pocket, but didn't pull it out. "One thing for sure. You aren't telling me everything."

"I've told you the facts. You can't print hunches anyway unless you do decide to work for those supermarket tabloids. What is it you're always saying? The truth makes the best story."

"The only story," Hank corrected. "Another of my granddaddy's lessons. Integrity and fairness in reporting the news, community service, and some stories to make them smile. That's what makes up a good hometown paper. Throw in a body on the courthouse steps and everybody wants to buy a copy. I printed a hundred extra copies but still sold out yesterday."

"You didn't shoot Rayburn just to up circulation, did you?"

"I hope that's not one of your hunches." Hank's smile was a little uneasy.

"Hey, I'm joking." Michael laughed. "Don't look so nervous. You'll make me suspicious."

"Just don't go joking like that with Little Osgood or Buck. They'd have me in the slammer before you finished saying 'circulation,' because you were right about that picture in the paper. Little Osgood called me from the hospital as soon as he came out from under anesthesia to raise Cain about it. He wants a retraction."

"How do you print a retraction of a picture?"

"I haven't figured that out yet." Hank twisted his mouth as he thought about that. "Maybe I could get them to pose shaking hands or catch a shot of Buck taking Paul flowers at the hospital."

"You've got more chance of finding real gold on Main Street."

"Yeah, that's what I figured. So guess I'll just have to take the heat." The editor's grin was back. "That's another thing my granddaddy taught me. Learning to take the heat was high on Granddaddy's list. Right up there with trusting your hunches."

All the way back to the office, Michael wished he had some hunches to trust, or maybe he wished he didn't have any hunches. That he could just let Rayburn's murder slide into that great pit of unsolved crimes. What was it they said? If there wasn't a suspect in custody within forty-eight hours, the murderer might never be apprehended.

Michael would keep trying to find out what happened, but it might be good to also start thinking about ways to make folks feel safe in Hidden Springs again.

Betty Jean looked up from listening to Lester's school crossing stories when Michael came in the office. "Paul called again. You owe me. I didn't give him your cell number."

"What now?"

"He wanted to know if you'd searched around the courthouse and parking lot again yet or figured a place to drag the lake." Betty Jean's lips twitched as she barely kept a smile off her face. "Says you know the lake better than him from living on it and so he wants you to say where. He has some people lined up to start in the morning."

"The man's nuts." Michael rubbed his forehead as though to get rid of a headache. A headache named Paul Osgood.

"You won't get any argument from me," Betty Jean said. "But you're still going to have to come up with a place to start. What you figure? You can get over the whole lake in a year, give or take a few months."

Michael sighed and looked at Lester. "You go

fishing a lot, Lester. Where's an out-of-the-way place but one that's close to the road? No need making this too hard to start."

Lester thought a minute. "How about that spot out on Perry Lane? The lake's real deep there, and you can park right by the road on top of the cliff in this little pull-off. You could fish right out of your car if your line was long enough. 'Course, it's steep down to the lake, but not so steep you can't climb out with your fish."

Michael knew the place. While it wasn't on the main road out to the interstate, it wasn't far off it. "Sounds as good a place to ditch a gun as any. Tell you what, Lester. You go on out there tomorrow morning after your crossing duty and supervise things."

"You mean it, Michael?" When Michael nodded, Lester stuck out his chest and fingered his holster flap. "Well, then you bet I will."

Michael bit his lip to keep from smiling and told Betty Jean to let Paul know the location.

"You know they aren't going to find anything." She gave him a look as she picked up the phone.

"They can not find something there as good as anywhere." Michael turned back to the door. "And tell Paul I'm searching the grounds right now."

She started to punch in the number, then stopped. "Wait a minute, Michael. Reece Sheridan called."

"Alex cancel her visit?" Michael tried to tamp down the disappointment that rose up inside him at that thought.

"He didn't say anything about her. He wanted us to check on Joe's cat. Said he wasn't feeling so hot and Janelle's still home with her little boy. He's worried he didn't put out enough food for Two Bits. He said Joe's spare key is up on the top brace of his barbershop pole. I would've done it, but I can't reach that high."

Joe's cat started yowling as soon as Michael put the key in the lock. The sound raised the hairs on Michael's neck, and he pushed the door open quickly, figuring Two Bits must be hung in something or hurt somehow. Joe would be heartbroken if anything happened to that cat.

The smell hit him in the face, but he still couldn't quite believe it. Joe was slumped on the floor in a pool of blood between his barber's chair and the sink, a pair of scissors sticking out of his neck. The cat stood on Joe's legs, blood on his paws and his fur ruffed up as he yowled again.

Michael stared at Joe's body and wanted to yowl along with the cat. Nobody was going to feel safe in Hidden Springs for a long time to come.

⚜ 21 ⚜

Finding a body on the courthouse steps had been bad, but Rayburn had been a stranger. His murder was little more than a puzzle in need of a solution.

Joe was one of them. That changed everything. Michael would still have to solve it or at least try, but now he dreaded the answer he might find. Whoever stuck those scissors in Joe's neck was also one of them.

With a heavy heart, Michael pushed the door closed behind him and moved carefully across the shop to squat down beside Joe. Two Bits stopped yowling and fixed mournful eyes on Michael.

Joe stared at him too, his eyes set, vacant. Michael should have been able to stop this. He should have made Joe tell him what he knew about Rayburn's death, but now whatever answers the man had were forever lost to Michael.

"I'm sorry, Joe." Michael touched the man's arm. It was cold. The killer must have been waiting for Joe when he came in that morning, but how did he know Joe would be back today? Even Reece hadn't known that. Unless Reece was the murderer.

Michael jerked back from the thought. Reece could no more have stuck those scissors in Joe than Michael could have himself. But somebody had. Somebody Joe knew. Michael shut his eyes a moment and tried to quell the sick feeling rising inside him. He wanted to go back to rumors about the mob.

He covered Joe with the black plastic cape the barber kept draped across his chair waiting for his next customer. The cat stepped onto it and circled twice. The plastic crackled under his feet before the cat curled up on the cape.

Michael pulled his eyes away from the body and surveyed the room. Bloody paw prints crisscrossed the worn floor, but there were no shoe prints. In fact, nothing was out of order except Joe and his bottle of combs and scissors, which were spilled down in the sink. Even the cat was where he liked best to be. In Joe's lap.

Joe's fingers peeked out from under the black cape. They grasped no bit of cloth or paper that might supply a clue. No name or initials had been traced out in blood on the floor. There was nothing.

Michael looked up at the ceiling. He wanted to say a prayer for Joe. For them all. Death seemed to demand it, but he didn't know what to pray. It would do no good to pray what he wanted, and that was to see Joe sitting in his chair stroking Two Bits the same as any other day. A terrible sadness swept over Michael as he looked back down at Joe's body.

"God help us," he whispered.

At the sound of Michael's voice, Two Bits looked up at Michael and mewed pitifully as if the cat realized Michael wasn't going to be any help after all.

"If only you could talk, Two Bits," Michael said softly.

Michael unclipped his radio and called it in.

This time was different. The sheriff was there in two minutes, his face rigid and grim as he barked out orders to Betty Jean on the radio. Chief Sibley showed up minutes later and slumped down in one of Joe's waiting chairs, a sickly green cast on his face.

When Betty Jean came over to get Two Bits, tears streamed down her cheeks. Michael wanted to hug her, but he had his hands full, holding on to the frenzied cat.

"He's not happy," Michael told her. "And he needs his paws washed."

Betty Jean stared at the blood on the cat's fur and Michael's uniform. "This can't be happening."

"What can't be happening?" Judge Campbell stepped up beside Betty Jean.

With a sudden yowl, Two Bits twisted and jerked free of Michael's hold, hurled through the air, and landed on the judge's chest with all his claws extended.

"What the . . . ?" The judge knocked the cat off him.

The fall dazed Two Bits, and Betty Jean scooped

up the cat before he recovered enough to run away. She cooed at him. "There, there, baby. It's going to be all right." She glanced up at Michael. "I better get him away from here."

"Right." Michael nodded at her, then looked at the judge. "You all right, Judge?"

"What got into that cat?" The judge dabbed at a scratch on the back of his hand with his handkerchief. "I never saw Two Bits act like that."

"Joe's dead." Michael didn't know any easy way to say it. "Murdered."

The judge opened his mouth, then shut it without saying anything. He moved past Michael to peek through the door at Joe's body. All the color drained from his face, and he didn't even look at Michael or make the first booming comment. Instead, he headed straight back over to the courthouse.

Sheriff Potter came out of the barbershop to watch him cross the street. With a sad shake of his head, he said, "The judge and Joe were good friends."

That was the problem. Joe was everybody's friend.

Even Hank looked truly distressed when he came running down the street, this time with camera in hand. He took a picture or two of the outside of the barbershop, but he didn't even attempt to get a picture when Michael and Buck helped Justin load Joe's body into the hearse.

Justin's face was a funny gray color and his hands trembled so much he had to try three times before he got the hearse door closed and locked.

The coroner looked over at Michael. "I haven't felt this bad about carrying somebody off since I took in your mama and daddy after the wreck. There are some things that just shouldn't happen." He shook his head. "Tell Alvin I'll get him the report as soon as I can, but the cause of death is pretty evident."

"How evident?" Hank asked Michael after Justin drove the hearse away.

Michael didn't see how it could hurt to tell him. Everybody in town would know before the next issue of the *Gazette* came out anyway. "Scissors in the neck. Hit the jugular, I'd say."

Hank blanched a little. "I always did tell Joe he kept those scissors too sharp. 'Course, I was worried about me losing a piece of ear. But a murder weapon? No way."

Michael didn't say anything. What was there to say or even do? Joe was dead, and Michael didn't have the first clue as to who did it or why.

"Where's Two Bits?" Hank fingered his camera.

"Why?" Michael gave him a hard look.

"Oh, I don't know. I might take his picture. People like cats."

"I can't believe you, Leland. You'd do anything to sell papers."

"Not anything, but I'd take a picture of a

cat." Hank peered toward the barbershop door.

Michael blew out a breath. No need getting mad. Hank was just being Hank. "Two Bits isn't here. Betty Jean came and got him."

"I don't guess you could ask her to bring him back over."

"No." Michael stared Hank down.

"Just a thought. I'll find something else to shoot. The barber pole maybe." Hank raised up his camera. "Folks expect pictures, but it just isn't fun this time, is it? Two murders and the week's not even over yet. A fellow has to wonder who's next."

Hank snapped some pictures of the front of Joe's shop and the people gathering on the sidewalk. The same as last time, the storekeepers had abandoned their posts to check out what was going on. Some men out of Earl Lee's pool room next door still held their pool cues as they silently, almost reverently watched Justin take Joe's body away. A sprinkling of kids who must have been hanging out at the Grill after school was there too.

Then the same as before, Michael spotted Anthony at the back of the crowd, but this time the apron hanging around his neck proved he was where he was supposed to be.

Seeing the kid there made Michael uneasy. Michael had had a hunch Joe knew something about the murder, and now Joe was dead. Michael didn't just think Anthony knew something, he was certain of it. Did the killer know that too?

What had Hank said? Who's next?

Michael jerked his eyes back toward where he saw the boy, but Anthony was headed back up the street. The boy slowed down in front of the car parts store, but if he was tempted to lift something from the deserted store, he overcame it. He went on toward the Grill. Maybe Aunt Lindy was having some effect on the kid after all. Now if Michael could keep him alive.

When he canceled out on Karen for the play that night, she said of course she understood. She promised to pray for him and for Joe's family. She could get one of her church members to go to the play with her and maybe they could get together the next night. Michael forgot all about his promise to entertain Alex for Reece until after they said goodbye. He started to call her back but decided it could wait. Who knew what would happen by tomorrow night? He might have to break that date too.

He spent the rest of the afternoon talking to anybody and everybody who might have seen or heard anything. They all wanted to help, but nobody knew anything. He came across only a couple of wild rumors, because the townsfolk were having a hard time fitting Joe, a friend as comfortable as a pair of old shoes, into any of their theories.

By the time he got back to the sheriff's office it was nearly dark. The courthouse was empty except for Betty Jean rocking Two Bits back and forth in the sheriff's chair the way she might have a baby.

"What are you doing still here?" Michael frowned at her. "You should have locked up and gone home hours ago."

"I didn't know what to do with Two Bits. I thought about sticking him back in the evidence room, but I was afraid he'd freak. Poor kitty." She ran her hand over the cat.

Michael supposed the cat was the closest thing to evidence they had since no fingerprints were found on the scissors.

Betty Jean was still explaining. "So I asked Burton if he could keep him up in the jail, but he says he's allergic to cats. And I couldn't take him home. My cat does not share territory with any other animals." Betty Jean looked at Michael. "Can you take him home with you?"

"Jasper might be as bad as your Sandy. He's never been around cats." Michael sank down in his chair. He couldn't even solve the problem of what to do with a cat.

Betty Jean creaked the sheriff's chair back and forth a couple more times. "How about Reece? He sounded worked up over the cat this afternoon."

"Did you call him and tell him about Joe?"

"No, but I must've had to tell everybody else in Hidden Springs." She looked over at Michael.

"Even after I've said it a hundred times, I still can't believe it. I don't want to believe it."

"I know what you mean." Michael took Two Bits from her. "Anything go on here after I left?" The cat settled down in his arms without a fight.

"Not much. The chief left to go home and lie down awhile. And you know Buck. He has to be on the move looking for something, even if he has no idea what to look for."

"None of us know what to look for. So I guess the sheriff and the judge had to hash it out alone."

"The judge didn't come over." Betty Jean frowned a little.

"At all?"

"Nope. I never even saw him until after Uncle Al left. I thought he must have already gone home, but then I saw him going toward the back door. He didn't poke his head in to see why I was still here or anything. I don't think he even said boo to Roy, who was sweeping out in the hall."

"Maybe I ought to go by his house and make sure he's all right." Michael ran his hand over Two Bits. "You notice anything else out of the ordinary? Anybody you talk to on the phone act as if they knew something?"

"Nope. Nobody even knew Joe was back."

"Somebody did," Michael said.

"But who?"

"I don't know." Michael kept rubbing the cat. Two Bits was calm now, content to let them do what they willed with him. "But I aim to find out."

"I hope so, Michael. And soon." Betty Jean stood up and picked up her purse. "Oh, by the way, Paul's had a setback. Some kind of secondary infection. I don't know exactly what. I talked to him, but he wasn't very rational. Still raving about finding the murder weapon and dragging the lake, so Uncle Al said you'd better go on and let the divers play around out there tomorrow morning even if it is a waste of the county's money."

"All right. If I'm not here when Lester comes in from the school, remind him to go on out there."

They were to the door when the phone rang. Michael hesitated, but Betty Jean flipped off the lights. "If it's important, Sally Jo knows how to find you, and truth is, I can't talk to one more person today about Joe. Not even one."

"Okay." Michael shifted the cat to one arm and pulled the door shut on the insistent ringing.

The hallway was dim with only a couple of lights on over the exit doors and all the offices dark. "Maybe we should keep more lights on out here," Michael said.

"The place is spooky after hours." Betty Jean shuddered a little. "Fact is, that Blake kid scared two or three years off my life tonight."

"Anthony?" Michael was surprised.

"Yeah. I had to go to the ladies' room, and when I went out in the hall, there he was hanging around in the shadows. Gave me quite a start."

"What was he doing here?"

"I didn't have a chance to ask. He was out the front door before I got my breath back, but then later I saw him again."

"Where?"

"Just passing by the office. I had the door open. I think he went out the back way. Roy might have chased him out so he could lock up because it was late. Just after the judge left." Betty Jean looked up at Michael. "I figured maybe he was hanging around to see you."

Michael stowed Two Bits in the backseat of his cruiser and then made a quick turn around the courthouse in case Anthony was still hanging around. But there was no sign of him. Maybe Joe's death had frightened the kid enough to make him ready to come clean about whatever it was he knew about Rayburn getting shot.

Michael hoped that was it as he drove toward Reece's house. He'd tried to run the boy down earlier, but Anthony told Cindy he had something he had to do and left the Grill early. It was odd that his "something to do" was hang around the courthouse.

Then when Michael turned on to the street that led to Reece's house, things got odder when he spotted Anthony's old car parked in some deep shadows on the far side of Judge Campbell's house, where it couldn't be seen from inside any of the houses. What was the kid up to?

The car was empty, the motor cold. Michael looked down the street toward Aunt Lindy's house, but if Anthony was there, why park this far up the street? But where else would he be? Surely the boy couldn't be planning to break into any of these houses.

Michael started to walk around the street, but inside his cruiser, Two Bits started yowling. He'd have to take care of the cat, then find Anthony.

Reece came to the door, his lucky hat bristling with fishing hooks and lures still on his head. He was surprised to see Michael there struggling to hang on to Two Bits. "What's going on? I just wanted somebody to feed Two Bits, not bring him to me."

"You haven't heard." It was more a statement than a question.

Reece hadn't heard. He must have been fishing all day. He always said fishing was the best medicine he knew for when a fellow wasn't feeling so hot. He frowned at Michael. "Did Joe's sister pass on?"

"No." Michael knew no way to say it gently, so he just spit it all out in a wad. "Somebody killed Joe this morning in his shop."

Reece staggered back a step as if Michael had dealt him a body blow. All the breath went out of him as his face turned chalky white. "Joe? Dead?" He gasped, then clutched his chest as his legs sagged.

Michael kicked the door closed behind him, dropped the cat, and grabbed Reece before he could fall. He lowered the old man into a chair beside the door. Two Bits landed on his feet and scooted out of sight under the same chair.

Before Michael could decide what to do next, Alex appeared beside him and shoved him out of the way.

"What did you do to him?" She shot Michael an accusing glare before she searched through her uncle's pocket until she found a small medicine bottle. She placed one of the pills under Reece's tongue. "Take it easy, Uncle Reece. Breathe in and out. That's it. You're going to be all right."

Michael stepped back out of the way, more than a little overwhelmed as he was every time he saw Alex. She leaned over Reece, her tall, graceful body molded by her jeans. Dark hair curled around her shoulders. She wore little makeup, but she needed none to highlight her best features. All her features were best. She took his breath away.

Michael could remember the first time he realized Alex was not just pretty but shockingly beautiful. The next summer after the wreck, she arrived the second week in June as always, running across the yards to Michael's house to say hello. Michael had been outside throwing baseballs at the old tire he'd rigged up at strike level. He had looked forward to Alex coming for weeks. Had even practiced witty things to say to

236

her, but the sight of her knocked all the words right out of him like somebody had punched him in the stomach. She laughed at him that day as he stared at her, his mouth hanging open.

Even now, that was how he felt every time he saw Alex for the first time after she'd been away awhile. She still knocked all sensible words right out of him for a moment before he had a chance to get used to the way she looked all over again. He had learned to keep his mouth shut.

Aunt Lindy loved her. Said a person shouldn't discriminate against a girl because of the way she looked, and that Alex had what was really important—the mind inside the body. Aunt Lindy never came out and actually said it, but Michael knew she thought Alex could mother town founders with one arm strapped behind her.

Reece was breathing easier, and color was creeping back into his cheeks. Alex turned on Michael, sparks of anger flashing in her smoky-blue eyes. "What in the world do you think you're doing? You know Uncle Reece has a weak heart."

Michael held up his hands to fend off her words and didn't answer. She never listened anyway when she was in a rage.

Reece took up for him. "It's not his fault, honey. Somebody had to tell me about Joe."

"What about him?" Alex demanded, her eyes going to Reece, then back to Michael.

"Come on in the sitting room, Michael. You can

tell us what happened." Reece's voice was sad as he slowly got to his feet, then looked around. "Where'd Two Bits go?"

Michael leaned down and pulled the cat out from under the chair. His claws raked against the floor as he tried to hold his spot in the shadows. "He's had a hard day." Michael stroked the cat.

"Poor kitty." Reece reached for Two Bits and the cat gentled down at the sound of his voice.

"I don't much like cats." Alex frowned at the cat.

"Two Bits will grow on you." Reece led the way into the front room and settled in his shabby old brown recliner. He stroked the cat, then looked up at Michael. "Who would want to murder Joe?"

Alex sucked in her breath at the word "murder," and Michael was glad the word shocked her.

"Murder? Here in Hidden Springs?" she said.

"We aren't perfect, my dear," Reece said. "In fact, this makes two murders right downtown this week."

"Two?" Her penetrating eyes settled on Michael's face. "What are you doing about it?"

"I'd arrest somebody if I knew who to arrest." Michael looked back at Reece. "We found Joe's body this afternoon after you called about the cat."

"Who found him?" Reece saw the answer in Michael's face. "I'm sorry, Michael. That couldn't have been easy."

"No." Michael pressed his lips together a

moment. "Joe was a good, nice guy. I can't imagine Main Street without him."

"You surely have a suspect," Alex said. "Hidden Springs is too small for anyone to murder someone and get away with it."

"Whoever it was won't get away with it." Determination hardened Michael's voice.

"But you don't have a suspect," Alex said.

"Quit browbeating the boy, Alex, and let him tell us what he knows."

So Michael went through the bare details. Reece shuddered when Michael told them how Joe died, and Alex went a shade pale.

"That's about it. I spent the rest of the day finding out nobody knows anything except Two Bits, and he's not talking," Michael finished up. He looked at Reece. "Joe didn't tell you anything after the first murder, did he? Even a hint of what he might have suspected could be helpful."

"We talked about the man getting shot the same as everybody." Reece stared down at the cat for a long moment. "But come to think of it, I did most of the talking. I remember thinking at the time that Joe had something on his mind, but I thought it was because his sister was so poorly." He paused a minute. "You think he knew something then?"

"Why else would he be dead?" Michael said.

"That is the question." Reece sort of withdrew from them into himself. Even Two Bits noticed and raised his head to stare at him.

Michael waited a minute before he pushed him to talk. "If you know something, Reece, it's not the time to keep secrets."

Reece slowly stroked the cat again. "What few secrets I know couldn't have anything to do with this."

"That may be what Joe thought," Michael said. "He must have been trying to protect someone."

"I suppose that's possible, but if so, I don't know who or why. Perhaps Joe's death isn't even connected with this other man's death."

"That's pretty unlikely," Michael said.

Reece sighed. "Yes, I suppose so. But whoever it was surely didn't intend to kill Joe this morning or they would have brought a more trustworthy weapon along. Not many murders are committed with scissors."

"Murder weapons come in all shapes and sizes," Alex put in.

"And so do murderers, Reece," Michael warned him. "If you think of anything, anything at all, you let me know."

⤙ 22 ⤚

Michael didn't remember about Anthony until he got up to leave. A quick glance out the window showed the boy's car was gone. Michael had intended to listen for the car starting up, but

Reece's health scare put that out of his mind. Then seeing Alex sent him in a tailspin the way it always did. He hadn't heard a thing but her voice.

Alex walked him to the door, mildly apologetic for her brusque manner earlier. "I was worried about Uncle Reece," she said simply.

"You were right. I shouldn't have sprung the news on him that way."

"The news would have been a shock no matter how you told him. But I think he's all right now." She took a peek back toward the other room, where they could see Reece in his recliner, still stroking Two Bits.

"I hope so. It will help that you're here."

With their apologies out of the way, they moved to friendlier ground. At the door, she smiled. "I hear you're taking me out on the town tomorrow night. Does that mean Cindy's finest?"

"I think Reece had in mind something over in Eagleton."

"Poor Uncle Reece. He's under the mistaken assumption Eagleton is a city."

"The closest thing to one around here, and he doesn't want you to be bored while you're here."

"I've never been bored in Hidden Springs." When Michael raised his eyebrows at her, she shrugged a little. "I always manage to escape before that happens. How about you, Michael? Aren't you bored yet?"

"Not yet."

She shook her head at him. "I don't understand you."

"Me? I'm the easy one to understand. You're the exotic bird who flits in here now and again and makes all the locals go wide-eyed with wonder."

Alex laughed delightedly, the sound rippling through his memory all the way back through the blackness to his early childhood. It was a good laugh, one he'd once been willing to do almost anything to hear, from standing on his head as a six-year-old to reading law books in college just so he'd be able to talk to her about famous cases.

"I guess you know Uncle Reece is doing his best to cage me up down here for a while. He says the doctor told him to cut back his hours because of his heart, but he doesn't want to let his clients down." Every trace of smile was gone from her face now. "Do you think his health is really that bad or that he's just playing on my sympathies?"

"That was no act tonight," Michael said.

"No, but you know Uncle Reece. He never gives up on an idea, and he's been thinking Sheridan and Sheridan ever since I passed the bar." She peered at Michael. "That and other impossible plans he has for me."

Michael almost blushed. "It's just a dinner, Alex. He didn't ask me to propose or anything."

"Of course not." Her lips twisted up in a wicked grin. "I'm guessing that is Malinda's part in the plot. We both know you can never refuse her anything."

"I promise I won't propose."

"And that's supposed to make me happy?" Alex's grin widened.

"I don't know, Alex." He laughed. "But maybe it will me."

She laughed with him and shoved him out the door. "See how nice I am. I'm letting you have the last word, but you'd best be ready tomorrow night. It won't happen again."

He smiled all the way to his car, but then the weight of the day's happenings fell back on him. He still had work to do. And finding out what Anthony Blake was up to was priority one.

When he checked with Aunt Lindy, she said she hadn't seen Anthony. He never came between sessions, and he wasn't due back at her house until Saturday afternoon. Why did Michael ask? When he told her about Anthony's car parked down the street, she had no answers.

Then Michael stopped at the judge's house, but his wife said the judge had already retired for the evening. Did Michael want her to wake him?

"No, no," Michael said quickly. He'd never seen June Campbell when she didn't look ready to smile for a camera. Even at this hour the petite lady's silver hair was in perfect order and her rose-colored lipstick looked freshly applied.

The folks in Hidden Springs all agreed June was

the perfect wife for the judge. She smiled warmly and indiscriminately at everyone, and she always remembered to ask people about their grand-children, usually by name. Even better, she never refused a worthy request for her time, so she was a favorite of the charity organizations. She would be a definite plus in the judge's run for state representative not only as a beautiful, fragrant flower on his arm but because of the important connections she had forged through those extensive volunteer activities both here and in Eagleton.

"Did you need to talk to Wilson about poor Joe?" A look of distress crossed her face. "I can hardly believe such a terrible thing has happened in our town."

"It is hard to believe, but no, I was just worried about the judge. He didn't seem his usual self this afternoon."

"Joe's death was such a shock to him, you understand." June looked concerned that he might not understand. To Michael she always looked a little worried in spite of her meticulously maintained exterior, as if she was afraid she might hiccup or belch out in public and embarrass herself or, even worse, the judge. "As it was to me as well. It makes one rather uneasy, don't you think? Makes one wonder about their own safety."

"I don't think you have anything to fear, Miss June."

"I don't know." A frown etched lines on her forehead. "I had considered waking Wilson earlier, even though I really didn't want to worry him when he's already so upset. It was quite a relief, let me tell you, seeing your car across the street and knowing you'd have things under control."

"What do you mean?" Michael asked. Sometimes Miss June could talk in circles.

"I was quite certain I saw somebody out there in the shadows earlier this evening." Miss June fluttered her hands nervously in the direction of the bushes alongside her driveway. "It was a bit unnerving, considering the events of the week."

"What was he doing?"

"I'm not really sure." She produced a neatly folded tissue out of some hidden pocket and touched her lips. "Lurking is the word that comes to mind, although I'm not exactly clear about what one does when one lurks. However, it did make me decidedly uneasy, and I was in a definite quandary as to what to do until you stopped across the way at Reece's. His sweet niece has come to visit him, hasn't she? The two of you were always such good friends as children, weren't you?"

Michael suppressed a smile at the word "sweet" applied to Alex. "Yes, ma'am, but about this person you saw? Did you recognize him?"

"How could I? He seemed to be clinging to the shadows, you know, and I hardly dared step outside for a better viewpoint, now did I?"

"No, of course not."

"It's just so tragic. All of it. First that poor man showing up on the courthouse steps on Tuesday morning. What was his name?"

"Jay Rayburn."

"Yes, yes, that was it. Wilson says I couldn't have known him. That he wasn't from around here. Still, I've come across that name some-where. I have always made an effort to keep names in my memory. People do appreciate one remembering their name."

"You think you may have known Jay Rayburn?" Michael couldn't completely hide his surprise.

"It's not very likely, is it? I daresay Wilson is right and it's just a similar name I'm recalling. I knew a Jason Rathborne once. At any rate, I do sympathize with his family. Such a sad way to die, taken before your time like that." She rattled on, hardly pausing for a breath. "And then poor Joe. I suppose it's enough to make one start to jump at shadows, and Wilson has always said that I sometimes see dangers where there are none. I tell him I have to do the worrying for both of us, because he won't. Worry, I mean. He says things generally take care of themselves as long as a person is trying to do the right thing, and Wilson always does the right thing."

Michael tried to sift through her words to see if she'd said anything he needed to respond to, but while he was sifting, she went off on a new tack.

"I do appreciate you coming by, Michael, and I know you'll be able to handle whatever happens. It's so comforting to have a wonderful young man such as yourself protecting us, and I'm sure you quite scared whoever was out there away."

"Yes, ma'am. I hope so, but if you notice anything that gives you the least concern, you call me or Sally Jo." Michael touched her arm. "Don't hesitate a minute, do you hear?"

"That is reassuring, Michael. To know you'll come by to check out any problems. But no doubt I was simply letting my imagination get carried away earlier."

"That could be, but it never hurts to check things out." Michael looked at her a minute before he added, "And if you do remember where you might have heard Jay Rayburn's name, you will let me know, won't you?"

"Of course," she promised. "Wilson has just been so disturbed about it all. It's simply not the kind of thing one expects to occur here in our little town."

He agreed with her again, then thanked her as he began backing away with her words flowing after him down the porch steps. It had been awhile since he'd talked to Miss June one on one. When the judge was around, she let him do most of the talking, only smiling and nodding her support.

Michael couldn't keep from smiling as he remembered what Aunt Lindy sometimes said about June. "Words spill out of that woman like marbles dropped on a hard floor. You just don't know which direction they're going to roll or if they'll ever, please for mercy's sake, stop."

Michael made another round of the neighborhood but noted nothing in the least suspicious. Anthony was gone, and nobody else was out and about. Aunt Lindy would be in her rocking chair, grading papers. Reece and Alex would still be discussing Joe's death and the sad state of affairs in Hidden Springs. Miss June's front door was closed, and through a crack in the drapes he could see the flickering light of a television set. Michael rubbed his eyes and looked at his dash clock as he pulled out of the street. Ten thirty. He wanted nothing more than to go home, but he still needed to track down Anthony.

He drove by Anthony's house. The boy's car wasn't there, and Michael didn't have the energy to deal with the aunt. He'd talk to Vera tomorrow if he had to. Michael cruised around town, checking out all Anthony's usual hangouts, but he was nowhere to be found.

Finally Michael gave up and headed home. One thing for sure, Anthony couldn't hide forever. He'd find him, but he needed to do that before the killer decided the boy knew too much.

The next morning Michael made all the rounds again without luck and then waited at the school. Again he wasn't really surprised when Anthony didn't show up, but he was beginning to get worried. He almost wished they had arrested Anthony for stealing Bonnie Wireman's laptop and put him in jail. At least then Michael might be able to keep him safe.

Buck was waiting for him at the office to compare notes, but neither one of them had much. A state police forensics expert was coming in later to go over Joe's shop.

Betty Jean asked about Two Bits and then reported that Chief Sibley had called. He was going over to the hospital to be with Caroline. Seemed Paul was delirious.

"Nothing new about that," Buck muttered.

"Where's the sheriff?" Michael asked.

Betty Jean looked at the clock on the wall and then rolled her eyes at Michael. "Just because there's been a couple of homicides, you don't expect Uncle Al to change his schedule, do you? He's eating Cindy's biscuits up at the Grill."

"How about the judge?"

"Him too or I miss my guess," Betty Jean said.

"And the girl don't miss her guesses very often," Buck said.

Betty Jean gave him a sour look over her computer screen and went on talking to Michael. "Your kid was back in the hall this morning."

"Anthony?" Finally Michael was surprised.

"The very one. I told him he could come on in the office and wait if he was looking for you. That

249

made him flare up big-time. Said he wasn't looking for nobody, and why couldn't people just leave him alone?" Betty Jean's eyes settled on Michael. "He said he just came in to use the public john and when was that against the law." Betty Jean looked back down at her computer screen. "That boy has got a problem, but I don't think it has anything to do with needing to find the men's room."

"Did he take off?"

"Like a shot."

"You spot him again, Betty Jean, you radio me. I need to talk to him."

"You think he knows something?" Buck looked over at Michael.

"Maybe. Maybe not, but I don't want him to end up like Joe. Whoever we're dealing with isn't taking any chances."

"Could it be the kid? He seems to always be around," Buck said.

"What motive could he have?" Michael frowned.

"What motive does anybody in Hidden Springs have?" Buck said. "Admit it, Mike. We don't know enough to even come up with an interesting guess as to what's going on."

Michael couldn't argue with that.

"The most we can do is keep worrying the ends of these strings that don't seem to go anywhere until something starts unraveling." Buck pushed up out of his chair. "About the only good thing that's happened around here since Monday is Little Osgood's appendix busting like that. Now that was divine intervention if I ever saw it, and I guess you could say he's the only one we can be absolutely sure about striking off the suspect list. Everybody else in Hidden Springs is fair game till we know better."

"I liked suspecting the mob better," Michael said.

"I think you can forget that." Buck gave a sympathetic shake of his head. "I don't think Joe ever had much cause to get on the wrong side of the mob, but have you heard the new idea going around this morning?"

"What's that?"

"That it's some psycho killer who's knocking off people whose names start with *J*. Jim Deatin over at the auto parts store is talking about closing up shop and taking an extended vacation just in case."

"Spare us, Buck, and get out of here." Betty Jean glanced at him over her computer screen. "Some people have to work instead of sitting around yammering all day."

"Hey, we're working." Buck laughed. "Got to consider every idea in our quest to protect the public. To protect you."

"Wonderful. I feel so much better now that you're after psychos with a thing about *J* first names." Betty Jean made a face.

"It might not have to be a first name, Betty Jean, with this psycho *J* killer. Maybe you ought to go off with Jim. I hear he's been sort of lonesome since his wife up and left him."

Betty Jean calmly picked up her empty coffee mug and threw it at Buck. He caught it easily and set the mug back on her desk with a laugh. It was an old routine between them. "Guess I'll mosey on up the street and lean on Leland. I hear he's been out digging, and it's time he learned to share."

Michael wanted to leave the office and go lean on somebody too. But he didn't know anybody to lean on other than Anthony, who was staying out of Michael's sight. Besides, his desk was loaded down with routine work. Just because the town had been rocked by a couple of homicides didn't mean everything else screeched to a halt.

The phone rang almost continuously, but Betty Jean had her spiel down pat. No, there were no new breaks in the case. Yes, the sheriff had everything under control. Yes, that was an interesting possibility. No, she couldn't say whether the sheriff had thought of that yet, but she was sure he'd check it out. No, she didn't know when the sheriff would be available to talk to them. Even after the sheriff came in, she said the same thing.

The sheriff paid no attention as he creaked his chair up and back enough to get on everybody's nerves before he stood up and said he'd heard people were speeding out at the interstate exit.

Since he knew Michael didn't have time right now, what with the homicide investigation and all, to do much ticketing, maybe he'd go do some patrolling.

Betty Jean waited until he left to say, "Not to mention it's Friday."

"Friday?" Michael looked over at her, puzzled.

"Chicken and dumplings special out at the Country Diner. I'd go out there myself if Lester was here to cover the phones."

Michael thought about mentioning her diet but thought better of it. "You heard from Lester since he went out to the lake?"

"He's called in a couple of times. To hear him, you'd think they were going to find sunken treasure. He hasn't been this excited since the kids at school gave him that little trophy shaped like a whistle."

"How long did the sheriff say they could keep diving out there?"

"All day. You have to pay them for a full day whether they work that long or not. Uncle Al believes in getting full return for the taxpayers' dollars. By the way, you'll have to go out there this afternoon so Lester can come do his crossing guard duty. I promised him you would."

"Okay. I guess the city will have to pay for this since it was Paul's baby."

"Maybe so, but don't forget, city taxpayers vote in county elections too."

"Betty Jean, did anybody ever tell you that you are awfully cynical for a small-town girl?" Michael asked with a smile.

"Small town, big town. Politicians still want votes and voters still don't like to pay taxes."

The telephone rang again, and Michael went back to work on his report of the latest fender bender as Betty Jean started through her spiel. Suddenly she plunked the caller on hold, hissed at Michael, and pointed toward the hall. "There he goes."

Michael was out from behind his desk and in the hall in a flash. Anthony took off, but Michael collared the boy at the front door without ceremony.

"What's going on, Deputy?" The boy gasped as he attempted to pull away from Michael's hold. "I haven't done anything."

"Nothing but skip school again." Michael eased his hold on the boy's arm but didn't turn him loose. "It's time we had a long talk."

"So I skipped school. I keep getting sick." Anthony's face was closed tight. "What more do you want to know?"

"Whatever you know that you're not telling about what's going on around here. You don't want to end up like Joe."

"I can take care of myself." Anthony was stiff, but he stopped trying to pull free.

"Sure you can, kid. But we're still going to talk."

"Okay. You're the cop. If you want to talk, I guess I'll listen."

"Good choice." Michael tightened his hold on the boy's arm and propelled him back down the hall.

Stella Pinkston peeked out of the county clerk's office and giggled.

"She'll make a good witness when I take you to court for police brutality." Anthony dragged his feet on the floor.

"You're not taking anybody to court. Now be quiet and walk."

"What's going on out here, Mike?" The judge's voice hadn't quite gotten back to full boom, and his eyes were bloodshot with dark circles under them.

Before Michael could say anything, Anthony spoke up again. "Hey, Judge. Help me out here. Tell him to let me go."

The judge ignored Anthony and kept his eyes on Michael. "Shouldn't this boy be in school?"

"Yes sir. We're getting ready to discuss that," Michael said. "Don't worry. I've got things under control."

The judge nodded and retreated back into his office.

Anthony made a sound that was almost a laugh. "The judge doesn't look happy. Are you happy, Deputy?"

"For somebody who doesn't want to talk, you're

doing a lot of it." Michael pushed the boy into the sheriff's office.

Betty Jean was on the phone again. She looked up at Michael with relief. She put her hand over the phone. "Good. You didn't leave." Then she spoke back into the phone. "Stop shouting in my ear, Lester, and just calm down. I'll send Michael on out. He'll know what to do."

Michael shoved Anthony down into one of the chairs and stood guard over him. He wasn't about to let him slip away again.

When Betty Jean put down the phone, he said, "Don't tell me they actually found a gun."

"No. But they did find something."

"Not another body." Michael's stomach tightened.

"Sort of. A car. The divers say it's been there a long time, but they think somebody was in it. I guess I should say is in it. Or what's left of them."

Michael stared at her. "This has got to be a joke."

"You wish." Betty Jean reached for the phone book. "You're going to need a wrecker."

"I don't think that will do it. Better hunt some kind of crane."

Anthony stood up. "I guess that means you don't have time to mess with me, Deputy. What say we cut it short? I promise to go to school and do what good little boys are supposed to do and stay out of your hair. Let you get back to important things."

"You're not going anywhere." Michael stepped in front of him.

"Why not? You can't arrest me for skipping school."

"I'm not arresting you. Just holding you in protective custody for a while. We'll talk on the way out to the lake."

"I told you, Deputy. You can't make me talk."

"So far my problem has been getting you to shut up." Michael fingered the handcuffs on his belt. "Now, are you coming peacefully or do I get out the cuffs?"

Anthony shrugged a little. "I guess I wouldn't mind seeing what they found out there. Might be more fun than hanging around here. Besides, the guy at the paper has offered to pay me for any story leads I bring him."

⊰ 23 ⊱

Michael locked Anthony in the backseat of the cruiser to give the kid the chance to get in a more cooperative frame of mind. The boy squawked a little, but when Michael paid no attention, he slumped down in sullen silence. Michael didn't bother talking either as he headed out toward the lake.

They'd been on the road ten minutes when

Anthony broke the silence. "Why aren't you using your lights and siren?"

"Whoever's in that car will still be there when we get there."

"Who do you think it is?" Anthony tried to sound bored, but a little curiosity sneaked through.

"Nobody we know or somebody would have missed them a long time ago. Folks in Hidden Springs don't just disappear."

"That's not what I've been told," Anthony said.

Michael looked at the boy in his rearview mirror. "All right, Anthony. What have you been told?"

The boy's face shut down. "Nothing you want to hear, Deputy."

"Fine, but just so you know. The two of us are going to be constant companions until you tell me what I want to know. For your own safety." Michael flashed his eyes between the road and the boy. Not exactly the best cross-examination situation. "And don't try coming up with some cock-and-bull story, because I want to hear the truth."

A blaze of challenge shot through Anthony's eyes as he glared at Michael in the mirror. "Nobody in Hidden Springs wants the truth. They never have."

"What say we give it a try? You tell me whatever you know and that might help us both figure things out." Michael met the boy's eyes in the mirror for a second.

"It doesn't have anything to do with you." Anthony looked down.

"You need to let me decide that."

"Okay, I'll come clean. I did skip school and you want to know why?" Anthony scooted up closer to the barrier between the seats. "Because school stinks. Now you have the truth. Satisfied?"

"I hope you like it back there." Michael tried to sound like he was promising him ice cream cones and popsicles. "You may be there awhile."

"What if I have to take a leak?"

"We'll work something out."

"Maybe I won't. Maybe I'll just let go here in the backseat."

"Then you'll have to sit there in wet pants like a baby until we get back to the courthouse, where you'll be obliged to scrub the seat." Michael kept his voice cheerful and his eyes on the road.

Behind him, Anthony grumbled under his breath. Michael caught a few words now and again, but he ignored them. Let the boy grouse. Get it out of his system.

Michael turned off the main road and bounced through the ruts on the narrow gravel road down to the lake. A cloud of white dust chased after the car.

Some years back the county officials had talked

about blacktopping the road with the idea that people might build summer homes down along the lakefront or bring in camping trailers. The only problem was that they couldn't get Baxter Perry on board. Baxter owned most of the land along the road, and none of it was for sale. He wasn't about to let a bunch of tourists move into his best hayfields. He didn't care what anybody offered him an acre.

These days nobody besides Baxter used the road to the lake much except local fishermen and sometimes teenagers looking for a place to do things they shouldn't. Michael occasionally patrolled the road on Friday and Saturday nights just to keep the kids straight, and as Lester had said, it was a good fishing spot.

He felt funny now thinking about the times he'd sat on the rocks dropping a line down in the water, thinking how peaceful and serene the place was, when all the while somebody had died in a car below his hook. Maybe everything he'd always believed about Hidden Springs was a polished-up illusion, and Anthony was right. Instead of hunting for the answers, could it be he was hiding from the truth?

Michael glanced up in the mirror at Anthony huddled against the door, staring out the window. They made a pair. Michael didn't want to believe anything but good about Hidden Springs and Anthony nothing but bad.

The grappling fingers of the bushes along the road gave way to a wide clearing with a pull-off on the rock cliff towering over the lake. Lester's car was sitting right in the middle of the clearing, his blue lights flashing round and round. A beat-up red pickup was parked over close to the edge of the cliff with ropes and cables spilling out over the lowered tailgate. Lester and another man stood at the cliff edge, peering down at a boat floating on the gentle bluish-green waters of the lake.

"Stay put," Michael told Anthony.

"Do I have a choice?"

"No." Michael didn't look around as he opened the door.

"How about rolling my window down back here?" Anthony scooted up and grabbed the barrier between him and the front seat.

"No." Michael still didn't look at him. "The front windows are down. You'll be fine."

"I get claustrophobic in closed-up places, Deputy." Anthony raised his voice a little.

Michael finally looked around at him. "Then you'd better get used to it or start talking."

"I don't know what you want me to tell you." Anthony sat back and crossed his arms over his chest. He turned his head away from Michael.

"I think you do, kid."

Michael was glad to see Buck pulling up behind his cruiser. Buck had been around a long time, and if he ever worked on a missing persons report, he would remember.

Muttering a few choice words under his breath, Buck stepped up beside Michael. "Remind me to go in the front when we leave here. I've been eating your dust for a mile." He spit on the ground and then spotted Anthony in Michael's cruiser. "What's he doing here?"

"I'm just hanging on to him for a while. For his own protection."

"He got anything to do with this?" Buck gestured out toward the lake. "I mean, you don't think after all these years . . ." Buck left the thought dangling.

Michael looked at Buck, who was staring out at the lake now, and the uneasiness that had been with him all the way down to the lake suddenly had a name. The only missing person in Hidden Springs who had never turned up was Roxanne, but that had been over ten years ago.

"That's crazy," he said to Buck.

"Yeah," Buck agreed. "They say whether it was a man or woman in the car?"

"Not that I've heard."

Buck blew out a long breath. "Guess we'd better go see what they've got."

After they talked to the divers, Michael sent Lester back out to the main road to wait for the crane Betty Jean had managed to locate. When Buck asked him how he thought they'd get a crane down that sorry excuse for a road, Michael radioed Betty Jean to get Baxter Perry to come out with his chain saw.

Then with a sigh, he told her to call Justin and the sheriff. "The divers say the water's murky down there, but they're sure they saw a skull in the car."

It took a long time to get the car out. The sheriff came and left. Lester went to do his crossing guard duties at the school and came back with Hank Leland on his tail. Michael relented and let Anthony out of the car, but he or Buck stayed on the boy like a shadow as the afternoon slid by. When Anthony claimed to be starving, Buck got him a pack of peanuts and a lukewarm soda out of his stakeout stash.

Anthony gave him a look. "How come you're being so nice, Sergeant? You decided we look alike or something?"

"Don't get your hopes up, kid," Buck told him. "If you'd been mine, I'd have beat the you-know-what out of you a long time ago. Now eat and shut up before I forget you ain't."

Quitting time came and the divers went into overtime. The shadows lengthened, and Michael asked Betty Jean to call Karen and Alex for him. He didn't have a signal on his cell phone.

"Both of them?" she said. "And what do I tell them? Michael can't decide which of you he wants to see tonight?"

263

"Lay off, Betty Jean. It's been a long day. Just tell Karen I'll call her tomorrow and Alex that it looks like the big city is out of the question and even Cindy's finest is doubtful."

"You sound blue about it. You want me to tell her that too?" Betty Jean said.

"Would you cut it out? We're on the radio."

"Oh, sorry." Betty Jean didn't sound one bit sorry.

"Anything else going on?" Michael asked.

"Those forensic guys have been over at Joe's for hours. Maybe Buck should come in and talk to them."

Michael looked at Buck, who shook his head. "He'll check with them later. You can go on home if you want to."

"You know who it is yet?" Betty Jean asked. "The judge wanted me to ask."

"We may not know even after we get the car out. They say it's been down there a long time." Michael started to key off but then added, "Thanks for finding the crane, Betty Jean. You're a wonder."

"I've been telling you that for months." She gave a snort and broke the connection.

"Big date, Deputy?" Anthony said after Michael put the radio back in his belt. "I wouldn't want to mess that up for you. So whenever we get away from here, you can just drop me off at my car and you can take out your girlfriend."

"I told you, kid." Michael barely glanced at him.

"You're with me till I get some straight talk out of you."

"Whatever." Anthony shrugged a little. "It's your date."

Down below in the lake, the divers surfaced and began making upward motions. Then they clambered over the edge of their boat and scooted it well out of the way. The crane operator started cranking up the cable, and in a matter of moments, the car's bumper and grille broke the surface of the water. Hank lay down on his belly on the rocks close to the edge, busily clicking pictures.

"A Chevy," Buck said softly. "Can you tell a color?"

"It's hard to tell with the rust." Michael squinted at the car. "Red maybe."

Buck didn't say anything more as the car emerged from the water inch by inch. When it broke free of the water, he looked over at Michael. "Better put the kid back in your cruiser. We won't have time to watch him."

"Where could I go?" Anthony protested. "We're at the end of nowhere."

Buck ignored Anthony with his eyes hard on Michael. "Do it."

Michael looked at the car, then back at Buck before he took hold of Anthony's arm. "Come on, Anthony."

"What's going on here?" Anthony jerked loose from Michael and stared at Buck.

"Nothing, kid. Just do as you're told for once without raising a fuss." Buck didn't quite meet the boy's eyes.

Anthony stepped up close to Buck. "You think it's her, don't you?"

Buck didn't push the boy away as he looked him straight in the eye. "I don't know. It could be."

Anthony's eyes went to the car streaming water back down into the lake. "If it is, I have to know."

Buck put his arm around the boy's shoulders. "You'll be the first we'll tell, but just in case this is your mama, you don't want to see this. You want to remember her the way she was to you as a little boy. Not this way."

Anthony looked scared and near tears as he shrugged off Buck's arm and stalked toward Michael's car. Michael followed him, but at the car, Anthony said, "You don't have to lock me in. I ain't going anywhere."

When Michael hesitated, Anthony went on. "You have my word."

Michael wasn't sure he could trust the boy, but he was sure that he'd spoil any chance of ever reaching him if he didn't. "Okay, Anthony. On your word."

"Hey, Deputy," Anthony said as Michael turned back toward the cliff. "I used to keep a couple of little cars in the glove box to play with if I had to wait on Mama. You think they'd still be there?"

Michael looked around at the boy. Behind him,

the cable screeched and the car scraped against the rocks. He kept his eyes on Anthony's face. "I don't know, but I'll look."

Michael and Buck pried loose the door with a crowbar. It popped open with a loud creak, and more water and a couple of carp spilled out on their shoes.

"Careful," Justin cautioned behind them.

Michael wasn't sure exactly why they needed to be careful. There was nothing left but bones, and the years in the water and then the journey back onto land had disturbed them more than he and Buck ever could. The skull, like something out of a horror movie, stared up at him with green algae growing on its forehead and in its empty eye sockets.

Buck swore under his breath. "I wish I could go sit in the car."

"Female." Justin spoke briskly beside them. With rubber-gloved hands he picked up a leg bone. "About five feet four, slight frame."

He had a stretcher with a body bag pulled up close to the car. He handed Michael and Buck some rubber gloves. "Get every fragment you can. It's the least we can do for the poor soul after all these years."

"Do you think it's Roxanne?" Michael asked no one in particular as he pulled on the gloves with a snap.

"We'll have to use dental records to make a

267

positive ID," Justin said. "But Buck says the car's right, and the bone structure fits. I wouldn't be surprised."

They gathered the woman's remains, gently laying each find in the body bag, and the whole time he worked, Michael could almost feel Anthony breathing down his neck, even though the boy had stayed in the cruiser.

Instead, it was Hank peering over their shoulders to get a better view. He might have taken pictures if Buck hadn't looked up at him and growled, "You even think about snapping a picture, Leland, the camera goes in the lake whether you turn loose of it or not."

Hank took one look at Buck's face and lowered his camera. "I'll get a shot of the car when you're finished." He backed off a respectable distance.

Once Justin was satisfied there was nothing more to be disturbed or found, Michael reached across and pried open the glove compartment. A rust-encrusted revolver fell out in his hand. Right behind it were the two cars. He picked the biggest one up and scraped some crud off it until the shape of a hot rod appeared like magic under his fingers.

"What'd you find?" Buck asked.

Michael opened his hand to show the toy car. "He said it would be there."

"I always knew she wouldn't leave the boy." Buck looked as if his faith in motherhood had been restored.

Michael's hand closed around the toy. Lester was helping Justin load up his hearse yet one more time. "Accident?" Michael said.

"Who knows? I hope so, but can't imagine why she'd be out here by herself." Buck yanked off the rubber gloves and pitched them into the car. "Justin said her skull was cracked, but that could have happened on the way down. One thing sure, I don't think she drove into the lake on purpose."

"Did you know she had a gun?"

"No, but doesn't surprise me. Roxanne wasn't the kind to take chances or to trust somebody else to bail her out of trouble if it came along." Buck shook his head and clapped a hand on Michael's shoulder. "Look, Mike, maybe last week we could have worried this into a homicide, but fact of the matter is, even if we did, I don't know what we'd do next. The trail is cold. Stone-cold. And we aren't doing so hot figuring out a couple of murders that happened so close under our noses, we ought to be able to sniff out the culprit."

"Maybe you're right."

"Buck Garrett is always right."

"I thought it was Garrett always gets his man." Michael managed a little smile.

"That too. Now watch what you say. That pesky Leland is inching back over this way."

"You think you can keep him occupied while I go talk to Anthony?" Michael looked over at

Hank. "I wouldn't want his picture on the front page next week."

"Leland's going to have so much to put on the front page next week he may have to put out two of them, but go ahead. I'll take care of our newshound."

"I can trust you not to throw him in the lake?"

"Don't worry, Mike. I can be nice when I want to be."

To prove it, Buck moved between Michael and Hank before the editor got out his first question.

"Hey, Leland, quit playing favorites." Buck sounded like he was talking to a long-lost friend. "Keane's not the only one around here who knows what's going down. Why don't you ask me your questions?"

Hank practically dropped his pencil. "Is that before or after you throw me in the lake, Garrett?"

"What a joker." Buck let out a hearty laugh and put his arm around Hank. "Come on. If you want pictures of the car, now's the time before T.R. starts loading it up."

His eyes wide, Hank glanced back over his shoulder at Michael as Buck began steering him toward the car. "He's going to throw me over, isn't he?"

Michael tried to keep a straight face. "I think you're safe as long as you don't try to take his picture."

Anthony took the toy car from Michael without

a word. Michael sat down beside him and waited, not sure what to expect out of the boy. Sorrow, anger, disbelief. He was ready for any of that. He wasn't ready when the boy started laughing.

"All these years, she's been right here." Anthony looked over at the lake. "Right here."

Michael put his hand on the boy's shoulder and pulled him around where he could see his face. "You all right, Anthony?"

"Don't look so worried, Deputy." Anthony's laughter died away, but a smile stayed on his face. "The thing is, I always knew my mother wouldn't go off and leave me like everybody said she did. And she didn't, did she?"

"No, she didn't."

His smile faded completely away. "I guess that man was right. Somebody did kill her."

"What man?"

"That first guy. Rayburn. He told me somebody killed her."

Michael stared at him intently. "When did he tell you that?"

"The morning he got shot. He called the house before Aunt Vera even got up. She gave me heck about that. Said I'd better tell my friends to wait till a decent hour to be calling."

"You were the one meeting him at the court-house?"

"Yeah. He told me if I wanted to know more, to meet him in the parking lot at nine." Anthony looked straight at Michael. "He said he knew something must have happened to my mother back when she disappeared and that he wanted to help me find out what."

"How was he going to help you find out?"

"He said he'd tell me more when we met. That he was pretty sure who my mother had been hanging around with before she disappeared."

"Did he tell you who that was?" Michael asked.

Anthony's face closed up again. "Nope. Said that it might be better if I didn't know too much until he worked a few things out. That bad things happened to people who knew too much sometimes. I guess he must have known too much, huh, Deputy?"

"Could be."

"And Joe too. What do you think Joe knew?"

"I wish I knew."

"Well, now you know what I know." The kid leaned back and blew out a breath.

"Do I?" Michael studied the boy's face.

"I've spilled my guts. What more do you want?"

"Everything you know."

"I told you everything. The man called. Told me he figured something must have happened to my mother all those years ago. Wanted me to meet him so he could help me find out what. Then he was dead when I got there."

"Is that everything, Anthony?" Michael kept his

eyes steady on the boy's face. "I get the feeling there's more."

Anthony turned defiant. "Do I have to make something up so you'll be happy?"

"I only want the truth."

"Are you sure that's what you want?" Anthony narrowed his eyes on Michael.

"Try me." Michael didn't waver.

"Okay, Deputy, here's the truth. I told you what I know. That's it. The whole story. I don't know anything else." Anthony dropped his eyes back to the car in his hand. He pushed it forward a little. "How about that? It still almost rolls."

⛧ 24 ⛧

Michael gave up on getting Anthony to do any more talking and locked the boy in again. Anthony hardly seemed to notice as he rubbed the little car with the bottom of his T-shirt.

On the other hand, Hank wouldn't quit talking as he followed Michael around, throwing out question after question. How come Anthony was with Michael? Had Michael had a tip about the car in the lake? From Anthony? About it being Roxanne? If they didn't have a tip about the car, why were they at the lake?

Finally Michael turned and looked straight at Hank. "You're asking the wrong person. You need to talk to Paul Osgood. This whole operation was his idea."

"Can't. At least not right now." Hank stuck the lens cover on his camera and wiped the sweat off his forehead. "Last I heard, they weren't real sure Paul was going to pull through."

Michael thought maybe the editor was trying to pull one over on him to get an unguarded comment he could print. "You're kidding?"

"Nope, honest. He's in bad shape. Something about a mistake in medication." Hank looked at Michael with narrowed eyes. "You think our killer found out Paul knows something and found a way to slip him the wrong medicine on purpose?"

"That's crazy," Michael said.

"No crazier than this." The editor nodded toward the car they'd pulled out of the lake. "You finding Roxanne's long-lost car, and then her kid being here in your car. Come on, Michael. You don't expect me to believe this is just a coincidence. Something fishy is going on here, and it's my duty as a newspaperman to find out what." Hank pulled out his notebook and pencil.

"Weird things do seem to happen, don't they, Hank? Like the way you just happened to follow Lester out here."

Hank shut his notebook and stuffed it back into his shirt pocket. "I suppose coincidences can happen."

Michael didn't let him off the hook that easily.

"And I hear your information network has expanded to include mixed-up kids."

Hank had the grace to look a bit shame-faced. "I didn't offer the boy much more than an understanding ear."

"That's all, huh?"

"It could be I did say I might be able to help him hunt for his mother. It's not all that hard to find people nowadays. Not if you know how to search on the computer." Hank flicked his eyes over to the car they fished out of the lake and back to Michael. "Of course, don't guess I'd have had much chance of finding her in this case."

"Anthony's got enough problems without you playing with his head to get a story."

"Oh, give me a break, Michael. I'd pass anything he told me on to you."

"I mean it, Hank. Leave the kid alone." Michael gave him a hard look. "This isn't a game and I don't want to find any more dead bodies. Especially not Anthony's. And not yours either, for that matter."

Hank stopped in mid-reach for his notebook. His eyes widened as he hit his chest with his hand instead. "Mine?"

"You've been digging. You may have found out too much."

"You're giving me the willies, Michael." Hank looked around uneasily. "I won't even be able to drive out of here without locking my doors now."

"Good."

"I haven't really found anything out."

"But you like to sound as if you have, and the murderer may not want to take any chances."

"Do you think he murdered Roxanne too?"

Hank didn't seem to expect an answer since he left his notebook in his pocket. That was just as well because Michael had no answer to give him.

Evening shadows had darkened into night before they wrapped things up and headed back to civilization. Buck threatened to shoot out Lester's tires if he tried to go in front of him down the gravel road. So Lester had to settle for the spot behind the wrecker.

Justin and the divers were long gone, but that still left Hank and Michael behind Lester, with Baxter Perry bringing up the rear as though he had to close some invisible gate behind them. Lester's blue lights stabbed holes in the darkness as they made their way back to the main road and gave the whole thing the feel of a funeral procession.

The slow drive away from the lake gave Michael plenty of time to think about Hank's last question. While it had been nothing but the weirdest coincidence that they found the car while on a wild-goose chase thought up by a delirious man, that didn't change the fact that Rayburn had known Roxanne, had even professed to know she had been murdered.

What if she had? What if Rayburn had been blackmailing the murderer all these years and the murderer got tired of paying? That didn't explain why Rayburn asked Anthony to meet him at the courthouse. Or was Anthony even telling the truth about that? Or about Rayburn already being dead when Anthony got there? How much had Anthony actually seen?

Too much to let him go home and disappear into the night again. That was for sure.

Back out on the main road at last, the procession split up, with Buck heading one way, the wrecker turning back out toward the interstate, and Hank rushing for town to get his headlines in print. Hank told Michael this kind of news couldn't wait till next Wednesday. He planned to put out a special issue of the *Gazette* the next day.

Michael radioed Lester to turn off his lights and go home.

"Can't I wait till we get to town?" Lester asked.

"No, Lester. Now."

"Okay, Michael." Lester didn't sound happy, but he doused the lights. The air was calmer at once. "But if you need any more help tonight, you call me. I'll be right there."

In the backseat, Anthony laughed after Michael signed off. "That Lester's something. You don't watch out, he'll save the world instead of you."

"He might." Michael put down the radio. "As long as it gets saved, right?"

Anthony scooted up next to the grille between the seats. "Look, Deputy, I'm tired. How about letting me go home? I told you what I know."

Michael didn't bother answering. Instead, as soon as he had a strong cell signal, he pulled over and called Vera Arnold. He told her what they might have found in the lake and that he was going to keep Anthony with him for a while.

For once in her life, Vera was without words. There was such a long silence that Michael was almost ready to check his phone to see if the call dropped when she squeaked, "Roxanne?"

"Yes, ma'am, I'm afraid that's what it looks like, although no official identification has been made. Justin will call you in the morning with more information."

"I can't believe it," she finally said after another long silence. "I always figured Roxanne would come waltzing home one day dressed to the nines and dripping diamonds, and you say she's been in the lake all this time?"

"That's how it appears, but until Justin makes it official, it'd be best if you didn't share that news with anybody."

After he disconnected the call, he imagined Vera's hand hovering over her phone. He'd be surprised if she didn't succumb to the temptation, and by morning everybody in Hidden Springs would know they'd found Roxanne. It didn't really matter. Though it might not be official, the bones in the car had been Roxanne's. There wasn't much doubt about that.

Michael sighed and then scrolled down to Reece's number. Nobody answered. Maybe Reece had gone to Eagleton with Alex after Michael canceled out. Just as well. Michael was way too tired to match wits with Alex tonight. Still, her outsider's view of the town might let her see something in the whole mess that Michael was missing. And he had to be missing something.

He got burgers and fries at a restaurant's drive-thru window out at the interstate before he turned toward home. After Anthony made short work of the burger, he scooted up to talk to Michael again. "You said you'd let me go if I talked. I talked."

"I know." Michael kept his eyes on the road. "Sorry about that. But don't worry. I'll let you go to school Monday."

"How do you know I'll stay at school? You going to follow me around all day?"

"Maybe. Or who knows? Lester wants to help. He'd probably enjoy a day at the high school. Now eat your fries before they get cold."

"What about your big date tonight, Deputy?" Anthony sat back in the seat and slurped up his drink.

"Duty before fun."

"Are you saying kidnapping me is your duty?"

"Okay, kid, you want it straight? Here it is." Michael glanced in his rearview mirror, but he couldn't see the boy's face was in the shadows. "You've been working hard to get into trouble for some time now. I don't know why I care, but I do."

"Stop it, Deputy." Anthony groaned. "I'm gonna be sick."

"Yeah, I guess it does sound like a scene in a bad movie." Michael gave a short laugh.

"All we need is some sappy music." Anthony crumpled up the hamburger wrapper and bounced it between his hands. "How come you decide to pick on me instead of some of the other kids out at school?"

"Don't know the answer to that. Miss Keane says it's because I think we're alike." Michael gripped the steering wheel and stared out at the road.

"Me and you alike?" The boy snorted. "That's a joke."

"Yeah, a real laugher. But whatever the reason, here we are."

"But I need to get my car and go on home. Aunt Vera wants me to mow the yard tomorrow."

"Your car will be fine in the parking lot. And your aunt was fine with you staying with me tonight."

"I'll bet," Anthony said under his breath.

"Things work out, you can go home tomorrow." Michael kept his voice casual. "But tonight, like it or not, you're stuck with me. I aim to make sure you're alive to mow that yard."

"You think somebody wants to do me in?" Anthony sounded surprised.

"I don't know. I hope not, but I didn't think somebody would kill Joe either."

Anthony was quiet for a long minute as they turned down the lane leading to Michael's house. When he did finally speak, his voice had lost the cockiness. "So you think my father would kill me if it came to that."

The words settled in the air between them.

"Your father?" Michael peered over his shoulder at Anthony, but could only see his shape in the backseat out here away from the town lights.

"Who else would want to make sure that Rayburn didn't tell whatever he knew?"

Michael hesitated a minute. "Do you know who that is?"

"Nope. Aunt Vera says she doesn't know, but when she gets mad at me, she talks bad about Mama. Says she had lots of boyfriends."

"She shouldn't have told you that."

"Why not? I thought you were all about telling the truth." Anthony laughed, his cockiness back. "You know you're fighting one losing battle trying to keep me straight. A mother like that and a murderer for a father."

"Whatever else your mother did, she loved you."

"Maybe, but not my daddy. I think we can be

pretty sure about that. Especially if you think he's trying to get rid of me. Permanently." Anthony tried to sound tough, but he wasn't completely successful.

Michael concentrated on dodging the chugholes in the lane and kept quiet. He couldn't think of much to say.

After a minute, Anthony asked, "What happened to your folks, Deputy?"

"They were killed in a car wreck."

"I remember your mother. She was nice. She used to come and take me to Sunday school. Always gave me chewing gum." Anthony sounded like he might actually be smiling. Then his voice changed. "She never came after Mama left."

"That's when the wreck happened. That same year your mother disappeared."

"You mean the same year my mother was murdered."

"We don't know she was murdered."

"You don't know, but sounds like that Rayburn guy knew. Else why would he be dead?"

Michael let the question hang in the air without answering it.

Anthony didn't seem to care. After a moment, he asked, "Your folks didn't drive into the lake too, did they?"

"No, there was another car. My father swerved off the road and hit a tree." Michael stared out at the dark roadway and remembered how his eyes had jerked open when his mother screamed. The lights were coming straight toward them. "My parents were killed instantly."

"The people in the other car get killed too?"

"The other car didn't stop. Probably a drunk driver."

"So you say that happened the same year Mama disappeared?" Anthony fell silent for a moment. "Think that's kind of weird?"

The question surprised Michael. "Why?"

"Just seems odd you losing your parents and me losing my mother at about the same time." Anthony leaned up toward the front seat again. "When was the wreck?"

"Toward the end of June. The twenty-fifth."

"Mom disappeared—I guess I should say was killed—in June too. A couple of weeks after school was out." Anthony ran his fingers up and down the wire grille between the seats. "I was five. So you had to be sixteen or seventeen at least."

"Fifteen," Michael said.

"So what do you remember about Mama being gone?"

"I was away at camp most of June before the accident."

"Are you sure it was an accident?" Anthony sat back.

"What are you getting at, kid?" Michael glanced up at the rearview mirror, but it was too dark to see Anthony's face. He considered flipping on the overhead light, but he didn't. Sometimes talk was easier in the dark.

"Oh, I don't know. Just that everybody thought my mother ran off, but she didn't. So maybe whoever ran your folks off the road aimed for it to happen. Who knows? Maybe your daddy was my daddy and we're brothers or something."

"That would shoot down your theory that your father is the murderer. Since my father died in the accident." Michael gave up on seeing Anthony's face.

"Yeah, I guess we can rule that out. I wasn't all that excited about being your brother anyway. It's just a game I used to play when I was a little kid, wondering if this man or that man might be the one."

"Maybe it was Rayburn."

"I thought about that, but it didn't work with the other stuff he told me."

"What stuff?"

"All that stuff I told you already."

They turned the last corner to the log house. Light spilled out of the windows, and a car was parked in the drive.

"Looks like one of your girlfriends is here, Deputy." Anthony tapped on the window.

"Maybe it's the murderer."

Anthony laughed. "If you're trying to scare me, it's not working. It's that foxy lady who's visiting Mr. Sheridan."

"How do you know?"

"I saw her car last night."

"That's right. You were skulking around Keane Street last night. What were you up to anyway?" Michael pulled the car to a stop.

"I lost a hubcap. Thought I might have lost it there."

"It was sort of dark to be looking for a hubcap, wasn't it?"

"I've got good eyes."

"Sure you do. You've been seeing a lot, haven't you?" Michael opened Anthony's door.

"More than you." Anthony climbed out and stood face-to-face with Michael. Then he gave a short laugh and stepped away from the car. "But then it could be you see it, you just don't want to believe it. People around here want everything to match a pretty little picture of the town they carry around in their head."

"If that was ever true, the picture's been smeared up pretty badly the last few days." But Anthony was right. That did make Michael sad.

When Jasper bounded around the house to greet them, Anthony stopped in his tracks. "Does he bite?"

Michael grabbed Jasper's collar to keep him from barreling into the boy. The dog knew no strangers. "He's just excited to see you."

"Really?" Something changed in Anthony's voice as he leaned over to rub Jasper. "To see me? I've never had a dog."

Jasper licked his hand.

"Unless Alex found his dog food, he'll be ready for his supper."

"Alex." Anthony gave the dog one last pat, then straightened up to follow Michael toward the house. "Is that her name? What do you think, Deputy? Maybe that old lawyer uncle of hers is my daddy. That would make her my cousin, wouldn't it?"

Michael looked straight at Anthony in the light spilling out of the house's windows. "Reece isn't your father."

"Maybe not." Anthony shrugged. "But somebody is. Somebody you think might do me in to keep anybody from finding out."

⊰ 25 ⊱

When they went in the door, Alex laid aside the thick brief she'd been reading and uncurled from the couch. The table was set for two with white Styrofoam plates and red plastic cups. No sign of candles.

"Checking out the law for defenses against breaking and entering?" Michael asked her.

With an easy laugh, she pushed her silky dark hair back behind her ears and came to meet them. The sight of her sent the familiar rush of pleasure through Michael and started up a little buzz in his ears. Beside him, Anthony's eyes popped open wide.

"You don't see anything broken, do you? Unlawful entry perhaps, but not breaking. The door was unlocked. You have to pay attention to the letter of the law." She let her eyes touch on Anthony. "Bringing home your work?"

"You could say that." Michael glanced at the boy. "Anthony Blake, Alex Sheridan."

Alex held her long, slim hand out to Anthony and smiled. "Do you need a lawyer?"

"I might." Anthony clasped her hand. "I'm thinking about charging police brutality."

"Interesting." Alex flashed her eyes back to Michael.

"Don't get your hopes up, Alex. The kid couldn't afford your retainer fee. Besides, all I'm doing is trying to keep him alive to give me more trouble tomorrow."

"Bet you're wishing you'd let me take my chances about now." Anthony sounded very pleased with himself.

Michael ignored the boy's smirk. "Hope you brought enough food for three, Alex."

"No worry. We have an overabundance," Alex said. "Malinda called me up. Said she knew you'd be hungry, and since she had some kind of school thing, would I be so kind as to go by Cindy's and pick up the dinner she'd ordered for you and carry it down here? She even ordered chocolate pie. Knew I loved that. She was sure we'd want to talk over old times anyway. How could I refuse her?"

"Nobody can turn down that old lady," Anthony muttered.

Alex raised her eyebrows, and Michael explained. "She's tutoring Anthony."

"Consider yourself fortunate, Anthony." Alex gave Anthony a smile that surely made the boy's knees weak. "Just pull a chair up to the table while I dig out another piece of china." She turned back to the kitchen area to set out another Styrofoam plate.

Alex took the fried chicken, mashed potatoes, and green beans out of the oven while Michael filled the plastic cups with ice. It was somehow jarring seeing Alex in a kitchen. She didn't fit. She was courtroom drama, romantic restaurants, and walking on beaches at sunrise. Not kitchens.

When she pushed him aside to get a fruit salad and slaw out of the refrigerator, he said, "You actually seem to know what you're doing here in the kitchen."

"Hey, I can be homey." Alex sounded offended. "I can even cook if I want to."

"You? Cook?" Michael gave her a disbelieving look. "What can you cook?"

"Eggs. Toast. Popcorn in the microwave." She counted off on her fingers.

"You think she'll cook us eggs and toast for breakfast, Deputy?" Anthony settled in the chair against the wall where he could keep his eyes on Alex. He was obviously captivated.

Alex turned cool eyes on Anthony that made red bloom on his cheeks as he dropped his gaze to the table. "I didn't mean anything by that, Miss Sheridan."

"Of course you didn't." She gifted him with a forgiving smile.

Michael rescued the boy by changing the subject. "So what's going on?"

"Your friend Karen called. She tried your cell, but as usual, you didn't answer. She said the play last night was great and it was too bad you had to miss it, but of course, she understood." Alex peered over at him. "Don't look so worried. I didn't talk to her, just eavesdropped on your answering machine."

"I'm not worried."

Alex laughed. "Then Judge Campbell left a message." Her smile disappeared. "Didn't sound like himself. Has he been sick?"

"I don't know about sick. 'Upset' might be a better word. Miss June said he took Joe's death hard." Michael poured pop into the glasses.

"People are dead and the judge is upset." Anthony drummed his fingers on the table.

Michael looked at Anthony. "Have you had a run-in with the judge?"

"Not unless you call us talking to him today a run-in." Anthony shrugged and sounded bored. "Remember? When I asked him for help and he acted like he didn't hear me." Anthony looked at

Alex. "I don't guess he'd changed his mind about that help?"

Alex watched Anthony, a tiny frown etched between her eyes. "I think he just wanted to know what was going on."

"Who doesn't?" Anthony said.

Michael ignored him as he asked Alex, "Did you talk to him?"

"I picked up when he said who he was. It tore him up hearing my voice, I can tell you. He called me Karen twice." Alex gave Michael a sideways glance. "Karen here a lot?"

"Some," Michael said.

"Thinking about making it permanent?"

"If we do, we'll be sure to send you an invitation."

"A wedding invitation?" Alex sounded surprised. "Wow! Malinda didn't tell me things were so serious."

"Neither did I." Michael smiled a little. "But you're welcome to jump to any conclusions you want."

"A good lawyer doesn't jump to conclusions. She sifts and sorts through all the evidence to find out what really happened."

"Nobody around here wants to know what really happened." Anthony spoke up again.

Michael sat down at the table. He ignored the food and settled his eyes on Anthony. "Okay, kid. So tell me what you think really happened."

"I've already told you what I know, Deputy.

You're the one who has to figure out what happened."

"Hey, guys," Alex broke in. "Save the cross-examinations until after we eat. I'm starved."

Later, the food gone and Anthony asleep, in spite of himself, on the couch, Michael and Alex walked out on the deck. The nearly full moon cast silvery shadows across the yard, and the tree frogs were in full chorus. Jasper padded out of the house with them to lean against Michael's leg and nudge his hand for a pat.

"It's so beautiful here." Alex gazed out over the moon-kissed lake surface.

"Yes." Michael's eyes stayed on Alex.

"Karen's a lucky woman to be able to share this with you."

Michael ignored the implied question. "You'd like Karen."

"I doubt it." She sat down on the deck steps and Michael dropped down beside her. Jasper gave up on more pats and curled up on the deck behind them. "And I'm pretty sure she wouldn't like me thinking about holding hands with her guy the way we used to when we were kids. Do you remember that?"

"It sounds like a good thing to remember." Without hesitation, Michael reached over and captured her hand. It was soft and slender and at the same time strong as she curled her fingers around his.

"Do you ever wish we were kids again with no worries?"

"Kids have worries." Michael motioned with his head toward the house. "Just ask Anthony in there."

"What is it with the two of you?"

"He's tired of me being on his case." It was hard to think about Anthony with Alex's hand in his and so close to him that, when a breeze sidled up from the lake, a wisp of her hair brushed his face.

"He's hiding something." Alex turned toward Michael, her face enticingly close in the soft darkness.

"I know. That's why he's here." Michael made himself look away from her back toward the open door. He could see the top of Anthony's head on the couch. It might be good to keep his mind on Anthony. That might prevent him from doing something foolish, like put his arm around Alex.

She was quiet a minute or two. "Did you really pull his mother's body out of the lake today?"

"It was her car and Justin said the bone structure was right." Michael stared out toward the lake. So peaceful and beautiful in the moonlight, and yet for years it had hidden the tragic truth of Roxanne's disappearance.

"I remember when she disappeared." Alex stared back out at the lake too.

"You do?" Michael was surprised.

"Everything that happened that summer your

parents got killed has stayed burned in my memory. Maybe because before that I hadn't honestly realized bad things like that could happen to me or anybody I knew."

Michael shifted a little on the porch to look at her face in the moonlight. "Tell me what you remember."

He was sorry he had asked when she pulled her hand away from his to run it through her hair. He'd seen her do that a thousand times. Her way of gathering her thoughts. But even though he wanted to know what she remembered, he wished her hand was still in his.

"I didn't know you were away at camp until I got here that summer. I was so disappointed, but Uncle Reece said you'd be home in a week and he'd made plans for us to go fishing. Just the two of us. But even that fell through when Roxanne disappeared and he had to work out custody arrangements for Anthony. He was county attorney then."

"I'd forgotten that," Michael said.

"His term was up the next year and he didn't run again. Politics don't suit Uncle Reece." Alex made a face at him. "You know how he is. Doesn't want anybody upset with him. Anyway, Aunt Adele was outraged by the idea that a mother, any mother, no matter what else she did, could just go off and leave a little child alone like that. That was all she talked about."

"Everybody thought Roxanne just took off?"

"Nobody suspected foul play, if that's what you mean." Even in the moonlight, Michael could tell Alex's look had sharpened on him. "Do you now?"

"It's a definite possibility."

"Anything to do with these other murders, you think?"

"That is the question."

"A question in need of an answer, but some answers take time." She shifted over a little to lean against the deck railing.

If only she'd shifted over to lean against him instead. He tried to keep his mind on the questions in need of answers, but the question of what he was going to do about how he felt about her had a way of pushing all sensible thought out of his head. "And some never get answered."

"Right." She clasped her hands around her knees and stared back out at the lake. "Actually the talk I heard was more about her little boy. Anthony, I suppose, although I didn't remember his name. I was only fifteen at the time, an innocent in Aunt Adele's eyes. So she was careful about what she said about Roxanne around me. I heard whispers, but the rumors about Roxanne would not have been fit conversation for my young ears."

"Okay, so what did she say about Anthony?"

"Everybody talked about taking him in, even

Aunt Adele, but it was mostly just talk. Except with your mother. I think she meant it."

"My mother?" Michael turned to stare at Alex, but she kept her eyes on the lake.

"Yes, your mother was such a lovely woman. That very first day after they found Anthony alone at Roxanne's place, she was waiting when Uncle Reece got home. They stayed shut up in his office forever. Later, Uncle Reece told Aunt Adele that your mother wanted him to appoint her Anthony's guardian until Roxanne could be found, but I always had the feeling there was more to it than that. They both looked so serious when they came out."

"Maybe Anthony's right. Maybe we are brothers." Michael made an attempt at a laugh, but it sounded sort of hollow even to his own ears. Alex's words were dragging up too many sad memories.

Alex scooted around close to him on the step and touched his hand. "You don't remember your father very well if you can even think that might be true."

Michael curled his fingers around hers. "A lot of blanks never got filled back in after the wreck."

Alex squeezed his hand a little, then pulled it away again. "I know, but trust me. Your father worshiped your mother. His eyes never strayed from her. Anyway, after the wreck, everybody sort of forgot about Roxanne and what might happen to Anthony. They had a new kid to feel sorry for. You."

"Did you?" he asked. She was so close, her face inches from his.

"Did I what?" Her breath whispered toward him.

"Feel sorry for me." Michael's fingers tingled with the desire to brush a stray strand of hair back from her cheek, but he curled his hands into fists instead.

"I did." Alex's smile faded as the lake captured her gaze again. When she went on, her voice was soft. "Not just for you. For me too. I was devastated. They said even if you lived, you might never regain your faculties. 'Faculties.' What kind of word is that to talk about a teenage kid? I had to ask Uncle Reece what that meant. It wasn't good."

"They were wrong."

"I know." Alex looked at him, then quickly away again, as though she were having an attack of shyness. "But there was no way I could know that. Not then. That summer. I spent hours standing at the window staring at your house and wishing you'd suddenly appear on the porch and wave at me the way you used to. I wanted to run out and meet you halfway, but of course, you were in the hospital."

Michael didn't say anything. He was afraid if he did, she'd stop talking, and in fact she did pull back from him to hide her face in her hands. "This is embarrassing."

"I think it's fascinating." He leaned down in front of her and pulled her hands away from her face.

"You would. You don't have any juvenile memories to confess." She looked up at him. "Just keep in mind I was fifteen and thought I was in love with you."

"In love with me?"

"I told you it was embarrassing." She fanned her face with her hands and laughed a little. "Actually I thought you were in love with me too, and that we would get married someday. After all, you'd asked me to marry you every summer since we were six."

"I don't remember." That was a memory he fervently wished he hadn't lost.

"I know." She sounded almost sad.

"When you were trying to help me remember things later, why didn't you tell me?"

"I don't know." She ran her fingers along the edge of the steps. "By the next summer, everything was different. We weren't kids anymore."

"Did you ever say yes?"

"I don't remember." The corners of Alex's lips turned up as she looked out at the lake again. "Maybe the first time when we were six."

With his fingers on her chin, Michael gently turned her face back around until he could see her eyes in the moonlight. "And did we ever kiss?"

"A few little kid pecks. We were very young."

"Kid pecks? I don't remember. Show me what you mean." Michael moved closer to her. She leaned toward him, her lips incredibly warm and soft on his. Then his arms were around her, pulling her tight against him as his heart pounded till he thought it would explode inside him. At last, with effort, he made himself pull back and look down at her face. "We must have been pretty wild kids."

She laughed the way he'd hoped she would. He was about to pull her close again when Anthony stepped out on the deck behind them.

"Hey, Deputy, give me your keys, and I'll get lost."

Alex laughed again, not a bit embarrassed now as she extricated herself from Michael's embrace. "Don't worry about it, Anthony, the deputy and I were merely reminiscing about when we were kids."

"Some kids," Anthony said.

"Yeah, we were." Alex gave Michael's cheek a feather touch with her fingers that felt too much like goodbye as she stood up. "But all that was a long time ago. Another world almost."

Michael followed her back into the house, where she collected her briefcase and purse. "Maybe I should follow you out."

"Don't be silly. I'll be fine." She waved her

hand as though to brush aside his worry. She flashed Anthony another smile that made the color spill into the boy's cheeks. "Good to meet you, Anthony. Keep in mind that for the right causes, I waive my retainer fee."

"Great to know." Anthony trailed her to the door like a puppy dog.

Michael pointed toward the couch with a warning look. "Stay put or you might really need a lawyer."

Anthony's shoulders slumped, the sullen look back on his face. "Where do you think I'm gonna go? Swimming?"

"Not something I would advise." Michael stared the boy down.

Alex reached over and touched Anthony's arm. "Hey, the deputy's not so bad. You can put up with his company for one night."

"Like I have a choice." Anthony went back to the couch and plopped down hard enough to break some springs.

Michael ignored him and followed Alex out of the house. When they were off the porch, he said, "I had more questions."

"About when we were kids?"

"That was a good question." A little tremble went through him at the thought of kissing her again, but that moment had passed. She wouldn't welcome his kiss now. "I wouldn't mind asking some more like that, but no, I wanted to see what you thought about the murders. I was hoping you might see something I haven't."

She looked at him for a long moment. "I'll help any way I can. You know that, but it's late tonight. How about coffee at Uncle Reece's at ten tomorrow?"

"Sounds good."

"Like old times, only it used to be Aunt Adele's lemonade." She smiled and then grew serious again. "But I have the feeling I'm not going to be able to help you. I think this is one of those things you're going to have to dig down through the layer of years to figure out, and to do that, you need someone who knows what's been going on."

"Reece?"

"He might be a good place to start, but it could be you may be able to come up with some of the answers yourself. If you're not afraid to confront the questions." She kept her eyes on his face as she shifted her briefcase from one hand to the other.

"I don't know what you mean." Michael frowned.

"You don't want anybody here in Hidden Springs to be a murderer. None of us do. But because of that, you may be overlooking something."

"What?"

"I don't know." She opened her car door to place her briefcase and purse on the front seat.

Then she straightened back up to peek around him toward the house. "But I advise you to keep an eye on Anthony, because even if you've missed it, I don't think he has."

Michael glanced over his shoulder. The kid was at the door watching them. "You could be right."

"Always." She tiptoed up to kiss his cheek quickly. "There. That's the kid peck."

"I liked the other demonstration better." It was all he could do to keep from pulling her into his arms.

"I'll bet you did." Again her laugh sent sweet shivers up Michael's back. "But you caught me at a weak moment. It won't happen again." She got in her car and lowered her window. "Tomorrow at ten. I'll bake muffins."

"That's a scary thought."

"Worry not. I'll buy a mix." Another laugh and she was gone.

After her lights disappeared up the lane, he called Jasper and held the door open for him to go in.

The dog made a beeline for Anthony, who reached out to ruffle the dog's ears. He almost smiled but then caught himself. He pushed Jasper away to sit down on the couch. With a sly look up at Michael, he asked, "How much is my silence worth to you?"

"Silence?" Michael pulled a couple of blankets out of the hall closet and piled them on the couch.

"I think talk is what I've been wanting out of you."

"I mean about tonight. I could go by and see Reverend Allison. She's been after me to come to her youth group."

When Michael laughed, the kid couldn't hide his surprise. "Tell her whatever you want." Michael pitched him a pillow. "Now take off your jeans and shoes and go to bed."

"I'm going to sleep in my clothes."

"Sure thing. Except for your jeans and shoes. I'll hang on to them till morning." Michael held out his hand. "And Jasper barks anytime something rattles a door. Great watchdog."

"I'm not going nowhere, Deputy."

"Not without your shoes and jeans." Michael kept his hand reached out.

Anthony glared at him a minute, then shrugged. He kicked off his shoes and jeans and handed them to Michael.

The kid went to sleep right away. Michael could hear his low steady breathing, but sleep was a long time coming for Michael. He kept thinking about what Alex said about how he might know something that could point to the murderer. He replayed every word Joe had said to him, but there was nothing there. He went over in his mind the morning he'd found Rayburn on the steps, when things were still more exciting than threatening.

He cataloged the few bits of evidence they had.

Paul was right about one thing. It would help to find the gun. Michael had read the ballistics report, but maybe he'd missed something. It had come in after he found Joe, and his mind might not have been as clear as it needed to be.

Somehow in spite of the odds, it was all connected. It had to be. Even Roxanne in the lake all these years. Was that the secret somebody would do anything to keep from revealing? But Rayburn hadn't known that. He may have suspected someone had killed her, but if he'd known how, he wouldn't have waited all these years to tell. It was the secret before that. The secret that might be the reason Roxanne ended up in the lake. That's the secret he had to dig out.

⊰ 26 ⊱

The phone woke Michael the next morning a few minutes before six thirty. As he grabbed it to jab the on button, he got up to look through his bedroom door at the couch. Anthony hadn't moved since the last time he'd checked around five.

The judge's voice boomed in his ear. "I told that pretty Alexandria Sheridan to tell you to call me when you got home. How come you didn't?"

"It was late. I thought it could wait until morning." Michael wanted to add that it could have waited until a little later in the morning, but he didn't. Michael kept his voice low. "You talked to the sheriff, didn't you?"

"He says they found Roxanne's car in the lake and her in it." The judge's voice went down to an almost normal level.

"That's what it looks like."

"After all these years." The judge was silent a moment. "Did the boy tell you where to look?"

"The boy? You mean Anthony?" Michael shook his head to clear out the remaining cobwebs of sleep.

"Somebody had to tell you. If it wasn't him, who was it?"

"Nobody told us anything. It was just blind luck." Michael rubbed Jasper when the dog pushed his head up against Michael's hand.

"Luck?" the judge echoed. "I don't believe in luck, Michael."

"Didn't Sheriff Potter tell you? Paul had us out there searching for the murder weapon when the divers found the car."

"The murder weapon? Al didn't say anything about a murder weapon. You're not making any sense, Michael." The judge's voice got louder and Michael pushed the phone tighter against his ear to keep the sound from leaking out into the room.

"Look, Judge, it's a fact that not much is making sense, but I don't think we're going to be able to figure it out over the phone. I'll come by to see you later. Could be you can help me get the straight of it all. You remember when Roxanne disappeared, don't you?"

Again the line hummed with silence for a moment. Then he said, "Of course I remember. But all I remember is that she up and disappeared."

"Can you think of anybody who might have had reason to want her to disappear?"

"What are you trying to say? That somebody pushed Roxanne into the lake?" The judge didn't wait for an answer. "Look here, Michael, it's not going to do any of us the first bit of good to search for a bogeyman behind every bush. It was probably just an accident."

"Maybe so, sir, but things aren't adding up. Since Rayburn knew Roxanne, you have to wonder if it's all somehow connected."

"What makes you think Rayburn knew Roxanne?"

"He told Anthony."

"Are you sure about that?" the judge said.

"I'm sure."

"That does give the whole thing a new wrinkle." The judge huffed out a breath. "Could be Rayburn told the kid he was the one to push Roxanne's car into the lake and so the kid shot him."

On the couch, Anthony still hadn't moved, but now his eyes were open, staring at Michael. "I hadn't thought of that."

"Well, you better think about it and you better

keep an eye on that boy. Who knows what he might do next?"

"Don't worry, Judge. I'll take care of it."

"Just see that you do before somebody else turns up dead." With that the judge broke off the connection without even saying goodbye.

Michael punched the off button.

Anthony sat up. "Sort of early for the judge to be calling, isn't it? Or does he give you marching orders every morning?"

Michael didn't bother answering as he let Jasper outside and then waited for the dog to come back in before he headed for the bathroom. He looked at the shower longingly but settled for a cold splash of water in his face. No need giving Anthony time to slip out the door and hot-wire the cruiser.

He toyed with the idea of letting Burton lock the kid up in the jail. It wasn't as if he and Anthony were ever going to be on any kind of friendly terms no matter what he did. Michael simply needed to make sure he was out of harm's way until he figured out who the murderer was. The jail would do fine.

But then when Michael came out of the bathroom, Jasper was leaning against the kid's legs while Anthony stared at what was left of the little car. His cheeks were wet with tears.

The boy dashed them away. "I guess you're right, Deputy. I ain't so tough after all." When

Jasper nudged Anthony's arm, the kid stroked the dog's head a couple of times. When he pulled his hand away, Jasper curled up on the floor by his feet.

"She was your mother."

Anthony looked down and pushed the little car across his bare thigh. "When I was a little kid, every day I woke up, I thought that would be the day she came back. She'd have some big story about why she left. I never could think of any story good enough, but I knew she'd have one. Then when I got older, I gave up on her coming back, but there was always that feeling that she might, you know." He was quiet a minute before he went on. "I guess I can be sure it won't ever happen now."

Michael took a step toward Anthony, but stopped. "It's better to know."

The words echoed in his head. Aunt Lindy must have told him the same thing a thousand times as he tiptoed around the blackness, not sure whether he wanted to plunge in to pull out another lost memory.

Anthony stared up at him with challenge in his eyes. "Knowing stuff sometimes gets people killed."

"It does." Michael met his look fully. "Especially when they don't tell anyone what they know."

"I don't know about that. Rayburn told and he died."

"Joe didn't tell and he died."

"Looks like we're down to the tiebreaker. I guess we'll see which one of us is right." Anthony stood up and stretched.

"So it seems."

When Jasper scrambled up beside Anthony, the kid's face softened a bare bit. He ran his hand all the way down Jasper's back.

"You want to feed him?"

After a second's hesitation, Anthony stepped away from the dog. "Nah. He's your dog. You feed him."

"All right." Michael filled the dog's dish.

Anthony watched the dog eat for a minute, then said, "How about giving me back my jeans? I'm hungry, so I promise not to run away till after breakfast. Besides, it's not all that bad out here. Beats Aunt Vera's. Somebody's always yelling at somebody around there in the morning."

Michael picked up the jeans and pitched them toward him. "Take a shower if you want. Towels are on the shelf. But I'm afraid all I've got for breakfast are frozen waffles and cornflakes."

"That Miss Sheridan's toast and eggs sound better."

"She probably burns the toast."

"Yeah, maybe. But burned toast isn't that bad." Anthony laughed as he headed for the bathroom.

A couple of hours later, Michael unlocked the sheriff's office with Anthony still in tow.

"Looks like you're the only dedicated employee here today, Deputy." Anthony looked down the empty hallway. "I'll bet you even work on Sundays."

"Sometimes. Now be quiet for a while. I've got to look up some things."

"You still haven't figured things out, have you, Deputy?"

"One thing." Michael looked at him. "You talk a lot not to ever say much."

"Okay, okay. I'll just sit over here and count the little holes in the ceiling tile."

Michael's cell phone rang before he could make his first call. It was the sheriff tracking him down. "Justin says there isn't much doubt the remains we pulled out of the lake yesterday belong to Roxanne."

When Michael made a sound of agreement, the sheriff went on. "You let the kid go home yet?"

"Not yet."

"He tell you anything?"

"Not yet."

"You need to send him on home. The little twerp might bring some kind of harassment charges against the county and then what?"

"He'll be alive to bring them." Michael stared over at Anthony, who was pretending not to listen.

"Now, Mike, nobody's going to kill that kid." The sheriff sounded irritated. "What purpose would there be in that?"

"I don't know."

"Just do what I say, and we'll talk about it later. The state's sending some people in to poke around on Monday, and I don't want them to find anything out of the way to jump on."

"Whatever you say, Sheriff." Michael would figure out an excuse later for ignoring his orders. He changed the subject. "You heard from Paul this morning? Yesterday Hank said they weren't sure he was going to pull through."

"You don't say? I haven't talked to the chief for a couple of days. Guess you'd better check up on him when you get a chance."

Anthony watched him put down the phone. "You don't look too happy, Deputy."

"You can sit there and be quiet or see how you like it up in jail."

"Jail don't scare me."

Michael ignored him while he tried to track down Buck, but without luck. He wasn't surprised.

Next he called Chief Sibley. When he didn't answer, Michael called the hospital, where a nurse in the intensive care unit said Paul's condition had been upgraded from critical to serious. That was all the information she was allowed to give out concerning Mr. Osgood's medical condition.

Lester called in to say his mother wanted him to mow the yard, but if Michael needed him for

310

anything, the grass could wait. Michael looked at Anthony and considered bringing Lester in to watch the boy, but in all likelihood, Anthony could lose Lester in two minutes flat. So he told Lester to make his mother happy and mow the yard.

Alex called to say she was stirring up the muffins and should she plan on Anthony's appetite too?

"I guess you better, and why don't you see if Aunt Lindy will come over?"

"This is sounding more and more romantic." Alex laughed. "How about I ask the judge and Miss June too?"

"Do you have enough muffins?"

"Well, no, but I can send Uncle Reece down to the grocery to pick up some high-calorie, fat-laden sticky buns."

"Sounds perfect. I've got a couple of things to do here and then we'll be on over."

"How about Karen? Maybe I should call her since everybody else is coming."

"I doubt she knows much about when Roxanne disappeared. She's only been in Hidden Springs a couple of years, but hey, if you want to ask her, Aunt Lindy has her number."

With another laugh, Alex hung up.

Michael ignored Anthony's attempts to needle him and concentrated on the ballistics report on the bullet that had killed Rayburn. Something about the report kept bugging him. He finally spotted what it was at the bottom of the report. A matching ballistics report was already on file in the computer. Michael stared at the code, and didn't know how he could have missed it. That other report had been filed from this office.

Michael eyed the computer on his desk like the opponent it was. Betty Jean could pull up that old report from the database in four or five clicks of her mouse. Michael might do the same in an hour, but what the report said wouldn't matter that much. What he needed to know was where the gun was now. First place to check was the evidence room.

After he fished the key out of Betty Jean's desk drawer, he gave Anthony a hard look. "You stay put or else."

"Or else what?"

"You don't want to know."

Anthony shrugged. "I can stick around a little longer, I guess." He slouched down in the chair and closed his eyes. "I'll just take a little nap here while you finish up business."

"Good idea." Michael stepped across the office to unlock the evidence room. With the door propped open, he could keep an eye on Anthony.

Five Saturday night specials were lined up on the shelf with tags indicating the files that told their stories. Four of them were covered with the fine dust that filtered around in the old courthouse and settled on everything that wasn't periodically moved. No dust was on the fifth one, an old Smith & Wesson.

With a sick feeling in the pit of his stomach, Michael slid a pencil in the barrel of the gun to carry it back to his desk. The suspect list had just shortened.

"Hey, Deputy, you don't look so hot." Anthony sat up straight and stared at him. "You aren't about to end it all, are you? I mean, if you are, let me go out in the hall first, okay?"

"You're all heart, kid." Michael didn't even glance over at him. He kept his eyes on the gun and clicked over in his mind the people with keys to the office. Him, Betty Jean, the sheriff, Lester, Roy.

What was it Roy had said after Rayburn's body had been found? That his keys weren't on the right hook in the supply closet. That lengthened the suspect list to just about everybody in the courthouse. Not a list Michael liked considering.

"Is that the gun that did in that Rayburn guy?" Anthony peered over at the gun.

"What makes you think that?"

Anthony didn't answer. Instead he laughed. "Pretty smart, huh? Borrowing a gun from the sheriff."

"What makes you think this is the murder weapon?" Michael repeated his question, his eyes boring into Anthony's face.

"I know things." Anthony looked entirely too pleased with himself.

"The only way you could know that is if you were the one to use the gun and then put it back." Michael didn't let his stare waver from the boy's face. "Maybe that's why you've been hanging around the courthouse. Waiting to sneak in here and put the gun back."

"You know that didn't happen." The corners of Anthony's lips turned up a little. "How could I have gotten the gun in the first place?"

"I don't know. You tell me."

"I guess I'm going to have to, since you obviously can't figure it out. You see, it's like this. I came this close to seeing Rayburn get it on the steps out front." Anthony held his thumb and finger about an inch apart. "Whoever shot him went back into the courthouse."

"How do you know that?"

"I told you that Rayburn called me and wanted me to come meet him. He said nine, but since I was up already, I headed on down here. Wasn't hard to find his car in the parking lot where he told me to meet him. Took you awhile longer to find it."

"We were slow on that one." Michael kept his voice level. "Go on."

Anthony grinned. "To make a long story short, I got tired of waiting by his car, and I figured, how big is Hidden Springs. I couldn't miss him."

"So you found him."

"Not soon enough for him to tell me anything. I was coming up the side alley when I heard a popping noise. I didn't know it was a gun. Figured a car backfired or who knows what. Then I came around the corner and there he was. Slumped against the post and nobody else anywhere around."

"So why didn't you call the police?"

"Me? Call the cops? You got to be kidding. You see me in the yard with a hundred other people and you've been on my case ever since. Think what would have happened if I'd been the one to tell you about it." Anthony shook his head. "No way did I want to play that scene. The man was dead. Me yelling for the police wasn't going to change that."

"And you didn't see anybody else?"

" 'Fraid not."

"Lucky for you, I guess. They might have had an extra bullet." Michael glanced down at the gun and back at Anthony.

"Yeah. Lucky's my middle name." Anthony let out a short little laugh with no humor in it. "Anyway, the only way the shooter could have gotten out of sight that fast was by going into the courthouse. I decided it wouldn't be smart to follow the killer inside here to yell help. For all I knew, it could've even been you."

"What made you mark me off your suspect

list?" Michael's mind was racing and he didn't like any of the thoughts zooming around.

"Because I know who did it now."

"Who's that?"

"Dear old Dad. That's who and that ain't you."

"And I suppose you've figured out who that is."

Anthony looked smug. "I told you. The murderer."

"How about a name?"

"You wouldn't believe me if I told you."

"Try me." When Anthony just looked at him without saying anything, Michael stood up and went over to stare down at him. "I don't think you know anything. You've just been doing a lot of guessing and now you're afraid to find out if you're right."

"Me afraid?" Anthony snorted. "That's a good one. You're the one who's scared to look behind the door because of what you might find."

The telephone rang as they stared at one another. Michael ignored it. "All right, Anthony. Let's say you're right and that you have figured things out. What are you planning to do about it?"

Anthony looked away from Michael toward the phone and then at the door. "Before yesterday, I planned on hitting him up for some overdue child support payments. Enough so I could leave Hidden Springs behind."

"Blackmail him like Rayburn must have?" The phone finally quit ringing.

"Yeah, why not?"

"For one thing, Rayburn ended up dead."

"He was dumb."

"And was Joe dumb too?"

"I guess he wasn't smart enough. He's dead." Anthony's knuckles were white where he grasped the chair arms.

Michael reached behind him, picked up Betty Jean's phone, and set it on the desk right in front of the kid. "Okay. Call him. See if he'll pay off."

Anthony eyed the phone. "Money's not good enough anymore. Not now."

"What are you going to do, Anthony? Shoot him?"

"Maybe." Anthony flared up at him. "He killed my mother."

"Then you'd be a murderer too."

"Like father, like son, I guess." Anthony tried to laugh, but it came out as more of a sob.

"I don't think so, Anthony." Michael worked to keep his voice even. He didn't like what he was suspecting. "I think you want the truth to come out and that won't happen unless we catch him."

"You know who it is, don't you?" Anthony's eyes met his.

"Maybe, but nobody is going to believe us without proof."

Anthony looked from Michael to the phone. "So you want me to call him up and set a trap for him?"

"It's the only way we'll know for sure."

"Let me get this straight." Anthony's voice sounded a little shaky and he cleared his throat. "You aim to put me out there as bait."

Michael nodded. "You brave enough for that?"

"Being brave doesn't mean being stupid, because let's face it, Deputy. Your track record of keeping people alive is not all that good lately."

"You're right." Michael pulled the phone back. "It is too risky. I'll have to think of something else."

"So I can go home now?" The kid started to push up out of the chair.

"I didn't say that. We're going to be constant companions a little longer."

Anthony sank back down in the chair, muttering under his breath.

"My couch isn't that bad." Michael started to set the phone back beside Betty Jean's computer.

Anthony leaned forward in the chair and grabbed it away from Michael. "Oh, what the heck. Maybe I'll make that call after all. Looks like I won't ever get away from you any other way."

He punched in the number from memory.

·⋛ 27 ⋚·

It wasn't a good plan. Actually Michael couldn't call it a plan at all. It was just happening. Had been just happening ever since the gun in the evidence room made the impossible seem possible. Of course he could have still controlled what happened then. It wasn't until he put the phone in front of Anthony and challenged him to make the call that he lost control.

That was where he made his first mistake. At least his first mistake today. Heaven knew, he'd made plenty of other mistakes on this investigation before that. A soft drink can dug a hole in Michael's leg as he crouched out of sight in the back floorboard of Anthony's beat-up old Chevy.

First they should have talked about where to set up the meeting, but Anthony played his own game on the phone and ignored Michael's hastily penciled directions.

The stupid kid had pushed Michael's paper away and said, "At the lake. You know the spot. Where you last saw my mother."

Not exactly the ideal place to confront a desperate man. A man who would kill, had already killed more than once, to keep his secrets.

Now with the driver's side door swinging open, Michael peeked through the space between the seat and the door and caught a glimpse of Anthony on the rock ledge jutting out over the lake. Way too close to the edge. He was peering down at the water, thinking thoughts no doubt as murderous as the man he'd dared to meet him there.

That was another flaw with the plan. The boy. The major flaw. Michael had no idea what Anthony might do. He never should have put him out there as bait. He should have locked him up in the jail and come out here by himself to see what happened.

He knew proper police procedure, and here he was acting like some kind of crazy television detective scrunched in the back of an old car with a spotty radio signal and no cell reception out here, maybe no backup coming. No help. Nothing. Worst of all, he had no idea what the murderer might do. What if he just drove up and started shooting? Or he might try to run down the kid and, in the process, bang this old clunker with Michael inside it into the lake. Could be, he wouldn't come at all.

That was Michael's first hopeful thought since he deserted his patrol car and climbed into the backseat of Anthony's car. Maybe nobody would show up. Maybe he and Anthony were wrong. He hoped he was wrong. He had never wanted to be wrong so much in his life.

He felt as though he were sneaking up on the blackness to pluck out another lost memory, and this time when he looked at it, his life here in Hidden Springs was going to be shot to smithereens. What was it he had told Anthony? That it was better to know the truth. An easier thing to say when it was somebody else's truth.

Michael checked his watch. Ten thirty on the dot. The time the kid had thrown out on the phone. "See anything?" Michael whispered.

"No." Anthony's voice showed the first sign of uncertainty. "What time is it?"

"10:31." Michael peered at his watch again. "We've been here almost ten minutes."

"Ten minutes? Feels more like an hour." Anthony came over to lean against the car. "I guess we have to give him time, huh?"

"You know what you're going to do if or when he gets here?"

"Yeah, you told me a hundred times on the way out here."

Michael bit back the urge to go over it again with him anyway. Michael hadn't totally deserted his good sense. He had coached the boy on what to do if the trap worked. He had put out a call for Buck. Buck might be a Lone Ranger, but he had a knack for showing up when something was going down. He might already be out there on the main road watching for their suspect.

Michael shifted his body to keep his legs from cramping up. The seconds leaked by and dragged the minutes along behind them. He hated waiting like this. The slower the minutes ticked by, the more he doubted the wisdom of letting Anthony stay out in the open. The kid was altogether too exposed, too close to the edge in more ways than one.

His bad feeling about the whole thing grew worse when he checked his watch and saw it was 10:39, nine minutes past the appointed meeting time.

He thought briefly of Alex's muffins and felt closer to a smile than he thought possible. He might never know now whether she could really cook or not.

10:41. Michael scooted up where he could see out the window. Time to call a halt to this nonsense. The murderer wasn't going to show.

"Get down. You're going to blow it," Anthony hissed without looking around at him. "Some-body's coming."

Against his better judgment, Michael slid back down in the seat as he pulled his gun out of his holster. This was insane. He must have taken leave of his senses. Still it was happening now, and it was up to him to see that nobody else died.

Tires crunched on the gravel as the car slowly came toward them.

"It's him," Anthony said when the car broke into the clearing. "Dear old Dad."

It was all Michael could do not to sit up and

look. Even though he had decided there could be no other answer, he still had a hard time believing it. He needed to see it with his own eyes, but he stayed down and whispered, "Don't do anything stupid, Anthony."

"Like what? Stand out here and make a target?"

"Just do what we said," Michael said.

"Yeah, okay. Sucker him into admitting he knocked off Rayburn and good barber Joe, and then you'll burst out of the car like Superman and arrest him."

"Something like that." Michael gripped the gun harder.

"How about Mama? You want me to get him to admit that too?"

"Just stick to the plan and don't get shot."

The car slowed to a stop not far from them. The muscles in Michael's chest tightened and his hand holding the gun leaked sweat. He wondered how fast he could really burst out of the car. The whole thing was ridiculous. He wasn't even playing a competent crazy television detective. Not only that, he had the weirdest feeling he'd somehow been here before. As if he were replaying a scene he'd already done once.

A car door opened and then slammed shut. Maybe he didn't even need a verbal confession. Just showing up was admission of guilt enough.

"Hey, Pops." Anthony sounded unconcerned. "You bring the money?"

"I've got it." The man's voice was low, not the judge's normal booming tone at all.

Inside the car, Michael's every sense was heightened. He could not only hear but almost feel the judge stepping closer. *Keep him back, kid,* he shouted in his mind.

"Good," Anthony said. "Just put it on the ground and don't come any closer."

"All right," the judge said. There was a moment of complete, deep, and terrible silence. "Now what, son? Do you just take the money and disappear, never to bother me again?"

"Don't call me son," Anthony shouted, his control shattering like glass.

"Take it easy, boy. Fact is, we can agree on that. I never was that sure you were mine anyway. Could be your mama just settled on me because I had the deepest pockets and more reason to want to keep things hushed up than some of the others. Or who knows? She might have been holding several men around town up for a few dollars." The judge laughed a little. "That would have been a real joke on us all. Something Roxanne would have liked."

"You were the only one."

"How do you know?"

"Rayburn told me."

The judge laughed again, and inside the car, Michael tensed, ready to spring out of the car.

"Rayburn never told you anything. Rayburn didn't know anything to tell you."

"Then why did you kill him? Why did you kill my mother?"

The judge didn't answer him. Instead he said, "This all your idea, boy? How'd you get away from Michael?"

"The sheriff called and told him to let me go."

"Is that right?" the judge said. "And I didn't think Al was paying any attention when I told him it might cause trouble to keep holding you without any kind of charges."

"Keep your hands where I can see them." Anthony's voice went up a little.

"Or what? I don't see much way you're going to stop me doing whatever I want. It wasn't too smart of you to come down here all alone without a gun or anything."

"How do you know I don't have a gun?"

"How do you know I don't?" The judge's voice sounded definitely closer.

"What'd you do? Steal another one from the sheriff's office?"

"The sheriff's office?" The judge sounded suddenly wary. "What made you say that?"

Confession or no, Michael couldn't wait any longer. He pushed open the door and pointed his gun straight at the judge's chest. "Hold it right there, Judge." He managed to keep the gun level as he climbed out of the car.

The judge swore and shook his head. "Aww, Michael. I was afraid you were in there."

Michael stared at the judge while inside his head something clicked. The blackness parted, and he went back in time. He smelled the gas, the burnt rubber, the blood. He remembered the awful silence after the horrendous crash and how somehow the silence seemed the loudest. A face peered through the window at him. The face in front of him now.

"You killed them." Michael's words sounded flat to his ears.

The judge knew who he meant. His face changed, became almost sad. "Eva wouldn't give it up, but it was an accident. All an accident."

"Like my mother's car going in the lake was an accident?" Anthony spoke up.

"That's right. That was an accident too. I was going to give her the money she wanted, but she knew better than to expect she wouldn't have to earn it. Your mama, she could be a handful when she took a mind, so we were tussling a little there in her front seat. Nothing to worry about, but then she must have knocked against the gearshift. Silly woman left the motor running. I don't know what happened then. Maybe she hit the gas instead of the brakes. I barely got out before it went over." The judge looked over at the cliff. "We should have put some kind of guardrail down here years ago."

Anthony stared at the judge. "Why didn't you help her?" His voice was barely above a whisper.

"I wanted to, son. Really I did. That was one of the hardest things I ever did. Watching that car settle into the lake, but sometimes you have to think of what's best for the most people. Besides, there was no way I could get to her. No way to help. Even if she did survive the crash off the cliff, by the time I got back with help she'd have drowned for sure. I never was much of a swimmer."

The judge shook his head almost as if the thought still made him sad. He looked at Anthony and went on. "I thought a lot of your mama, and I watched the lake a good long time after the car sank, hoping she'd come to the top."

"But she didn't." Anthony's face twisted in pain as his voice grew louder. "You just left her in the lake and went home like nothing was wrong."

"I did what had to be done. It wasn't as if I could change anything. It had already happened."

"All these years you've lived a lie." Michael spoke up.

"Now, tell me, Mike. What good would it have done to tell anybody? I had plans for Hidden Springs. I couldn't let something like Roxanne stand in the way. It was unfortunate, but she was dead. There wasn't any reason for me to sacrifice my political career just so she could get buried in the ground instead of the lake. Dead's dead."

"And my parents?" Michael asked.

"I did hate that." The judge looked grieved. "The way things worked out and all. But Roxanne must have told your mother that I was the boy's daddy. Eva was a good woman, but she just didn't understand. She always thought things should be simple."

"And they weren't." An image of his mother smiling and straightening his collar popped into Michael's mind.

"They never are," the judge said. "They never are."

"So you left me for dead too."

"I thought you were already dead. Your eyes were open, fixed, and I couldn't see your chest moving. You looked like you'd gone on. I had to believe it was for the best."

"For the best," Michael echoed. He felt dizzy, the way he used to years ago after the wreck and something he saw or heard would make too many memories surface at once. At times then, he had wanted to walk back into the blackness and rest awhile. That was the way he felt now.

The judge kept talking. "It wasn't as if I aimed for any of it to happen. Instead, it was almost like somebody was taking care of things for me. First Roxanne. Then your folks. Don't you see? It all happened the way it had to."

Michael stared at the man in front of him. This couldn't be the man he'd lived next door to most of his life. The man who'd paid him to rake his leaves. Whose wife gave him cookies. The man who stepped in as a father figure after his own father had died. The man who caused his father to die.

"The way it had to." Anthony screamed out the words and dived toward the judge, swinging both fists.

"No, Anthony," Michael yelled, but it was too late. Quicker than Michael thought possible, the judge had a hammerlock on Anthony with a gun pointed at his temple.

Across the few feet between them, Michael's and the judge's eyes met. Michael still had his gun pointed at the judge, but now the boy was in between.

"Put the gun down, Michael," the judge said. "Slowly."

"Don't do it, Deputy. He's going to kill us both anyway," Anthony said.

Michael kept the gun pointed toward the judge. "No, he won't. He wouldn't kill his own son."

"I told you I never thought he was mine. Never." The judge's voice was steady and cold. "So put down your gun before I shoot him." His finger tightened on the trigger.

"Easy, Judge." Michael slowly lowered the gun and put it on the ground while he frantically tried to come up with a plan of action. He couldn't charge at him. Anthony would be dead before he got halfway there. "You can't get away with this." Michael looked out toward where the gravel road came into the clearing. "I've got backup coming."

The judge laughed a little as he pushed Anthony closer to Michael and the car. "I've been looking around corners more years than you can remember, son, and I can count on one hand with fingers left over the times I've let somebody surprise me. Fact is, I called Sally Jo and told her you didn't need backup after all. That you'd decided to take the day off to take Alex to Eagleton. That's why she didn't raise you on the radio."

"Why would she believe you?"

"I'm the judge. I run the county. Why wouldn't she believe me?"

"I had already called Buck. He'll be here."

"You do need to practice your lying, Michael. That's always been a failing you had. Too truthful. Too sincere. Too dedicated."

"Before today, I would have used those same words to describe you, Judge." Michael searched for the right thing to say or, failing the right words, at least some way to save the kid. He couldn't let the judge kill Anthony.

"I'm sure you would have, along with most of Hidden Springs. But lying so folks will believe your every word is a talent like anything else. One it appears I'm gifted with."

"You won't be able to lie your way out of this."

Michael's hand itched to grab his gun off the ground.

"Not with you, but unfortunately, you won't be around to hear the lies." Judge Campbell let out a sorrowful breath.

"What lies are you going to tell?" Michael needed to keep him talking.

"What difference does it make, Deputy? He's going to kill us." Anthony's voice was high and shrill. "Just shut up and let him get on with it."

The judge shoved the end of the gun barrel harder against Anthony's head. "Young people. No patience. Always in such a hurry."

"Let the kid go, Judge. Give him the money and let him disappear."

"And have to pay him over and over the way I had to Rayburn?" The judge's eyes narrowed. "I don't think so. Better to just wipe the slate clean. Besides, I can't let him go. He's the murderer, didn't you know?"

Anthony's eyes were wide and showing a lot of white. Michael tried not to show the same fear, to act as though they were discussing some minor happening in town. Not life and death. His death. Every minute he kept the judge talking was a little more chance for somebody to show up. Maybe not Buck, but somebody. He kept his voice casual. "I don't see how you can make people believe that. He's just a kid."

"But a kid who's always in trouble. Doing

things he shouldn't. It will all make perfect sense. The boy knocks off Rayburn because he finds out he killed his mother."

"What about Joe?"

The judge sighed a little. "Joe was hard."

"He saw you kill Rayburn?"

"I don't think he saw me, but he did see me coming in too early that morning. I don't know how Joe knew the things he did, but he recognized Rayburn as somebody he'd seen with me. Who knows when. But Joe never forgot anything that he ever saw happen in Hidden Springs, and then he was always putting two and two together and getting five."

"But this time he got the right answer." Michael eased a little closer to the judge and Anthony.

"Not right for him."

"I wouldn't ever kill anybody with scissors." Anthony spoke up.

"Desperation can make a person do things you can't imagine." The judge tightened his hold on the boy. "Besides, it doesn't matter what you would really do. Not as long as the folks believe you might have done it."

"So then the good deputy here finds out and I shoot him. Is that it?" Anthony said.

"That's good, kid. You're catching on," the judge said.

"But what about me? Who shoots me?" Anthony sounded merely curious.

"Why, you kill yourself, kid. Nobody will be too surprised. I think they'll be so relieved that it's all over, they'll hardly ask any questions."

"It won't work, Judge. You might as well turn yourself in." Michael did his best to sound confident as he held out his hand toward the judge. "Just give me the gun, slow and easy."

The judge actually smiled. "I'm sorry, Michael, but you've got to realize I'm going to be the next state representative. I've got things to do. Important things. You're a good boy and all, but the state needs me more than it does you. I can make things happen."

"You're nuts." Anthony tried to twist away from him, but the judge pushed the gun against his head.

"Could be, but I don't think so. Enough talk." The judge pushed the boy toward the car. "Time to get on with it, like the boy said. June will wonder where I am."

"Listen." Michael spoke up suddenly. "I hear a car coming. What are you going to do, Judge? Kill everybody in Hidden Springs?"

The judge hesitated, his eyes darting toward the road. Michael looked at Anthony's face. The kid was smart enough not to move his head, but he did blink. That was signal enough for Michael. With a yell that would have done the Confederate Rebels proud, Michael lunged at the judge, knocking his arm up. At the same time Anthony

333

dropped to the ground. The gun went off, the bullet whizzing harmlessly over their heads.

Michael grabbed the judge's arm before he could bring the gun back down. The judge was stronger than Michael had expected. For a moment, neither gave ground. With their faces inches apart, Michael said, "Give it up, Judge. It's over."

The judge backed up a couple of steps, then suddenly banged his head into Michael's.

For a second, Michael was dazed and his hold slackened. The judge whirled and began pushing against Michael.

"Watch out, Deputy," Anthony yelled. "He's trying to push you over."

Michael's feet slipped on the rock as he glanced over his shoulder. They were close, too close. Michael hooked a foot behind the judge's legs and they both went down hard with Michael on top. He banged the judge's hand that gripped the gun against the rocks. Bones crunched as at last the judge dropped the gun. Michael grabbed it and scrambled to his feet.

The judge sat up slowly, holding his hand. "We can talk about this, Mike. Work something out."

"I don't think so, Judge. You're under arrest for murder. You have the right to remain silent," Michael started.

"Stop it. Don't read me my rights. I know my rights." The judge glared up at Michael. "And weren't none of them murders."

"You stabbed Joe with his own scissors." Michael backed up out of reach.

"An accident. I didn't mean for it to happen. I just wanted to talk to him, but he wouldn't listen." The judge groaned as he pushed against the rock with his good hand to stand up. He got a few inches off the rock and then sank back down hard. He reached toward Michael. "Help me up."

"I don't think so, Judge."

"What's an old man like me going to do? You've already broken my good hand. I can't even stand up, and there's that Hank Leland." The judge looked past Michael toward the road. "You might know he'd be the one to spoil things."

Michael looked over his shoulder. Sure enough, Hank was bouncing along the rutted road in his old van. Michael looked back at the judge. Strangely enough, in spite of everything he knew the man had done, he felt sorry for him, or maybe he was sad for himself. "There's nothing I can do, Judge. It's over."

"I guess you're right. It is over." Tears filled the judge's eyes. He looked up at Michael. "I'd take it kindly if you'd just shoot me, Michael."

"You know I can't do that."

"Well, give the gun to the boy there." The judge's eyes flickered over to Anthony. "He wants to kill me. It'd give him a lot of pleasure."

"I don't think so." Michael didn't look at Anthony. "He's not a murderer."

"You mean like his father." The judge let out a sound close to a laugh. "You never know what you can do till you have to. That's all I ever did. What I had to."

Behind Michael, Hank's van stopped and a door slammed. The judge pushed against the rock with his uninjured hand and this time managed to get to his feet.

"Okay, Judge. Let's go." Michael motioned with the gun toward Anthony's car.

The judge didn't act as if he heard him. Instead, he was staring at Hank. "That idiot has his camera out. I can't do this."

Without warning, he turned away from Michael and hurled himself toward the edge of the cliff. Michael grabbed for him and managed to catch his jacket, but the judge was already too close to the edge. He embraced the pull of gravity. Michael teetered on the edge and might not have recovered his balance in time if Anthony hadn't grabbed him and yanked him back.

Behind them Hank snapped pictures.

❧ 28 ❧

Anthony clutched Michael's belt as the judge fell, arms and legs flailing against the air as though he'd changed his mind and wanted to climb back to safety. Then he slammed onto the surface of the lake below. The water swallowed him like a hungry mouth.

Michael closed his eyes after the judge disappeared under the water. He was suddenly very aware of the sun on his face and the slight breeze touching his skin.

"You think it killed him?" Anthony asked.

"Yes." Michael opened his eyes and stared down at the lake. Was it wrong to be glad for the feel of pulling in breath when he'd just seen death? Death that could be laid at his door because of his cockeyed plan.

Anthony turned loose of Michael's belt and stepped closer to the edge to peer over at the widening ripples in the water below. "And that, ladies and gentlemen, was my father."

"Not in any way that counted." Michael wanted to jerk the kid back from the edge.

Hank came up behind them. "I don't believe it. Was that the judge? It looked like he jumped." Then as if Anthony's words had just reached his ears, he went on. "Did you say he was your father? Wow, what a story!" He pulled out his notebook and pencil. "The big boys will be after this one. They'll have to give me a byline."

Michael turned and punched Hank in the jaw. Hank fell with a heavy thud, his pencil and notebook skittering away from him on the rocks as he instinctively protected his camera.

Hank scrambled up to a sitting position and felt

his chin gingerly while he worked his jaw back and forth. "Hey, why'd you do that?"

Michael didn't bother answering him. Instead he turned to Anthony. "You okay?"

"Better than you maybe." Anthony eyed Michael as though he'd sprouted horns or three eyes. Maybe both.

Michael pulled his phone out of his pocket and held it out to Anthony. "Here. Drive out till you can get a signal. Call Betty Jean and tell her the judge went over the edge. She'll know who to call. Her number is in the contacts."

Anthony took the phone. "What are you going to do?"

Michael stepped away from him toward the edge of the cliff. "I'm going down to pull him out."

"I thought you said he was dead."

"He is."

"Then it's too late to save him," Anthony said.

"It's been too late for that for a long time." Michael walked along the cliff edge until he found the spot where a steep path wound down to the water's edge.

Anthony trailed after him while Hank grabbed his notebook and pencil and scrambled to his feet, still rubbing his chin. He came after them but stayed well back from Michael.

"Maybe I'd better stay and help you. You might drown down there by yourself." Anthony looked past Michael toward the lake.

"You saying you care whether I drown or not?" Michael didn't look around at him.

"No, but you drowning wasn't part of the plan."

"Lots of things weren't part of the plan."

Hank came up behind Anthony. "Go ahead, kid, and do what he says. I'll help him."

"Help him what? Drown and then take pictures?" Anthony looked from Hank to Michael and back to Hank. "Or he might drown you."

"Naw, he wouldn't do that, and he's right. He has to pull the judge out. He owes it to Miss June."

Michael looked around at Hank for the first time since he'd hit him. "She called you?"

"Yeah." Hank took his camera from around his neck and placed it carefully on the ground. He eyed Michael a minute and then pushed it farther away from the edge. "She tried to disguise her voice, but she's called me a million times to put the screws on me for free space for this or that community service ad. There wasn't any way I could not recognize her voice." Hank stopped and looked past Michael down toward the lake. "But no way was I expecting this."

"I'll go then, I guess," Anthony said.

"That's what I told you to do, but don't drive crazy. There's no emergency now," Michael told the boy before he started toward the path.

Hank waited a minute and then followed him. Loose dirt spilled down the path as their feet slid on the incline. They were halfway to the bottom when they heard Anthony's car starting up.

"I'm sorry I slugged you." Michael stopped to regain his balance after he slipped on a loose rock. Below them, the ripples in the water lapped against the shoreline.

"Good newspapermen are supposed to get slugged now and again. Proves they're doing their job." Hank lost his footing and slid toward Michael. Michael put a hand out to stop him. "Of course, it would have been better if the boy had had the camera. That would have been some shot. Mild-mannered deputy sheriff swinging at dedicated get-the-news-this-time-every-time newspaper editor whose mouth was surely hanging open."

"It'll kill Miss June if you print any of those pictures." Michael leveled his eyes on Hank. "Especially since she's the reason you're out here."

"Maybe. Maybe not. I'm thinking she might have felt worse if I hadn't got here in time." Hank held on to Michael's arm to keep from sliding against him. "Wonder why she called me instead of the sheriff."

"I guess the old girl's got more going for her than we thought. She knew you'd follow up on the tip, but she couldn't be that sure about the sheriff."

"You think she knew all the time?"

"I think maybe she might have suspected it after

Rayburn. She said she remembered the name."
Michael turned and slipped the last few feet to
the lake's edge.

"That's more than any of the rest of us did. Or is
it?" Hank followed him down.

"Anthony knew." Michael unstrapped his gun
and laid it on the ground. "I didn't figure it out
until today."

"You going to give me the scoop?"

Michael looked at him. "You going to lose those
pictures?"

"Come on, Michael. That's asking too much."

Michael stripped off his uniform without saying
anything.

"I'll find out what happened anyway," Hank
said.

"Not from me." Michael dived into the cold
water and swam out toward where the judge's
body had risen to the surface. Behind him, he
could hear Hank yelling something, but Michael
didn't bother trying to hear him. He didn't want
to listen. He didn't want to think. He couldn't
think about it yet. He just had to keep doing what
had to be done, one thing at a time.

He dragged the judge's body out and laid him on
the rocky bank. It hurt him to see the man's slack
face with lake water and blood dribbling out the
corner of his mouth. He'd never seen the judge's
face when it wasn't full of purpose, whether he
was arguing somebody around to his point of

view, pushing a pet project, or winning a vote. He was, by turns, earnest, intense, hearty. Whatever the occasion called for. Now it seemed some occasions had called for murder.

"I still just can't believe it." Hank stared at the judge's body as Michael pulled his uniform back on. "Maybe Rayburn. That's hard enough to believe, but are you saying the judge killed Joe?"

Michael buckled his gun holster back around his waist. "I don't think you heard me say anything."

"I can't promise to delete those pictures, Michael."

"He jumped because he couldn't bear to see the picture you'd take." Michael sat down on a rock and tugged on his socks and shoes. He kept his eyes away from the judge's body.

"He jumped because he couldn't figure any other way out." Hank fingered the notebook in his pocket but didn't pull it out. "What was he going to do? Kill you and the kid too?"

Michael glanced up at Hank, who was studying him with narrowed eyes. He could almost see the gears turning in the editor's head as he tried to figure it all out. Michael carefully tied his shoelaces, then stood up. "You got anything in your van we can cover him up with till Justin gets here?"

"I should've gone with the boy and let you take your chances drowning, Keane." Hank headed back toward the steep path. He looked back to say, "I've got an old raincoat in there, but I'm not climbing back down with it."

"You can pitch it down."

After he covered up the judge's upper body with Hank's raincoat, he sat down to wait for more help to arrive. He could have climbed back to the top, but even as sad as it was there beside the judge, it was better than up on top with Hank and his questions. He might give Hank some answers in time, but not now. Not with the wounds so raw. Hank could wait.

He looked out over the lake and tried not to think about anything except how blue the water was and how the breeze swept ripples in front of it across the surface. He wished for his rowboat so that he could just get in and row out on the lake away from everything.

Above him, he heard tires on the gravel, car doors slamming, and voices. He couldn't make out their words. He didn't want to. The sound of the voices told enough, sort of like an opera he'd seen once where, in spite of not understanding a word anybody onstage was saying, he still knew the story was a tragedy.

The rest of the day was one thing after another that he didn't like. Helping Justin and the sheriff carry the judge's body back up the cliff. Worrying about having to give the sheriff CPR when his face turned blotchy purple before they got to the top. Then answering his terse questions once the sheriff could breathe again.

He didn't like not seeing Anthony there anywhere. He didn't like the white, tight-lipped look on Justin's face or the way Hank kept scribbling in his little notebook.

He didn't like the way the sun was warm and bright as if nothing in the world was wrong.

He especially didn't like it when the sheriff said, "Somebody will have to tell Miss June." And everybody looked at him.

After that was decided, they all left him alone, as if he had been set apart for some sort of a sacrifice and they were all afraid to get too close for fear they might become part of it too. Even Hank gave him a wide berth.

They were wrapping things up and the sheriff was ordering Michael to drive the judge's Cadillac out to save the taxpayers the cost of a wrecker when Buck did finally show up. He came barreling down the gravel lane so fast that Lester's car behind him was almost lost in the dust he raised. Both of them had their lights flashing.

"The keys might not be in the judge's car." Michael kept his eyes on the two cars speeding in and didn't look at the sheriff. He sincerely hoped the keys weren't in the judge's car.

"Look at those idiots!" The sheriff made a sound of disgust when Buck slammed his car to a stop right in the middle of the road. Lester jammed on his brakes and skidded sideways off the road. "That's all we need. Two totaled police cars."

The sheriff glared at the two men piling out of the cars before he turned back to Michael and went on talking as though there had been no interruption. "The judge always leaves his keys in his car. You know that. He says you don't have to worry about car thieves in Hidden Springs."

"Just murderers."

Buck rushed up to them without even looking back at Lester. His face was white and his lips were in a grim line. "Man, am I glad to see you, Mike. Sally Jo said you called for backup. I was heading out when she canceled the call. Then Lester radioed me that somebody got killed down here, but he didn't know who or how." He glanced over at the sheriff. "What's going down?"

Instead of filling him in, Sheriff Potter started yelling at him. "What's the idea of coming in here like gangbusters and slamming on your brakes like that? You trying to see if Lester's air bag works?"

"If he had any sense, he'd have known I was going to stop." Buck matched the sheriff's anger word for word.

"That's the point." The sheriff stepped closer to Buck and went up on his toes to get right in his face. "The boy hasn't got any sense. You should know that."

Buck stepped away from the sheriff and held up his hands in a gesture of surrender. "You're right, Sheriff. I wasn't thinking straight."

"I reckon that's understandable. Considering." Sheriff Potter blew out a breath. "I better go make sure he's not hurt." The sheriff started over toward Lester's car sitting sideways in the ditch beside the road. He looked over his shoulder at Michael and Buck. "You boys don't go anywhere till I see if we can get him back up on the road. You might have to push."

"We could call a wrecker," Michael said.

"We aren't calling no wrecker. Waste of taxpayers' money." The sheriff stalked on toward Lester standing in the road, wringing his hands.

"Who rammed a nest of hornets down his pants?" Buck looked around. "And where's the kid? He's okay, isn't he?"

"I guess so. I sent him for help and he didn't come back. Decided he did his part, I guess." Michael hoped the boy had the good sense to go home.

"That's a relief. When I saw Justin, I was afraid the kid had done something stupid like jumping or maybe getting murdered." Buck wiped his forehead. "But Justin is here for some reason, not to mention that vulture Leland." He looked across to where Hank was taking pictures of Lester's car in the ditch.

"Betty Jean didn't raise you on the radio then?"

"Betty Jean? It's Saturday. I told you Sally Jo was the one who radioed me. When I called back in to be sure you'd canceled the backup call, she said the sheriff was fishing. The judge told her you were entertaining that Sheridan lady. Lester was mowing his grass, and last she heard Little Osgood wasn't going to die after all." The veins in Buck's neck were beginning to protrude, and his voice was getting louder with each word.

Across the way, Hank heard Buck and started their way. Buck lowered his voice. "So just cut to the chase and tell me what happened, before Leland gets over here with that camera."

"It was the judge. Roxanne met him out here. He somehow got out of the car before it went in the lake. Said the whole thing was an accident, but he didn't think it would look good on his political résumé to admit he was around when it happened. Rayburn had been blackmailing him for years because he thought the judge was Anthony's father and suspected there was something fishy about Roxanne's disappearance. For some reason Rayburn called Anthony and arranged to meet him. Who knows why? Before that happened, the judge shot him. After that, the judge was just doing maintenance with Joe."

Michael glanced over at Hank, who stopped in his tracks when Michael looked his way. "If it hadn't been for Hank showing up, the kid and me, we would have probably been part of the maintenance too. But when the judge saw Hank and knew there was no way out, he jumped. I couldn't stop him."

Buck's eyes widened, then narrowed as he tried to take it all in. "That has to be the wildest story I ever heard. The judge? Our judge?"

"Yeah. Our judge." Michael stared out toward the lake. "And now the sheriff wants me to drive his car out of here and go tell Miss June. What am I going to tell her, Buck?" He looked back at Buck. "What can I tell her?"

"That's a rough one for sure." Buck shook his head. "But you'll think of something. You're good at that sort of thing."

"I've never had to do that sort of thing before." Michael stared at him.

"It's part of the job."

"Then maybe I should turn in my badge and gun and walk out of here."

"And then what, Mike? Then what?"

"I don't know."

Buck clapped his hand down on Michael's shoulder and squeezed. "You aren't a quitter, kid, and Hidden Springs needs you right now."

"I thought Hidden Springs needed the judge."

Buck shook his head as if he couldn't quite take in everything Michael had told him. "Who'd have thought it?"

Hank had edged close enough to overhear them, but he stayed a few steps back from Michael, his hand on his camera. A trace of black was beginning to color his cheek.

Buck glanced over at Hank. "How much does he know?"

"Nothing from me," Michael said.

"Oh, come on, Michael." Hank moved closer. "I probably won't print the pictures. I have to live here too, you know, but I want to see them. Besides, I could file assault charges."

Buck looked surprised again. "Assault charges? Against who? Mike?"

"File them then." Michael turned away from both of them to walk toward the judge's Cadillac.

Hank called after him, "And you have to admit, it helped. Me showing up. I might even have saved your life. You ought to be grateful for that."

Michael ignored him as he got into the judge's car. The keys were in the ignition. The judge's smell leaped off the leather seats to surround him. The console beside the bucket seat spilled over with appointment reminders the man would never keep now. A couple of ties were thrown across the backseat, and a Styrofoam cup half full of coffee was in the cup holder. Michael closed himself off to all of it, started the engine, and turned the car around.

Lester's car was still in the ditch, and the sheriff tried to flag Michael down as he passed. Michael didn't care. He just drove the Cadillac out of there without looking to either side.

He practiced on Aunt Lindy. She turned pale but didn't come close to fainting. She had questions in her eyes, but she didn't ask them. He didn't tell her about the judge being the one to run his parents off the road. The rest was enough right now. More than enough.

"I'm not sure June will be able to bear it." Aunt Lindy walked across the yard with Michael toward the judge's house.

When Miss June didn't answer the doorbell, Aunt Lindy pushed open the door that wasn't locked and called out to her. She didn't answer, but they went on in to find her sitting in a flood of sunshine on her glassed-in back porch. Ferns of all types spilled out of pots in every available spot, with the fronds seeming to reach toward the little woman in their midst. A large wooden rocking chair with brown corduroy cushions sat beside her neat wicker rocker. Miss June was humming softly as she kept her hand on the other rocker's arm and made it rock along with her.

"June," Aunt Lindy said after they stood in the doorway a moment without her noticing them there.

Miss June looked up at them with a bright, brittle smile. Every silver-gray hair was in place, and her dark pink lipstick perfectly matched one of the flowers in the silky blouse she wore. She didn't look at Lindy but straight at Michael. "Oh, there you are, Michael. I knew you'd come."

Michael tried to remember the words he'd practiced to tell Miss June, but they were gone without a trace. Aunt Lindy stepped in. She went over and sat beside Miss June in the big rocker. Michael followed to stand awkwardly in front of them.

"That's Wilson's chair." Miss June was still smiling, but the effort it cost her was beginning to show.

"He won't mind." Aunt Lindy put her hand over June's on the chair arm. The two women rocked together another minute before Aunt Lindy said, "Wilson's gone, June."

"Gone?" Miss June stopped rocking. Her smile trailed away. "You mean dead, don't you, Malinda?"

When Aunt Lindy nodded, Michael thought Miss June looked relieved as she began rocking again. She leaned her head back and closed her eyes. After a moment, she said, "Wilson always knew the right thing to do."

Michael thought about all the things the judge had done, and for a few seconds he could barely keep them from exploding out of his mouth. But then Miss June opened her eyes and looked directly at him, almost as if she heard his unspoken words. Michael saw past the fluffy blanket of lies she was pulling up over herself for appearances to the painful truth she knew inside.

He swallowed hard and managed to say, "Sometimes it's hard to do the right thing."

She pressed her lips together and nodded so slightly Michael wasn't sure it was an acknowledgment of his words or just the motion of the rocking chair.

⊰ 29 ⊱

The days passed.

Sunday morning, people in Hidden Springs got up and headed out to their respective churches the same as always, but when the Christian Church members arrived at their door, Joe wasn't there to shake hands with them the way he had been for more years than anybody could remember. Across the street at First Baptist, the judge and Miss June's spot, the fifth pew from the back, remained empty. Five-year-old Benny Upton tried to sit there, but his bottom barely brushed the seat of the pew before his mother jerked him off it. At both churches, the hymns, even the lively ones, sounded like funeral dirges, and the sermons on faith at First Baptist and forgiveness at the Christian Church sort of slid off the congregations without leaving much discernible trace.

Karen reported that she didn't try to preach a sermon at the Presbyterian Church. She decided to read comforting Scriptures and invite others to talk. A few spoke about how much they were going to miss Joe. Nobody mentioned the judge, though some said they were praying for Miss June. Michael didn't go to services at any of the churches. He sat on his back deck with Jasper and stared out at the lake. Monday was soon enough to have to talk to people.

Monday morning Miss Willadean showed up at the courthouse at nine on the dot the same as always. She barely paused at the county clerk's office and came on down the hall to peek in the sheriff's office. Betty Jean looked over her screen at the little woman and asked, "Can we do something for you, Miss Willadean?"

The woman hesitated, then stepped into the office. She was wearing a dark gray suit and a black hat covered in netting. Her somber colors were only broken by her cherry-red lipstick and the dark pink peony bloom she carried. She seemed reluctant to speak, which was far from normal for Miss Willadean.

Michael stood up. "Is everything all right outside, Miss Willadean?"

"Oh yes. Nobody on the steps. Nobody at all." Her free hand fluttered to her hat, where her fingers danced nervously across the black netting.

Michael glanced at Betty Jean, who shrugged and started working on her computer again. Michael turned back to Miss Willadean. "That's good."

"Yes, yes indeed. Good." She gave her hat a last

pat and dropped her hand back down to touch the peony bloom. She stepped forward, then back, as if unsure of which way she intended to move.

Michael didn't know whether to offer her a chair or usher her out of the office. "That's a pretty flower." He hoped that would help the old lady focus.

She looked down at the peony as though surprised to see it in her hand.

"Did you bring it for Neville?" he asked.

"No, of course not." She frowned a little. "He says flowers make him sneeze."

Michael started to say something, but Miss Willadean suddenly found her voice and her purpose. With determined steps, she came across the room to lay the peony on his desk. "I brought it for you. Because, well, just because it looked so lovely on the bush in my yard and I thought you might need a flower this morning. You know, after everything last week."

"Why, thank you, Miss Willadean." Michael picked up the flower.

"You're very welcome, I'm sure." She pushed back her jacket sleeve to check her watch. "Where does the time go? I best be on my way."

After she tottered out of the office and up the hall, Michael breathed in the peony's spicy fragrance.

"What do you know about that?" Betty Jean looked over at him. "People can surprise you."

"Some surprises are better than others." Michael stuck the peony stem down in a half-empty water bottle.

That afternoon, Joe was buried. Every business in town shut down as people packed the Christian Church to pay their last respects.

Tuesday morning Hank got the *Gazette* out a day early in spite of shutting down for Joe's funeral on Monday. Miss June's copy disappeared off her porch before she had a chance to see it.

At the sheriff's office, Michael glanced at the headlines over Betty Jean's shoulder. JUDGE CAMPBELL DEAD spread across the top in large black type with SUSPECTED OF MURDER in smaller type under it.

"I don't see why Hank had to put out the paper early. Tomorrow would have been soon enough." Betty Jean stared at the picture of Judge Campbell smiling at them off the front page, looking as if he'd just announced he was running for office.

"Then don't read it till tomorrow." Michael went back to sit at his desk.

Betty Jean looked over at him, then without a word folded the paper and stuck it in the drawer. "Now if I could just stick that in the drawer." She glared at the phone when it started ringing.

Tuesday afternoon the judge was buried. Michael was a pallbearer. He hadn't known how to refuse Miss June. Reverend Simpson, obviously in shock himself over the death and even more so the life of one of his most faithful deacons, stumbled through a funeral service that couldn't have been a comfort to any of his listeners. While the organist played a mournful hymn, Michael took his place beside the sheriff and the four other men selected to carry the judge's casket to the hearse and on to its final resting spot in the cemetery.

It was one of those perfect spring days. The sky looked freshly washed, and the air smelled sweet after the stale flower scent that pervaded the funeral chapel. Michael stood under the graveside tent and listened as Reverend Simpson, a bit more in control now, went through the motions at the graveside. Perched on one of the folding chairs, her sister on one side of her and Aunt Lindy on the other, Miss June wept quietly into her lace handkerchief. She looked frail and very tired in her black dress. Michael could almost feel the people gathered under the tent, closing ranks around her to protect her from the truth. Or perhaps to protect themselves.

Then there was Hank, standing to the side, sneaking down a word now and again in his wretched notebook. At least he'd had the decency to leave his camera in his car. Michael didn't know yet whether Hank published any of the pictures he took on Saturday. None were on the front page.

Hank caught Michael looking at him and gave a

slight shrug before scribbling another few words in his notebook. Michael hoped it was nothing about the deputy sheriff as pallbearer. He turned his attention back to the preacher's words.

"Our brother made mistakes as we all make mistakes. Yet he was a loving husband, a good friend."

Michael stopped listening and once more looked around. Betty Jean dabbed a pink tissue to her eyes. The preacher droned on as if trying to make up for his earlier ineptness by delivering the deluxe graveside service.

Miss Willadean had found a position next to the tent where she had a good view of Miss June so she could properly report the widow's deportment to her friends who hadn't been able to attend. But Michael thought of the peony on his desk in the sheriff's office and forgave her. The county's six magistrates in their dark suits made a forbidding line behind Miss June as they shifted back and forth on their feet, obviously wishing the ordeal over.

Michael wished it with them as he let his eyes slide over their heads to the back of the crowd, and there was Anthony. Since Saturday, Michael had made a few attempts to find the boy with no luck. Anthony had left Michael's cell phone in Aunt Lindy's mailbox on Sunday, but Aunt Lindy said it must have been while she was at church. She reported he hadn't been at school. Nobody knew where he was, so Michael was relieved to see him still in Hidden Springs.

Anthony didn't try to duck out of sight when Michael looked his way. Instead the kid pointed at Michael, then at himself, and finally at the coffin under the tent. Michael knew what he meant—that it easily could have been the two of them in coffins under the tent instead of the judge.

Then, as Reverend Simpson mercifully began his closing prayer, Anthony actually smiled and raised his hand in a kind of salute before heading away across the graveyard. Michael wanted to go after him, but he was closed in by mourners. By the time the preacher said amen and whispered the expected final words of consolation to Miss June, Anthony was out of sight.

Michael couldn't follow him anyway. He had to play out the role he was in. He spoke some bland, meaningless words to Miss June. She smiled and patted his arm as if she'd been comforted before she let Justin and her sister hustle her back to the limousine. Aunt Lindy went with them.

Alex moved under the tent to help Reece stand. The last week had aged him, and he leaned heavily on Alex's arm as they made their way toward his car. Alex's cheeks were wet with tears, and the tip of her nose was red. Michael caught up with them.

Alex swiped the tears off her cheek with the

back of her hand. "I can't believe this. I just can't."

Michael didn't say anything, but when Alex leaned against him, he put his arms around her.

"Take care of your uncle," Michael whispered before he turned her loose.

"I'm leaving tomorrow."

"So soon?" Michael said.

Reece spoke up beside her. "She has cases to take care of. Life doesn't stop just because something bad happens."

Alex tried to smile at Michael. "You still have people to put in jail, and I still have people to get out of jail."

"We just keep playing the game. Is that what you're saying?" The words felt heavy in the air between them.

Alex looked at him a long moment as her eyes grew even sadder. "We keep playing the game."

As he watched them walk away, he wanted to chase after her and ask which game. Professional or personal. But he stood rooted to his spot, still playing all the games, even though he was beginning to wonder if he knew the rules anymore.

When beckoned, he went across to drive the limousine carrying the pallbearers back to the funeral home. There he loaded up Miss June's car with the plants and flowers that hadn't gone to the gravesite. Then he drove Miss June and her sister home. Aunt Lindy followed in her car. The sister, Claire, a slightly larger and untidier version of Miss June, had come down from Ohio, and as Michael drove, the two women compared facts about the people at the funeral, some of whom the sister hadn't seen for more than thirty years.

At the judge's house, after Michael carried in the last pot of flowers, he ignored Aunt Lindy's frown and made his excuses. He wanted to track down Anthony, but once he was finally back out on the road, Anthony was again nowhere to be found.

⊰ 30 ⊱

Malinda watched Michael walk up the street to her house where he'd left his cruiser. She had hoped he would walk to Reece's house, spend some more time with Alexandria. Alexandria was good for him. She pushed him. She loved him. And Michael loved her.

Not that either of them would admit it. They danced around each other like they were afraid to touch. It had been that way ever since the accident.

The accident that turned out not to be entirely an accident. A deep sadness welled up inside her. Michael had told her the entire story Sunday afternoon. How Wilson kept trying to cover his tracks and, in the process, destroyed so many lives while he denied wrongdoing. If Michael hadn't been the one telling her, she might not have believed it. Not of the man she'd known since they were both children. The man who had been a substitute father to Michael in many ways. The man who had stolen Michael's parents from him.

Malinda rubbed her forehead as though that might eliminate the confusion of thought inside her head. She liked things being black-and-white with clear answers. But life wasn't that way. It was no wonder Michael wasn't his usual self. He would be feeling the same confusion. The same betrayal. He needed to talk about it to someone.

When Michael started up his cruiser and drove past Reece's house without slowing down, Malinda let out a long sigh. Across the street, Reece's front door opened and Alexandria stepped out on the porch to stare after Michael's car. If only Malinda could get them to see how foolish they were to not reach out to one another. They were both so sure their disparate lives made love impossible. But didn't they know that nothing was impossible with prayer and the Lord?

Great is thy faithfulness. Each morning new mercies, and the Lord knew how desperately they needed those mercies on this day.

Malinda sighed again, and June spoke up behind her. "Is Michael all right?"

"Yes, of course. He's sad as we all are, but he's all right." Malinda turned from the window. She was a little ashamed to be dwelling on her own sorrows when June's had to be much deeper and harder to face. She reached for June's hands. "Thank you."

June grasped her hands. She stared at Malinda with dry eyes. June looked like a fragile rose, but underneath was steel. "I am so very sorry," she said.

Malinda knew what she meant, that June had guessed about so much more than had been spoken between them. She squeezed her friend's hands. "Yes. So am I, but time will pass and the memories will be easier."

"One day at a time is all we're given." June pulled her hands free and brushed away a tear that had slipped up on her.

"Each day his mercies."

"Yes, I am depending on that." June turned back down the hallway. "Claire is setting out some food. You will stay and eat with us, and Claire thinks others might stop in to help the day pass. Perhaps Alexandria and Reece. I'm sorry Michael couldn't stay."

"Yes, so am I." Malinda glanced back at the window and sent prayers after Michael.

❧ 31 ❧

The next morning Michael quit playing the game. He ignored his uniform hanging on the closet door and pulled on blue jeans and a T-shirt instead. He threw some food into a cooler and pulled out his camping gear from the back of the closet. He loaded it all plus Jasper and his fishing rods in his motor boat and took off across the lake.

He'd have to pay for his disappearance, but he didn't care. The night before, he had turned the ringer on his phone off. He had listened to the messages when he got up, but he didn't return any of the calls. Not Karen's or Aunt Lindy's. Not even Alex's when she told him to call to say goodbye before she left.

Sheriff Potter's voice had been in there too, but after the "Hey, Mike," Michael had fast-forwarded through the rest of his message.

It was nice out on the lake with Jasper. When the dog jumped in the lake for a swim, Michael threw out the anchor and jumped in with him. The water was cool, but once back in the boat, the sun warmed him while he dried off.

He'd forgotten about the little island until it was in front of him. Maybe he had never remembered it since the accident, but as he steered toward land, memories came flooding back. When he was a kid, he felt like Columbus discovering this place. The little island had trees and wildflowers, a spring, and a rock overhang where he could get out of the rain. It was as good a place as any to hide out for a while.

On the third or maybe the fourth day, he wasn't surprised to spot another boat headed toward the island. He was lying on the top of the highest boulder watching a red-tailed hawk make circles over the lake. Jasper was stretched out beside him, a satisfied puff of air escaping the dog's mouth every little bit. Other boats had passed by the little island, mostly tourists busy with their own plans. They sped past, smiling and waving. But this boat headed directly toward the island. Someone local must have spotted him.

"The jig is up, Jasper." Michael sat up and watched the small fishing boat. The dog raised his ears and barked a couple of times just to keep things interesting.

Michael had never planned to stay on the island forever. He just needed time to think it all through, but it seemed easier not to think about it. Not to worry about what was next. Just enjoy the fishing and the sunshine. The birds and the lap of water against the shore.

He squinted toward the boat still a good ways off. Only one person in it, but it wasn't the sheriff. Not that Michael had expected him to come after him, even if Aunt Lindy had insisted someone do so. Maybe Buck, but the person didn't look big enough for Buck. Besides, Buck had one of those fast fishing boats. This was just a little dinghy with an outboard motor like Michael's. The sheriff might have sent Lester after him, but it couldn't be Lester. Too close to school crossing time. Then again, this might be Saturday. He had lost track of the days.

Still, if it was Lester, he'd have his hat on. Michael couldn't imagine Lester doing anything remotely official without wearing his uniform. Michael played with some other names. Paul Osgood? He might be recovered enough from his surgery to hunt Michael down and demand a full report of the murders. Hank Leland? He could want a picture of the dropout deputy sheriff for next week's *Gazette*. Anthony? The kid might be searching for a place to hide from the world himself.

That was as far as he got when he recognized the boat. Reece's. But it wasn't the old lawyer piloting it. When Michael stood up on the rock, Jasper started wagging his tail and scrambled down off the rocks. After staring a moment at the boat steadily drawing nearer, Michael followed Jasper down. Nobody could hide forever. He wasn't even sure he wanted to.

"Hello, Huckleberry." Alex cut the motor and threw Michael the rope to pull the boat up on the bank.

Michael smiled. He should have known. Who else would come after him?

"How'd you find me?" he asked as he helped her out of the boat.

She didn't answer right away as she greeted Jasper by scratching his neck. Then she straightened up and looked at Michael. "It wasn't hard. Don't you remember? We ran away here once when we were kids. Your dad came after us before it got dark and made us go home. I cried all the way."

"I don't remember," Michael said.

"One of the lost ones, I suppose. A shame." Alex pulled a face. "It was one of our best adventures."

"I thought you had to go back to the big city." He pulled her boat farther up on the bank and tied the rope to a tree.

"I did. Got my people out of jail." She looked at him with raised eyebrows. "I hear you didn't put your people in."

"Aunt Lindy send you to get me?" Michael walked with her up the bank to a level spot.

"Your amnesia must be kicking in again. Not Malinda. She said you'd come back when you were ready, and if you weren't ready, there wasn't any use trying to make you. That there were some things a person had to work out on their own."

"Then what are you doing here?"

"I'm not really sure." Alex flashed a smile at him. "Maybe it's just because I'm so competitive. I mean, it's panic in the streets in Hidden Springs. Or should I say street."

"Panic? Surely no more bodies on the courthouse steps."

"Maybe panic isn't quite the right word." She dropped down on a rock ledge and patted the spot beside her. "Sit."

He did as she said. "Then what is the right word?"

"Worry? Concern?" She hooked her hair back behind her ears. "Actually, I wouldn't doubt if there are a few folks who are wondering if you might not be dead, murdered even by the real murderer since everybody knows it couldn't have been the judge in spite of what that Hank Leland put out in the paper. Let's face it. Paper will lie still and let you write anything on it, and nowadays with folks using computers, well, who knows what the truth is anymore?"

"Not me." Michael leaned back and looked up at the sky.

She glanced over at him but let that pass. "Fact is, Paul Osgood, now that he's on the mend, is one of those not sure of the story Hank wrote up. At least he's not going to close the case till he hears the story straight from your lips, and Betty Jean says he's real anxious to hear the story straight from your lips. She says he's about to drive her batty. Anyway, he's sort of made it a contest to see who can find you and bring you in first."

"Then I guess Buck's not looking." In spite of himself, a smile tried to wake up inside him.

"Not so Paul will know anyway." Alex picked up a rock and tossed it down toward the water. "See how good I'm getting at figuring out all this small-town political stuff?"

"What about the sheriff?" Michael pulled his eyes away from the sky to look at her.

"He's mad as all get-out at you, but a little worried too that you might not come back and do all his work for him. Lester is having trouble taking up the slack, and Betty Jean told me she had to hunt the sheriff down at the Grill half a dozen times since you deserted your post. Sheriff Potter is not a happy camper." She peered over at him. "Are you?"

"Don't I look like it?" Michael let his grin slide out on his face. He was glad to see a person again. Especially this person.

"You look awful. Your nose is going to peel and your hair looks like you stuck your finger in a light socket. And your beard. Did you know there's a spot of gray there?" Alex pointed at his cheek.

"Probably dirt." Michael rubbed his hand across his beard. "If I'd known I was going to have company, I'd have shaved."

"Did you bring a razor?"

368

"No."

Alex laughed. "Oh well, I'm a sucker for the wild, rugged type."

"You're a hard woman to figure." Michael kept his eyes on her face. "I thought you liked the city slicker type."

"And I thought you liked the preacher type." Alex didn't quite hide the question lurking behind her words. "You have to admire a woman with the moxie to take on pastoring a church in Hidden Springs."

"Karen is an exceptional woman."

"You had about ten messages from her on your machine before the tape ran out, and a note on your door." Alex looked down quickly. "I didn't read it, of course."

"You could have. Karen and I are just friends. Nothing serious."

"Are you sure she feels the same way?" Alex peeked up at him. "She sounded awfully concerned on those messages."

"She's a preacher. A good pastor. She's supposed to be concerned about her members. And her friends."

"And what about you? Didn't you think about how you might be worrying your friends?"

"Okay. So I'm a bum."

"You won't find many who'll give you an argument on that right now." Alex bit her lip but couldn't quite hide her smile. "But I've been known to defend a bum now and again. Charity work."

"Did you bring food? That's the charity I need right now."

"Tired of fish?" She laughed and pointed at the boat. "Of course I brought food."

Two ham sandwiches later, Michael leaned back against a tree and opened another soft drink as he watched Alex feed Jasper half her sandwich. The dog finished it in two gulps and then lay down with his head in her lap. Michael was envious.

For a while they talked about how blue the lake was and which fish were biting, but then they seemed to run out of words. Alex kept her eyes on Jasper as she stroked the dog's head. Waves lapped up against the shore when a boat passed far out in the lake, but neither of them gave it more than a passing glance. High above their heads two buzzards drifted along on the air currents. That's what Michael had been doing, just drifting whichever way the wind blew him the last few days. But maybe now it was time to start dipping his wings to give himself some direction.

As if Alex read his thoughts, she said, "You can't stay here forever."

"A week's not forever."

"Nothing's going to be different in another week."

"I might be."

Alex considered that a moment. "Do you want to talk about it?"

"There's not much to talk about."

"I think there is." Alex used her best lawyer voice. She pushed Jasper's head off her lap and came over to sit cross-legged directly in front of him. "And I'm not leaving till you talk."

"Good. I didn't want you to leave anyway."

A smile played around her lips, but she wiped it away with one of her hands. "How long were you planning on us staying?"

"How much food did you bring?"

"Not nearly enough, the way you and Jasper eat."

"I've been aiming to go on a diet." Michael kept his eyes on her face. "That other time, did we go skinny-dipping?"

She let the smile surface this time. "That's something I guess you'll never know."

"Not unless you tell me."

"We went swimming."

"Let's go swimming now." He sat up and pulled off his shirt.

"Okay. Swim now, but then we'll talk." Alex stood up and stripped off her jeans and shirt down to a black one-piece suit.

He laughed. "Alex. Always prepared."

She shrugged. "I thought I might get some sun while you packed up your camping gear." She waded out into the water. Jasper splashed along beside her. "Ooh, the water's still cold."

"Wakes up the senses." Michael stepped into the lake beside her.

"Mine don't go to sleep." She grinned over at him and splashed on through the water until it was deep enough to plunge in.

They laughed and swam the same as they must have when they were kids, but just as that fun had had to end then, this fun did too. They climbed out and lay in the sun to dry off. She didn't push him to say anything, and maybe that was why after a while Michael started talking.

Alex reached over and held his hand when he told her about the judge being the one to cause the wreck. She squeezed it tighter when he got to the part about remembering the judge peering through the window at him and then leaving him to die. He told her everything, even about his crazy plan that almost got him and Anthony killed and how Miss June's phone call to Hank Leland might be the only reason he was sitting there beside her now.

When at last he'd said it all, Alex waited a moment and then asked, "Now what?"

Michael had been staring up at the sky the whole time he talked, but when she spoke, he turned his head to look at her. "I don't know. That's why I'm here."

Alex sat up and stared down at him. "The

trouble with you, Michael, is that you expect everybody to be good."

"I know better than that." He didn't shy away from her eyes.

"You know it, but you don't want to believe it. You went off to the big city and saw things happening there that you couldn't do anything about. Terrible things." Her still damp hair hung down over her cheeks. "So you thought you'd come back to your private little corner of the world where nothing bad ever happened, or at least nothing very bad."

"What's so awful about that?" He reached up to push a stray strand of her hair away from her eyes.

She shoved his hand away impatiently. She didn't like anything interfering when she was winning an argument. "Nothing, except you're a little old to believe in fairy tales. People here in Hidden Springs are like people anywhere else. Some good. Some not."

"Maybe you're right. I shouldn't believe in fairy tales." His eyes probed hers. "How about angels? Can I believe in angels?"

She looked at him for a long moment. "You can believe in angels."

"I don't want to just believe in them. I want to kiss one of them." He reached up to run his finger along her cheek to her lips. She didn't shove his hand away this time.

"I'm not an angel."

"Close enough." He wrapped his hand behind her neck and gently pulled her down toward him until their lips were touching. Then the wind and sun seemed to become part of their embrace as everything else faded away.

❧ 32 ❧

Not until much later when the shadows began to grow long and deep did Michael at last start packing up his camping gear. Alex pulled her jeans on over her swimsuit and asked the same question she'd asked earlier. "What now?"

He stopped and looked up at her. "I don't know. Do you think I'd make a good fishing guide?"

"You make a good policeman." She buttoned up her shirt and produced a comb from somewhere to rake through her hair.

"You always told me that any Tom, Dick, or Harry could go around getting shot at."

"So, maybe I was worried about you." She shrugged a little as she sat down to tie her sneakers.

"Were you?" He sat back on his haunches and watched her.

He thought he knew her so well, but now it was plain his lost memories kept him a step behind her. He remembered all those letters she wrote him while he was in a coma. When he was able to read again, he'd pored over them until he almost absorbed the words. But could be, if Aunt Lindy hadn't thrown them out, he should read them again. Alex's teenage words might tease more memories out of the dark. He wanted to do more than simply remember events. He wanted to recapture the feelings.

She took an extra long time tying her laces, but at last she looked up. "I was worried about you. Policemen wear guns and get shot at." She made a face. "It could be that I didn't have the proper perspective on law enforcement careers at the time."

He kept his eyes steady on her. "Is that lawyer speak?"

"Oh no, that would require more words. Billable words." She twisted her lips to hide a smile.

"How about plain old Alex speak?"

"Okay." She looked down at the ground. "So, I was young, and I had this idiotic idea you might go to law school with me."

"You never told me."

Her eyes came back up to his. "No, I guess I didn't. Would it have made a difference?"

"A big difference. I wouldn't have gone to law school, but I might have gotten up the nerve to tell you how beautiful I thought you were."

"You can tell me now."

"Now's no good. Now you already know you're beautiful."

"Didn't you know? Beautiful women are always the last to know." Alex flounced her hair and laughed. "But we're talking about your problems, not mine, remember? I asked my question first. What now?"

Michael turned his attention back to his gear and concentrated on rolling his sleeping bag as small as possible. "I'll think of something."

"Hold everything and don't think of anything yet. Not until I show you something." Alex went to Reece's boat and came back with a large manila envelope. "I hope it didn't get wet."

"A treasure map?" Michael raised his eyebrows as he took it from her.

"Not exactly. Hank told me to give it to you. Said that if this is what it took to get you back, then he was willing to make the sacrifice. Although he figured he might as well go on and print the pictures since everybody in Hidden Springs already hated him for putting the truth about the judge in the paper."

Michael stared at the envelope. "Did the AP pick up his story?"

"He got his byline, but he didn't know the whole story, just the latest installment. He guessed about Roxanne, but said he didn't have enough concrete evidence to print."

"He found the gold speck and then didn't dig is what you're saying."

"Gold speck?" She had a puzzled frown.

"Hank told me last week that a good news-paperman had a sixth sense about finding the right place to dig for gold. Or news in his case."

"Then I guess he decided to let the gold stay buried. He said Miss June could be a pain with her requests for free space for this or that charity event, but he liked the old lady. Plus, he said he had to think about Anthony. That the boy had problems enough without him adding to them."

"Has Anthony left town?"

"Nope." Alex pressed her lips together and shook her head a little. "Malinda says he was at school every day since the judge's funeral."

"You're kidding." He raised his eyebrows at Alex.

"Nope," she said again with a smile. "Actually, I ran across him before I came out here."

"Where? I tried to find him for three days with no luck."

"He wasn't a bit hard to find. He was sitting right there on your front steps when I drove Uncle Reece's truck out to your house to put my boat in the water. He gave me a hand getting it in the lake."

"Now I know you're lying."

"A good attorney may evade the unfortunate truth from time to time, but she never lies."

"Was he okay?"

"Looked okay to me. Claimed he'd come down to see if maybe you'd broken your leg or something, since you hadn't been on his case for a few days. I think he misses you."

"Misses you maybe. Not me." Michael snorted.

Alex pointed at the envelope. "Look at the picture."

Michael pulled the picture out of the envelope. Hank had blown it up to an eight by ten. Michael's gut wrenched as he stared at the judge leaning toward the air, panic twisting his features until, if Michael hadn't known for sure it was Judge Campbell, he might not have recognized him at all. Michael was grasping the judge's jacket, but even in the picture it was obvious he had no way to save the judge. Instead, it appeared Michael was about to lose his balance and pitch off the cliff along with the judge.

He might have fallen except for the third person in the picture. Anthony. Anthony was grabbing Michael's belt with a look of desperation as he yanked Michael back from the edge.

Alex peeked over his shoulder at the picture. "Hank says this picture could make him some money. Maybe even win a Pulitzer or something." She shivered and turned her eyes away from it. "I don't like looking at it."

Michael felt down in the envelope and pulled out the memory card. "Hank could have already downloaded it on his computer."

"He knew you'd think of that. So he said to tell you that sometimes friends had to trust one another. Especially in a little town like Hidden Springs."

"Huh." Michael stared at the memory card. "Everybody's full of surprises." Then he studied Anthony's face in the picture again. "Did you show Anthony the picture?"

"No."

"Good." Michael tore the picture in two, then again and on until it was a handful of glossy squares of paper. He dropped them and the memory card on what was left of the campfire.

After they melted into the ashes, he looked up at Alex. "I guess I owe Hank one."

"Don't worry. He'll be collecting for years." Alex reached for his hand. "Are you ready?"

"I don't know, but it's time to go. You've still got people to get out of jail, and I've still got people to put there."

And kids to pull back from trouble's edge. He didn't say that last aloud. But maybe that was what he'd been hoping to find here on the island. A reason to keep playing the game of life.

Michael didn't know what was going to happen next, but he had the feeling there would be other kids. Other Anthonys. Other Hallies.

Alex looked up at him. "Your boat or mine? Or each in our own boats?"

"Mine. We'll tow Reece's." He wanted her in his boat. In his life. "You are beautiful, you know."

Her smile was tinged with sadness. "I can't live in Hidden Springs."

"I know."

"And you can't not live here."

"I know." He soaked up the sight of her. "But right now, you're here and I'm here."

"Are you saying not to worry about what next? Just grab what now?"

"Sounds good to me."

"And to me." She tiptoed up to kiss his cheek. Then she took his hand and let him help her into his boat.

⚛ Acknowledgments ⚛

All I've ever wanted to do is write stories, but I've had fun going down different storytelling paths at times. I couldn't do that if I wasn't blessed with readers like you who are willing to follow me down those story trails. You've traveled through the years in my Shaker village of Harmony Hill. You've shared the adventures of Jocie and friends in my Heart of Hollyhill books. Then you went farther back in time to Rosey Corner to share the lives of the Merritt sisters. Some of you even went to 1855 Louisville for *Words Spoken True*. And now I've created Hidden Springs where mysteries happen. So thank you all for reading.

I also thank my publishing company, Revell Books, a division of Baker Publishing, for letting me tell the stories in all these different places. Thank you, Lonnie Hull DuPont, for your help in making my stories better. Thanks also to Barb Barnes for her careful editing, line by line, to keep my mess-ups to a minimum. Thanks to Lindsay Davis for her readiness to help anytime I ask her. I appreciate the whole Baker team and the great work they do on my covers and in turning my stories into books.

I am blessed to work with a wonderful agent,

Wendy Lawton, who is always looking around the next storytelling bend and encouraging me to do so as well. Her encouragement and prayers mean so much.

Thanks, too, to Tony Likins, who tried to guide me into the modern era of local police forces. Any mistakes I made are my own and no reflection on him.

Last of all, I thank my family and my Lord. Blessings on top of blessings. *Great is thy faithfulness.*

⚜ About the Author ⚜

A. H. Gabhart is a pseudonym for Ann H. Gabhart, the bestselling author of more than twenty novels for adults and young adults. *Angel Sister*, Ann's first Rosey Corner book, was a nominee for inspirational novel of 2011 by *RT Book Reviews* magazine, and *Love Comes Home*, Rosey Corner book three, was the 2015 Selah Book of the Year. Her Shaker novel, *The Outsider*, was a Christian Book Awards finalist in the fiction category. She lives on a farm not far from where she was born in rural Kentucky. She and her husband are blessed with three children, three in-law children, and nine grandchildren. Ann loves reading books, watching her grandkids grow up, and walking with her dog, Oscar.

Ann has fun connecting with readers on her Facebook page, www.facebook.com/anngabhart, where you can peek over her shoulder for her "Sunday mornings coming down" or walk along to see what she might spot on her walks or laugh with her on Friday smiles day. Then come visit Ann at www.annhgabhart.com to check out her books, blog, and more.

Center Point Large Print
600 Brooks Road / PO Box 1
Thorndike, ME 04986-0001 USA

(207) 568-3717

US & Canada:
1 800 929-9108
www.centerpointlargeprint.com